Praise for *The Ruins of Lace*

"Stunning…as beautifully fashioned as the sought-after lace, this story is sure to impress."

…s Weekly

"Compelling…I couldn't st …uthor of
…*and Before Versailles*

"*The Ruins of Lace* is an intriguing tale about a time and place full of great beauty and fraught with great danger. Iris Anthony intertwines the delicate threads of character and plot to form a story as complex and lovely as the lace at the heart of this ingenious book."

—Gillian Bagwell, author of *The Darling Strumpet*
and *The September Queen*

"A wonderfully resonant tale, delightful and unique…Desperation and dire straits, hard choices between compassion and immorality, between propriety and legality, and the meanness of such a world are well written and sharp enough to make the reader squirm as Anthony unfolds the lengths of her narrative. Well done. This story is a treasure that will doubtless call the hand to pull it from the shelf to read again."

—Mark Lehnertz, store manager,
Tattered Cover Book Store, Denver, CO

"Spun of intricate, multiple threads, *The Ruins of Lace* reflects the very fabric whose story it tells: a gorgeously wrought tale of two women bound to the cruelty and beauty of a forbidden perfection, and the dangerous intrigues of the lace prohibition in seventeenth century France. Iris Anthony has delivered a stunning achievement!"

—C. W. Gortner, author of *The Queen's Vow*

"Iris Anthony has managed to create a story that is atmospheric and driven at the same time, which is quite rare in my experience. By creating such vastly interesting and deep characters, as well as changing viewpoints, I'm getting the best of all worlds. In short, this book is every reason to go to bed early at night and every reason NOT to sleep once you get there."

—Shawna Elder, Iowa Book, Iowa City, IA

"I loved it...lovely historical fiction about a topic that is not commonly written about."

—Suzy Takacs, The Book Cellar, Chicago IL

"Iris Anthony's *The Ruins of Lace* is a fascinating tale, as intricately woven as her subject matter, about the contraband lace trade in France during the seventeenth century, when fortunes were won and lost over a bit of trim. In this exploration of greed, exploitation, and the meaning of honor, Anthony's characters leap to vivid life, drawing the reader into their destinies, reminding us that we are all complex beings capable of cruelty—and that we also have the power to resist the dark impulses within."

—Sherry Jones, author of *Four Sisters, All Queens*

"*The Ruins of Lace* is a period tale as artfully and skillfully woven as the exquisite length of lace at its center. With tears and laughter, I followed distinctively drawn characters from cloister house to chateau to a smuggler's hut deep in the forest—even to a wooden crate inhabited by an abused dog—all the while fascinated with each twist and turn of the story. This book was a pleasure to read."

—Brenda Rickman Vantrease, author of *The Heretic's Wife*

"An exquisite book, as intricate and enticing as the lace from which it draws its inspiration. I read far too late into the night and finished it the next day only to regret reading it so quickly. This is definitely a keeper to be savored. Whoever Iris Anthony is, she's a gifted writer with what is to be hoped is only the first of many wonderful stories to tell."

—Sara Poole, author of *Poison* and *The Borgia Mistress*

the RUINS of LACE

of

IRIS ANTHONY

sourcebooks
landmark

Copyright © 2012 by Iris Anthony
Cover and internal design © 2012 by Sourcebooks, Inc.
Cover design © Eileen Carey
Lace illustration by Shane Rebenschied
Cover photo © Mark Owen/Trevillion Images, CollaborationJS/Arcangel Images

Sourcebooks and the colophon are registered trademarks of Sourcebooks, Inc.

All rights reserved. No part of this book may be reproduced in any form or by any electronic or mechanical means including information storage and retrieval systems—except in the case of brief quotations embodied in critical articles or reviews—without permission in writing from its publisher, Sourcebooks, Inc.

The characters and events portrayed in this book are fictitious and used fictitiously. Apart from well-known historical figures, any similarity to real persons, living or dead, is purely coincidental and not intended by the author.

Published by Sourcebooks Landmark, an imprint of Sourcebooks, Inc.
P.O. Box 4410, Naperville, Illinois 60567-4410
(630) 961-3900
Fax: (630) 961-2168
www.sourcebooks.com

Library of Congress Cataloging-in-Publication Data

Anthony, Iris.
   The ruins of lace / Iris Anthony.
      p. cm.
   (pbk. : alk. paper) 1. Lace and lace making—Fiction. 2. France—Fiction. I. Title.
   PS3601.N55587R85 2012
   813'.6—dc23

                         2012003466

         Printed and bound in the United States of America.
                 VP 10 9 8 7 6 5 4 3 2 1

A NOTE TO THE READER

THE SEVENTEENTH CENTURY WAS THE AGE OF THE musketeer and fabulous royal wealth. It also was an age of poverty, despair, and unconscionable cruelty. There were those who made lace—and there were those who wore it. While some people paid fantastic prices for the privilege of buying lace, others were forced to make it under the most miserable of circumstances.

Girls were taken into convents at the age of six to learn the trade. They worked long hours with no fire and no light, as ashes and soot might have soiled the lace. It was rare for a lace maker to reach thirty before she had gone blind and permanently hunched from her work.

In 1636, King Louis XIII of France prohibited lace, both foreign and domestic. Those found possessing it were subject to confiscation of the lace, a 6,000-livres fine, and banishment from the kingdom for a period of five years.

Lace was smuggled through Europe for more than two centuries. Smugglers were creative, using hollow loaves of bread as well as coffins and dogs to move lace from Flanders into France. During one fifteen-year period, more than forty thousand dogs were killed by bounty hunters as they tried to cross the border.

Though lace is created from many threads, it is fashioned

from just two simple movements: the twist and the cross. This story, like a length of lace itself, is woven from many strands that are twisted and crossed, first overlapping, then intertwining. To try to follow each thread directly through the pattern of this story would be to miss the pattern maker's intention, just as following one thread through a piece of lace would be to ignore the beauty of the whole.

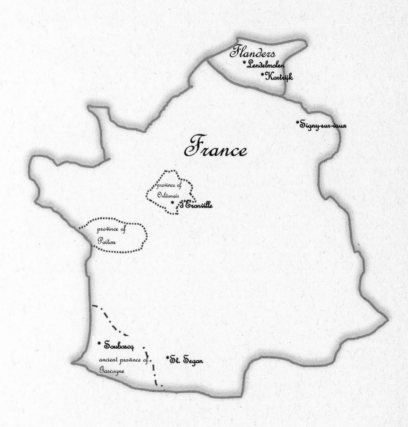

Flanders
•Lendelmolen
•Kortrijk

•Signy-sur-vaux

France

province of
Orléanais
•Éronville

province of
Poitou

•Souboscq
ancient province of
Gascogne

•St. Segon

1636

DURING THE REIGN OF LOUIS XIII, CALLED THE JUST

CHAPTER I

Katharina Martens

LENDELMOLEN, FLANDERS

*I*T HAD BEEN TWO MONTHS NOW. TWO MONTHS since my eyes had betrayed me. The darkness had come upon me so gradually that there had been no fear, no panic. Even now I could still discern shapes and colors. Though the details and textures of my lace were lost to me, my fingers told me what my eyes refused to convey.

I had spun an endless pattern of roses and leaves intertwined, bordered by a path of scrollwork. Every day I had lingered between those blossoms and lost myself in the maze of those scrolls. Every day for over three years. It took time to fashion a lace as long and as fine as this one.

I wriggled my toes within my clogs. At least I thought I did. I could no longer feel them. They had gone numb from autumn's chill. I shifted on the bench, hoping it would bring some life back into them. If not, they would waken with a tingling in the time it took to walk from the workshop to the chapel. By the time I finished with prayers, they would be well again. In winter it was worse. They woke from their sleep with a hot, dull ache.

Autumn.

Winter.

Spring.

Summer.

I had cycled through the years in much the same way I cycled through my bobbins and my pattern. One season, one set of bobbins, one rose after the other, and in the end, I found myself back at the beginning. As a child, cast upon the good graces of the abbey, I had been a fumbling novice at my craft. But now I was a skilled lace maker.

Lace is created from thread. Threads. Many of them. Twisted and crossed, looped and whorled, knotted and woven. But lace is formed from the absence of substance; it is imagined in the spaces between the threads. Lace is a thing like hope. It lived, it survived, and it was desired for what it was not. If faith, as the nuns said, was the substance of things hoped for, then lace was the outline—the suggestion—of things not seen.

Lace was my life. My solace. It was lace that gave my life meaning. And in the working out of my intricate patterns, I had also worked out my salvation. Twenty-five years I had been making lace. Twenty-five blessed years.

As I sat there with my pillow in my lap, the threads performed their intricate dance, leaping and jumping in a counterpoint about their pins. Each group of bobbins clattered to their own rhythm before I dropped them to the pillow to pick up the next. With a twist or a cross, more than two hundred threads danced around the circle before I dropped the last group and started once more with the first.

It amazed me, as it always had, that I should sit with my bobbins, day after day. And that they should perform their dance with so little help from me. Like the fairies my sister used to speak of, they completed their magic seemingly undirected and undeterred by human hands. Except, I *did* direct them. I *did* move them. In fact, they moved only at my command. But once I set them into motion, they seemed to dance alone. I used to watch, breathless, every day, waiting to see what they would create.

I knew, of course.

They would create the kind of lace they created every day, the lace that was named for the abbey: Lendelmolen. That was the only kind of lace we had been taught to make. We'd seen the other kinds. Sister had showed them to us so we could understand how superior our patterns were. But this lace, this length, was different. It was to be fabulously long. Six yards. The exquisite scrolls and roses and leaves had been inscribed by a pattern maker upon a parchment. Pins now marked that design, securing the pattern to my pillow.

But there was a difference between knowing what the bobbins would create and watching them go about their work. It was in the watching that the magic happened.

Of course, I never spoke of the magic. Not to the nuns.

Not to anyone.

Nowhere, at any time within the walls of the abbey, could I speak. Unless it was to God. And even then, we were to speak in whispers. God was a jealous god. He needed our hands. He needed our thoughts…and our voices. They were reserved, all of them, every part of us, for him.

And why should it have been any other way?

Except…I had never heard the voice of Mathild. And I had sat beside her as we worked, for twenty-five years.

Those first years, the years of learning, had been the most difficult. Learning what was expected of us and learning what was not. Learning how to please the Sister in charge of the workshop. Learning how to avoid a beating or a whipping.

And those first whippings…they came so unexpectedly, so brutally, for a sin no greater than a dropped pillow or a missed stitch. So viciously and so cruelly, a girl would be stripped to her waist and punished right in front of us. In front of all of us.

It served its purpose, I suppose.

It goaded us into concentration. But unavoidably, I too dropped my pillow. I too missed a stitch. And strayed from the pattern. I did not think often of those times. So much sadness, so much misery. I had sought the skirts of the Holy Mother herself on one occasion, hiding behind her statue in the chapel. Once I had been coaxed away from her, I was lucky to have survived the beating I was given. But it was then, in the midst of those dim-lit days and lonely nights, that I was taught how to make myself useful. It was then I learned the secrets of lace. And how could I truly despair when I knew, every day upon waking, that in the workshop my lace awaited?

I could survive a scolding, could suffer through a beating, always knowing I had my lace. I couldn't mind stinging buttocks or a bloodied back when my fingers were left untouched for work and my eyes could still see. It was the times when they rapped our knuckles that were the worst. For then we were left bleeding and bruised, forbidden to leave the workshop, but forbidden also to work. If punishment was doled out for failure—failure to concentrate, to keep the lace clean, to master the skills—the lace itself offered its own sort of reward.

To see it created.

To watch it unfurl.

To glimpse a pattern perfectly followed, perfectly accomplished.

I would rather have been whipped to the grave than been kept from my work.

But that had been back when I could see. Now that solitary pleasure had been denied me.

Perhaps in those early days, now that I think on it, I had heard Mathild speak once or twice. But I did not remember her words. To speak brought certain punishment. And so, we had avoided each other's gaze to avoid the temptation to talk. And soon we began, all of us, to sleep with an arm across the face…to ensure that, even in sleep, we would remain guiltless.

But I *had* seen Mathild smile.

And once, I had even seen her wink.

But speak? I could hardly remember those few words.

When would I have heard them? At prayers, we whispered our petitions to the Most Holy God. At meals, we ate. During washing, we washed. And when making lace? Making lace required everything we had. And by the time we collapsed onto our beds, there was nothing left within us. We were quickly consumed by sleep.

Of course, I had heard others talk.

The nuns spoke all the time.

I knew the voice of my teacher: Sister Maria-Clementia. She spoke very little, but when she bent over my pillow to inspect my lace, her "Well done" was like a song of a thousand words. And her "Rework this" could echo through my mind for days. There was no great need for words here. Not when so very few would do. And even when I talked to God, there was little to say. I said, "Thank you," for it was he who had placed me here. I said, "Help me, please," for who did not need help with such difficult work? But mostly, I said…nothing. For what could a poor girl say to such a great and holy God that did not begin and end with gratitude?

But…I had a secret.

I stored up words. I hoarded them, treasured them.

Words were my vice, my greatest weakness. Since I had discovered their great rarity, I remembered every one I heard.

They formed a pattern in my head, and in the spaces between them, I imagined the lives of their speakers. My one regret is how few of my mother's I remembered. But I could not have known, not while she was living, how precious few she would be able to give me.

She had talked often…so many lovely words. They came back to me sometimes in my sleep, like a length of *punto in aria* lace. Vast spaces of nothing, and then, suddenly, the outline of an intricate pattern. It was all the more beautiful for its spare design. Her words had the lightness of a butterfly. They were always dancing. Always followed by laughter. At least…that is how it seems to me now.

But perhaps I have distorted the pattern in transferring it to my memories. For what followed after her death was so… bleak. When she had been alive, there were words, nothing but words, in our house, and then after…silence reigned over all.

I remember only two words from my father. Perhaps he gave me more than those two…certainly he probably did while my mother was living.… but the only two I remember are the last ones he spoke to me.

Fare well.

Only those two words remain, and they are underscored by sorrow. They hang heavily in my heart. He died five years after I was committed to the abbey. Those two words are all I have left of him, but two words are not enough to make a pattern.

Fare well.

Was it a blessing? A wish? A hope?

Perhaps it was a sort of benediction. I do not know.

My sister, Heilwich…well, she has words enough for the both of us. And the words she gives me are more than enough to last the week between her visits. She speaks of her life, of the priest whose home she keeps, of her good works. Her pattern is *torchon*. Regular, repeating. Competent. Her design makes a sturdy lace. Not fancy, not frivolous. Respectable. Dependable.

And I imagine her life to be just that way.

But I have more than just family from whom to collect words.

I have the people walking by the workshop, past the abbey wall, on the street outside.

There is one man who walks the streets, shouting every day. He sells fish. And he does it especially loudly on Fridays. He shouts everything about them. How large they are, how fresh they are. He sells sole and plaice. Eels and herrings. Sometimes they cost more, and sometimes they cost less. And sometimes he sells something called a mussel. But only in the winter. I've always wondered what it looked like, a mussel.

But then, I had always wondered what he looked like as well.

His words were not fancy; they created an ordinary *malines* design. His pattern was the same, day after day, fish after fish. There were few holes, few gaps, from which to pattern a life apart from the street beyond the wall. I imagined he woke with fish and he worked with fish, and when he slept, he dreamt of fish.

It was what I did too…only with lace, of course. I understood a life like his. Except…How did he come by them? That great variety of fish? And how did he carry them? For certain by cart, for I could hear the wheels tumble across the cobbles. But…how? Tossed together in a great pile? Separated into baskets?

And where did he live?

What did he wear?

9

The holes in his pattern were tiny, but they were there, nonetheless. His was a life set upon a platform of a fine network of threads.

There was also a woman who shouted in the streets beyond the wall. But she didn't shout about something. She shouted *at* something. Was it a child? She shouted at someone called Pieter, who always seemed to be making a mess of things.

But what kind of mess was it?

Was he a child who rubbed his hands in the ashes of a fire…and then spread the soot about the house? That would make a mess. The worst kind of mess I could imagine.

She also shouted at someone else called Mies. And Mies always made her late.

But late to what? Where was she going, this woman who seemed to have nothing to do but walk the length of the streets, shouting all day? What was Mies doing to make her late, and how could Mies do whatever it was all day long, every day? And if it was always the same thing Mies did, then why did the woman not stop it from being done?

There was a pattern to this woman that made no sense, huge holes in the design of her life. Hers was a lace made of cutwork. Not dainty, not fragile. Without subtlety, it was bold in the extreme. A pattern without any elegance at all, and one which kept repeating. That lace was one of my least favorite kinds.

There were others out there on the street besides. I could hear them walking and running. And hear the sounds of their voices talking. But those people did not shout, and so I knew nothing of the actual words they said.

There were babies who cried.

And once, there had been a shriek. A howl.

The wordless sound of grief: black lace. The worst kind

to make. The kind I made as a child, new to the abbey. After being dyed its dark color, it would not show soiling. We could make it imperfectly, for the color hid our sins. We made it fast, though never for commission. It was for immediate consumption. For who could know when a soul might die?

No one thought of black lace—no one wanted to think of it—but somehow, we never seemed to be able to make enough of it. But to make a lace no one ever wanted? Those days, those laces...they were sad. And so was that howl.

So at times, I suppose, one word...one wordless sound... could create a pattern. It could tell a story...but some laces are not worth imagining.

Far better, far better, to keep my thoughts to what I knew. And what I knew best, the only thing I knew at all, was lace. The abbey had been kind enough to take me as a child from my motherless family, even though I knew how to do nothing at all. They had fed me; they had taught me. They had allowed me a chance to redeem myself. To prove myself worthy of the life I had been given. And so I worked, I labored, as one who would not be ashamed. *Nee*: one who could not be ashamed. When God looked down on what it was I had done, I knew the only thing he could say was this: *well done.*

My eyes strained through the darkness, trying—and failing—to discern one thread from another. In a short time we would be allowed a candle, but for now, my fairy dance continued, unaided, unfettered, by my lack of sight. As we worked, we waited. Waited in anticipation, just as we waited in the chapel to receive the Host.

Soon, Sister placed a single candle on a table before us. And then she began positioning the condensers. Clear glass balls filled with water, they focused the candle's light and then sent it forth. Around the table she went, adjusting each one so it cast a narrow beam of light upon each pillow.

With much gratitude, we repositioned our work into that light.

When I could still see well, it had been more difficult to work after the shadows of night fell. The pillow had to be constantly adjusted to follow the flickering of the candle's light. Now, it didn't matter. I could work in darkness as if it were the brightest of noondays. I had memorized my pattern. But still, I had to concentrate.

Think too much, and I would muddle up the bobbins. Think too little, and I would lose my place in the pattern. In my head, I sung a little tune the sisters had chanted when I was a child. And quick as that, the dance regained its rhythm and its grace.

I sung it to myself over and over, again and again. Who knows how many times I sung it, until at last, Sister said the word: *Done.*

My prayers that night were wordless.

My supper, tasteless.

My sleep, dreamless.

CHAPTER 2

Heilwich Martens

KORTRIJK, FLANDERS

I HAD BEEN SO CLOSE LAST MONTH! I'D HAD EVERY Spanish real the Reverend Mother had demanded. She had glanced up from her table as I entered the room, her coronet making her head look as if it were about to take flight.

I touched a knee to the floor. "Reverend Mother."

"And you are…?"

"I am Heilwich Martens. Of Kortrijk."

"Heilwich Martens…"

"I work for Father Jacqmotte. At Sint-Maartenskerk."

"Ah. A priest's woman." The Reverend Mother nodded, sending a shiver through her veil.

"I came to speak to you about my sister. I wish to take her home with me."

"Sister—? Which one?"

"*My* sister. My own sister. Katharina. She makes lace." I withdrew the pouch from my sleeve and set it on the table before her. The coins inside it betrayed their presence with a clink.

The Reverend Mother's hand snaked out and clasped the pouch, loosened the thong that bound it, and poured the contents out upon the table. "Katharina, you say? I am told she is our best lace maker."

I was surprised the Reverend Mother knew her, but isn't

that what Katharina had told me herself? That she was the abbey's best lace maker? An undue sense of pride kindled within my veins. I felt my chin lift.

"We have come to rely upon her skills."

Katharina had told me that as well.

"The skills we have spent many months, many years, in fact, perfecting."

Ja. I knew quite well how many years there had been between Katharina's leaving our father's house and my own visit to the abbey this day. Twenty-five of them.

"This is not enough to compensate us for our expense in training her." She gathered the coins and dropped them back into the pouch.

Clink.

Clink.

Clink.

Clink.

Clink.

She secured the thong and pushed it back across the table toward me.

"But…but…last time we spoke, this is the price you named!" And I had worked and saved for five years to gather all of it.

"That was several years ago, was it not?"

"*Ja*, but—"

"Did you think we would stop teaching her in the intervening time? Stop feeding her? Clothing her? Providing a place for her to sleep? A chapel in which to worship?"

"*Nee*, but—"

"Surely you can understand we must be compensated for all we have invested in her."

"But she is not a…a…piece of property or a…a…cow! She's a girl! And she's nearly gone blind from all of the lace you've made her make!"

"Blind? Truly? I shall have to investigate."

I shut my mouth up tight as a cooper's barrel. I had said too much. Or perhaps…perhaps I had not said enough. "*Ja!* She's hunched as an old woman. And very soon you'll throw her out of your abbey, just as you always do to those too blind to be of use." If the abbey could not see her worth, the men who lurked at the abbey's gates would. A girl did not have to see to be persuaded to open her legs to paying customers.

"And what would you have us do? Keep girls who can provide no assistance in exchange for our very great generosity? We would soon have to shut our doors."

"If you won't take my money, could you send for me before you turn her out?"

"For what purpose?"

"So I can take her home."

"You mean keep her here until you are able to come fetch her?"

"*Ja.*"

"As if we were some kind of lodging house?" The crook of her brow above her eyes told me her answer before she even spoke it. "Kortrijk is quite a walk, even if the father would let you come. I cannot do this. If I did it for you, then every family would expect the same."

"How much more do you need?"

She named her price.

It was much more than I could ever hope to earn, even if I had five more years in which to do it. Katharina was as lost to me as our father and mother. I had told her I would rescue her, but I couldn't do it.

I did what I could. I shamed the men who lingered by the gate into leaving, though I had no hope my words would drive them far. I shuddered to think of Katharina having to throw herself upon their mercy. I gave a silver coin to an urchin, as well. "If you see a girl come from the abbey, one of the lace makers, come tell me in Kortrijk. I work for Father Jacqmotte at Sint-Maartenskerk. The church with the great tower. Her name would be Katharina."

"Katharina."

"*Ja.*"

"And if I do? If I come tell you…?"

"Then I will give you another one of these." I took a second silver coin from my purse and held it out so he could see it.

His good eye gleamed as he reached for it.

I enclosed it within my fist. "And what is your name? Remember, I work for a priest. I'll tell him if you lie to me or if you cheat me."

The hand withdrew as he eyed me for a moment. Then his frown relaxed and, finally, he spoke. "Pieter. My name is Pieter."

I had done what I could, but it had not made my heart feel better. It still didn't, even three days later. Katharina should have been me. I should have been the one the abbey had taken. I was the older sister, after all. Katharina could easily have been placed out for work somewhere. She was a child of the sun, all golden hair and gleaming smiles. But I was not the one the abbey chose. They had taken one look at my short, stubby fingers and had not even let me enter their gates. It wasn't what we had planned. Not at all. It was me who was oldest. Me who ate the most. But in the end, it was Katharina they had taken and me they had left behind.

Several years after Katharina had gone, Father died, and the parish priest had taken me in. The elderly housekeeper showed me how to sweep a wood floor and how to manage a kitchen. Father Jacqmotte taught me how to care for the needs of the sick and how to lay out the dead. I did all the work—I did everything—but it still did nothing to beat back the knowledge that it was all my fault.

It was my fault Father had died: he had placed into my bowl the food intended for his own mouth. And it was my fault Katharina had become what she was: a girl who had found her age too early. Back bent, fingers gnarled from her work.

But in the priest's house, I had served the penance for my sins. I had worked my short, stubby fingers to the bone these twenty-five years to regain that which had been lost…only to discover my work had been in vain. It had not been enough.

I had not saved enough.

I might have paused by the River Leie, sat down upon the bank, and wept into my apron for sorrow at what life might have been, but there was too much to be done in the life that was. There were wicks to be trimmed and accounts to be looked over, supper to be prepared and vestments to be mended. There was old Herry Stuer to be visited. His pallet to be changed and water dripped into his mouth.

And for certain, the girl who looked after him would stick me with his care for the rest of the forenoon.

But I was the priest's woman. Such things, such generosity of time and of spirit, were expected of me. A gentle hand, a cool head, a ready smile…when all I wanted to do most times was shriek at them all and dash them over the head with my broom.

I turned from the river, jabbed at my tears with the edge of my apron, and sniffed the rest of them back down. It was too late for sorrow, and tears helped nothing.

CHAPTER 3

Denis Boulanger

THE BORDER OF FRANCE AND FLANDERS

I DON'T KNOW WHY I BOTHER."

Was the lieutenant asking me a question? Did he expect an answer? With him, sometimes it was hard to know. And the sun had barely just peered into the sole window of the shack. It was a tough job pleasing the lieutenant before he'd eaten the day's first meal.

"You understand what your job is."

Another statement that seemed as if it might be a question. So then I must answer it. "*Oui*, Lieutenant." It was to assist the *douaniers* with their work. To help them by guarding the border with the Spanish Netherlands and to assist in the collection of import taxes.

He looked down his long, crooked nose at me. "Then why aren't you doing it?"

Ah. Now there was a question. A true question. But it was a question I did not understand. "I am…I mean, I thought—?"

"Do you know what passes across the border? Every single day?"

"*Oui, chef*." I did. People. Sometimes animals. And carts.

"Hundreds of people cross the border every single day." He'd raised his hands, slicing at the air in front of me, setting in motion the lace that hung like cobwebs from his wrists. "And do you know what they carry with them?"

That was a question that really didn't sound like one. It didn't seem as if he truly wanted an answer. So I kept my mouth shut. That was easiest. How I wished he would stop talking, so I could stop standing at attention.

"The people who cross the border here are liars, cheats, and thieves. Every single one of them."

Every single one? I found that difficult to believe. The old granny I had given my arm to just the other day? Surely she wasn't a liar or a cheat or a thief. And that young mother with the three children, one of them just a babe in her arms? She had looked as if she might dissolve into tears at any moment. That's why I had helped to hurry her through the line. For that was my job, after all: to aid the *douaniers*.

"Do you know whom they're trying to cheat?"

Well. That was an easy question to answer. My mother had always said cheaters cheated only themselves. Although… hadn't they first to cheat someone else? Before they cheated themselves? Isn't that what cheating was?

"Denis!"

"*Oui, chef!*" I pulled my chin in even closer to my chest, making it touch the top button on my coat.

"Every blessed day, thousands of livres of merchandise cross this border. And do you know what's wrong with most of it?"

I guessed—I supposed—an answer was expected. "That it comes from the Spanish Netherlands? From those Flemish?"

"Those dirty, rotten, stinking Flemish. *Oui.* And those dirty, rotten, stinking Spaniards."

"The dirty, rotten, stinking, *filthy* Spaniards."

"You've a way with words, Denis Boulanger."

"*Merci, mon chef.*"

I'd always liked words. They were so particular as to their meaning. No one word could ever quite substitute for another. It wasn't like the army, where it didn't really matter what you looked like or where you were from. Where the next man could do the job just as well as you.

"But the fact that all of those goods come from Flanders and those *débectable* Spaniards doesn't really concern me at all. Do you know what concerns me?"

I could guess, but I wasn't sure I would be right. It was safest not to answer.

"What concerns me is those dirty, rotten, stinking Flemish are smuggling contraband across our border every single day."

I'd heard that. The lieutenant had said that. He'd said it nearly every day for these six months I'd been posted here.

"And do you know who helps them?"

Well—*non. Non,* I didn't.

"We do. We French do. We French conspire with those dirty, rotten, stinking Flemish to cheat our own King out of the tariffs he deserves."

Not *we* French. I mean, *I* didn't. And the lieutenant didn't. *Some* French. That was the better way to say it. *Some* French do.

"But do you know what's worse, Denis Boulanger?"

There were many things that were worse. So many things that were worse. It was difficult to choose just one.

"What's worse is some people even try to smuggle in things that are forbidden. Did you know that?"

"*Oui, chef.*" I knew that.

"Every single day, people try to bring things into France that don't belong here. Things the King, *our* King, doesn't want here."

He had come to stand quite near me. His tips of his boots touched the tips of my own.

"*Oui, chef!*"

He scowled. "*Oui, chef? Oui, chef!* You know this?"

"*Oui, chef.*"

"Then why don't you do something about it!" He yelled the words so loudly they hurt my ears. So forcefully his spittle landed on my face.

I couldn't keep from blinking. And falling back from his assault. "I do, *chef.* I mean, I try."

"You haven't tried hard enough. Do you know how many times you've intercepted contraband these past six months?"

I nodded. I did. I knew exactly how many times.

"None! Thousands of livres in goods are smuggled across this border daily, and you've intercepted none of it!" He shook his wrist in front of my face. "Do you know how old this lace is?"

"*Non, chef.*"

"Six months old. And do you know why?"

"*Non, chef.*"

"It's because you haven't brought me any that's newer!"

"I haven't...I've never seen any."

"Never seen any. *Bon.*" He turned on a heel and strode to his desk.

I wished I could do that. Turn on my heel and do it so quickly it looked like my foot was nailed to the floor. I'd tried. Many times. But I'd only ever made myself stumble.

"Never seen any. Never going to. I'm going to send you somewhere else. Lots of places to choose from. We're a country at war with these dirty, rotten, stinking Spaniards. So... do you think you could kill someone?"

"Kill someone?"

"With that musket."

"Why?"

"Why what?"

"Why would I want to kill someone?"

He sighed. Took up a piece of paper and began writing. "I

have here, in my hand, your new orders." He signed them with a flourish as he spoke.

"*Chef?*"

"You're leaving. I'm done with you. You're a disgrace to your King."

"But...I...I *would* catch them. I would arrest those smugglers if I could only tell which ones they were."

"The trouble with you, Denis Boulanger, is you've no imagination. Do you know how contraband crosses the border? How *lace* crosses the border? Because that's what we're looking for—*lace*. Do you know how lace crosses the border?"

I nodded. He'd explained it many times.

"Lace crosses the border in hollow loaves of bread. It crosses the border pinned to a woman's underskirts or the inside of a man's breeches. It crosses the border in boots and books. It even crosses the border in coffins."

Coffins? I didn't think I believed him. I was quite sure, in fact, that I didn't.

"It crosses the border with men and women. With children and dogs. With the young and with the very old. It crosses the border with *people*."

Oui. I knew all of that. Every day I looked for lace. That was what I was supposed to do. But how could I know who was smuggling it? "Just—give me more time! I'll find some lace. I promise."

He folded his arms in front of him, leaned on the table's top. Frowned. "I've been giving you more time for six months now."

"Please."

He scowled. "Fine. One more month. It's hard enough as it is with the war going on. Be warned, if you don't find any"—he waved the orders above his head as he dismissed me with his other hand—"then you're done."

. CHAPTER 4 .

The Dog

RURAL FLANDERS

I HAVE TWO NAMES.

One of my masters, my bad master, calls me Chiant. But I refuse to come when I hear it. That must be why he keeps me in the box that has no holes.

The other master, the good master, calls me Moncherargent...or sometimes just Moncher...and I like that best of all. When he says Moncher, he speaks it in a whisper. He says it in a sigh that feels to my ears the way his hand feels as he strokes my fur. *Moncher, Moncher, Moncher,* he says as I sit in his lap by the fire.

He frees me from my burden of lace, and he feeds me all I want and then just a little bit more. And he gives me milk to drink. Cream he calls it. And it's that cream I miss the most. Especially now, as I wait in the box. Especially now that I am Chiant once more.

I wish I knew how to keep from being sent away by the good master.

I was so careful last time.

I didn't yelp. I never yelp. Not at the good master. Not after that first nap in his lap. And never after my first taste of cream.

No. I had not yelped.

I had not nipped, either. Not at him. I could never bite the hand that tended my wounds. That fed me and caressed my fur.

No. I had not nipped.

But had I whined?

Perhaps.

I pushed to my feet and set my nose to work, trying to sniff out a hole. A big one. One bigger than the cracks through which the ants came in. If I could just find a hole, then I could make it bigger. And then I could get a taste of the rain my ears told me was falling on the box. And perhaps, if I were lucky, then I could find a way out. And I could run to my good master. And maybe this time I could stay.

But it was no good. I could not see, and surely if there were a hole, there would be light. What's more, my nose never failed me. And it had sniffed no moving air. No scent of forest or wind. The only thing I could smell was my own filth.

I pressed my back against the corner and curled myself into a ball.

No. There was no way out.

I whined.

I could not help it. The memory of fires and laps and cream was too fresh in my senses. I could feel the warmth. Taste the milk.

I whined again.

Yes. Perhaps I had whined at the good master. But could I not be forgiven such things? And how else was I to tell him what had happened to me? How else was I to make him understand? To keep him from sending me away?

For if he knew, surely he would not return me to the bad master.

If only he knew.

If only people could talk.

I woke.

How long had I been asleep?

I raised an ear. Took a listen.

The rain had stopped.

I let my ear flop back down against my head. I didn't like the rain. I couldn't hear the birds sing, and the squirrels weren't about their business. Someday...one day... perhaps one day I could pause for just a moment on my race through the forest. Maybe one day I would be able to see what those squirrels were doing. And know why those birds were singing.

But just now...just now I needed to think.

I needed to figure something out.

I wish I remembered what it was.

Something whined.

Something that sounded a lot like me.

I lifted my ear once more.

Nothing.

My stomach growled.

Maybe the whine had been me.

I was so hungry. But the only way to cure hunger was to not think about food. I would not think about the meat the good master fed me. And how it was always warm, and how the juices trickled down my chin. And I would certainly not think about the cream. I would not think about cream so thick I could almost chew it. Cream that coated my throat with lovely fat as I drank it. No. I could not think about cream.

I licked my nose, hoping for a drip or two.

Nothing.

It was dry. Dry as my mouth. Worse even.

I closed my eyes. I did not know why I had bothered to open them. I couldn't see anything, open or closed. The only thing to do was wait. I would not think about food. Or drink. I would not think about my belly or how it gnawed at me from the inside. Or the fleas that gnawed at me from the outside.

I rolled onto my side. The hunger shifted within me. I would rather be too hot or too cold than too hungry. There was no escape from hunger.

☙

I woke.

But I woke with fear.

If only I could see.

I lifted an ear.

Silence.

There was, perhaps, a wind. And underneath it…a sound. I put an ear to the floor of the box. Underneath the sound of the wind…the sound of footsteps.

I curled into myself. It would go easier that way. And I made sure to tuck my nose beneath my paws.

"Chiant, pain in the ass! *Espèce de crétin!* I am coming. I come for you…"

My box slid out from underneath me. I splayed my legs to keep from bouncing against its walls. I began to growl but stopped it up in my throat. If I said nothing, if I did nothing, perhaps he would think I had escaped.

The box rose up at one corner and tipped over onto its side. I closed my eyes. Open or closed, I could see nothing. And if I could not see him, then perhaps he would not see me. Memories of other shouts, other shakings, tried to invade my thoughts, but I did not let them.

Again the box turned over. This time; the top ended up on the bottom. And all my filth ended up on top of me.

Something struck the box. Something hard, something sharp. This was it then.

I pushed off my feet, crouching. If I shoved off hard, if I acted quickly, then perhaps I could make my escape now. The last time I had tried to dodge him, but this time I would run straight toward him. I would aim for the place where his knees stuck out. And if I could not run through them, then I would scamper up over him.

I pulled my ears in toward my head.

I could hear the wood splinter.

With a squeal of nail against wood, the wall came off. I was blinded by beautiful light. And I was struck by a switch. It must have been a switch. Only a switch could tear through my fur that way. Only a switch could lay open bare flesh.

Too late I remembered I must protect my nose.

Too late I remembered to curl into a ball.

Too late I remembered my plans for escape.

Too late. I was too late. I was always too late.

"Chiant! *Tu m'fait chier! Quelle chierie!*"

As he stood there over me in his shimmering gray clothes with his glinting cap, I gave up.

I rolled onto my back.

He struck me anyway. "If you didn't bring us such a sum of silver, I'd kill you now and be done with the bother."

Why could he not see I had surrendered? That I meant no threat?

"*Cher argent*, all that lovely money you bring us!"

I turned my neck so he could see the length of it. Perhaps this time he would kill me. I would gladly give up fires and laps and cream for the pleasures of oblivion.

But still he beat me. Still the switch searched out every hidden place.

As I lay there in the mud, I looked up at the sky. I imagined birds. I imagined the squirrels that would return with the warmer season. They would jump along the top of the house, carrying things between their teeth. Maybe someday they would carry me away, too.

I woke.

I was back in my box.

I was shivering, but I was also hot.

I sniffed at the air. The air was cold.

If the air was cold, then it was I who was hot.

I was hot, and I hurt.

I hurt all over.

I tried to whine but gave it up, putting my tongue to work instead. I tried to lick my wounds, but my tongue would not obey. It had no moisture. Even if it had, my fur clung together so tightly I could not reach the sores. And so I gnawed at the knots. I pulled the fur from my skin with violent tugs. And then I lay down on my belly, put my head on my paws, and settled down to wait.

I do not know how long I waited. When I heard the master return, I could barely lift my head. I did not have the strength. He pried the wall off my box and raised it on end, dumping me out on my head.

I was too tired, too miserable, and too sick to complain.

But outside the box in that light, after a while, I could see again. Even if my eyes did not work quite so well as normal.

The master leaned in close to take a look at me. Reached out a finger and poked it at my eye. "*Emmerdeur!* I should have taken better care. You cannot run for me if you go blind."

I wished I could see better. If I had any strength, if my

eyes had been working, I would have chomped at his nose and torn it from his face.

He threw a pail of water at me.

I put out my tongue to lap it up.

"Stop! It's for washing, not for drinking!" He threw three more pails at me and dabbed something onto my eye with a stick before shoving me back into the box.

There was the peace of silence then.

And the knowledge that if I could survive, eventually I would be free, running through the forest on the way to the good master. And this time, I would try to be so good he would never send me back.

CHAPTER 5

Lisette Lefort

Château of Souboscq
The province of Gascogne, France

I SAW IT AGAIN, IN MY DREAMS. THAT EXQUISITE, fabulous lace. I marveled at the meticulous and perfect regularity of its pattern, the gorgeous repeating roses. My fingers itched to stroke its luster. And, oh, how I admired the lavish folds of those cuffs. They reminded me of *Maman*, and I wanted them.

I wanted her.

She too had worn cuffs of lace. They had not been so grand; there had hardly been a flounce to them at all. But seeing that pair brought to mind her cool, gentle touch and the way her hands always seemed to be dancing along to the rhythm of her words.

But *Maman*'s hands had been stilled when she died of lung fever. And her cuffs had been entombed with her. She lived now only in my dreams.

Such sweet, though fleeting, dreams.

I watched as my seven-year-old self entered our guest's chamber, shuffling through the rushes on the tips of her toes. I saw her kneel beside the visitor's trunk and slowly open the lid. I heard her gasp with delight at the magnificent treasure nestled inside.

She ought never to have done it.

She knew she had no right to inspect a visitor's belongings.

And there had been many visitors to the château through the years, many guests stopping for a night, as was customary, or even a week's lodging on their way to or from Bordeaux. So many nobles with their sparkling coats and shimmering gowns.

But this visitor was different.

He was a noble, to be sure, a count. And he was the most beautiful person that young girl had ever seen, with shiny locks of dark hair falling in curls past his shoulders, and rings glittering from his fingers. He wore blue rosettes on his heeled slippers, and a hat that was both larger and floppier than her cousin, Alexandre's. He was all dark and very tall.

He'd caught the little girl's gaze a time or two as he talked in the entrance hall with her papa, but he had promptly disregarded it. And then he had proceeded to ply her papa with news from the court. Though she had asked after the Queen, the man told her women were of little importance, and her papa had hushed her. When she drifted from the hall, neither of them noticed. It was that which had driven her to the guest's room. She wasn't used to being ignored. And becoming a woman like her *maman* was the only thing she'd ever wished to do.

She was quite sure the guest wouldn't like her looking over his things, and that's exactly why she had done it.

But now, she paused at the trunk with her fingers hooked over its edge as she stared at the lace.

The bishop had worn this sort of cuff when he said Mass on Easter day. It spumed from the cuffs of his alb like a froth on fresh milk. She stretched out a hand toward it... should she?

I watched as she bit her lip in thought.

In that gossamer world of dreams where time twists and space shifts, I was everywhere and nowhere at once. I saw the back of her head, watched that mass of golden ringlets

34

tremble as she reached into the trunk. At the same time, I saw the glint of longing in her eyes as her hand hovered above the lace.

The two cuffs were set into a bowl made by a pair of gloves. As she slid a hand beneath them, they released their perfumes of jasmine, orange blossoms, and carnations, scents so cloying she almost gagged.

Perhaps they would dissuade her...but no. I felt tears of frustration prick my eyes.

The little girl merely coughed, took in a deep breath through her mouth, and turned toward the lace once more. The scents had done nothing to deter her. But though she wanted to touch the cuffs, though she was prodded by a nearly irresistible frisson of desire, she did not. Not at first, in any case. But soon, the inevitability of what must happen began to invade my dream.

I tried to call out. I tried to make that young girl stop. To turn, at least, and listen for one moment to reason. But she would not be swayed. She would not be swayed because of what she saw. It was so...beautiful. So lovely. A yearning to hold it, for just one moment to possess her mother once more, took hold of her.

You must not do it! Even in my dreams I felt that old, familiar weight of despair. I felt, again, the loss of all the lovely things we possessed no more: the tapestries and the Turkey carpets, the collection of enameled boxes and the jeweled crucifixes, the pairs of silver candlesticks. All of those humble comforts that had been luxuries to us, all those prized family treasures the little girl had caused to disappear.

She dipped her hands into the trunk, and they came out clutching the lace cuffs. They were even more glorious, more magnificent than she had thought. A pattern of leaves and petals, intertwined with a filigree of scrollwork, repeating again and again and again. A circle that never ended, a pattern so finely detailed that it seemed to undulate across the fine mesh into which it had been woven. She ought to have put them back right then. If she had put them back right then, none of the misery that had followed would have happened.

But she did not.

After slipping them over her wrists, she closed her eyes and imagined those cuff-draped hands to be her beloved *maman*'s. She wrapped her own arms around herself and pretended it was the embrace of her mother.

Sois sage, *be good, my sweet angel.*

It's too much trouble to be good, Maman.

But it's only the good who marry well, ma chérie, *the bad always get what they deserve.*

Then I shall be the most good girl who ever lived.

If only you had lived, *Maman!*

The little girl embraced herself one more time, and then she opened her eyes and made the sign of the cross. The lace swayed in the air, just as the bishop's had. She swept her hands up and down, back and forth, watching it ripple, taking great satisfaction in the fact that it seemed to weigh nothing at all.

Weightless.

Spotless.

Priceless.

I wanted to lecture her. I wanted to plead with her. I wanted more than anything to beg her not to do it. If only I could have explained what would happen. But though my mouth was open, no sound issued forth. Though I tried to run to her, though I wanted to take her in my arms and spirit her away, my limbs would not move.

Now, she pretended she was to marry. Pushing the cuffs farther up her arms, she smiled at a groom she would never have. She imagined marrying above her station, to a prince, perhaps. Or at least to a count. She glided across the room, chin held high, shoulders pushed excruciatingly far back. She curtseyed to the King and then to the Queen. She danced what she thought was a courante. But after a while, she tired of the game, and she ached with the rigid posture she decided marriage protocol required.

Much better, perhaps, to marry Alexandre, whom she would not have to impress.

She considered returning the cuffs to the chest and searching out her cousin. She even turned and started across the room. But then she stopped.

I knew what would happen next. I did not want to watch it, but I could not close my eyes.

What was it that possessed her? What sort of familiar spirit was it that told her if she held her arms out straight like posts and then rotated them, those cuffs would spin around her wrists faster than the miller's wheel? And what made her note the lace, when set in motion, looked like the stream in the forest as it flowed over the rocks?

Around and around and around.

Faster and faster and faster.

Until…One of them took flight.

We both watched—she in astonishment, I in dread—as that cuff flew across the room and then skidded to a stop in the fireplace. There was no fire. There would be no fire until later that evening. But there had been fires. Any number of fires over the years had left the hearth a deep and sooty black. The girl approached that place, heart in her mouth, bent down, and plucked the cuff from the dingy gloom.

It was…mostly clean. Except for an area at the edge upon which it had slid through the ashes. There, it had been soiled, the scrollwork thrown into dark relief.

I watched the girl's chin tremble and her face pucker as she thought of the *maman* who could neither comfort her nor right her mistakes. I also saw the moment when she realized it would do no good at all to cry. She had touched something that did not belong to her. She had gone where she was not supposed to go. Even her dear *maman* would have scolded her. She knew she must not be found out. She must hide the evidence of her sin. If she could do that, then no one would ever know.

I felt her guilt. I knew her panic. How could she rid the lace of its stain?

She tried to rub it along the hem of her skirts, but it succeeded only in smearing the soot's dark edge. Perhaps…if she cut off the part that had been soiled, then no one would ever know.

No—a thousand times no!

She dropped the cuffs back into the trunk and furtively shut the lid before leaving the room. But she would be back. She would take her shears from her workbasket, she would conceal them in the folds of her skirt, and she would return to the guest's chamber.

Was there no other way for this dream to end?

There she was. And here she came, padding through the rushes toward the trunk. She lifted the lid. She pulled out the lace. She picked up the shears.

Don't!

She set the edge of the lace between their sharp, cold, heavy jaws.

No!

Carefully, so carefully, lip caught between her teeth, she cut away the decorative fringe of the pattern, severing the soiled part from the rest. She secreted the evidence in her slipper, hiding it with the sole of her foot, and then she put the rest of the lace back inside the trunk. As she pulled down the lid once more, she was confident no one would learn of her transgression.

But she didn't know then what I knew now.

She didn't understand how quickly a life can fray. How a single thread come undone can cause the unraveling of everything else around it.

But that was not the worst of the dream. The worst of it was this: I woke wanting the same thing I had wanted back then. I woke wanting *Maman*. I woke wanting to touch that lace. And I knew if I had it do all over again, I would do the very same thing. The worst was knowing I could not have done anything other than what I did.

The Count of Montreau didn't care that it was an accident. "She didn't mean to." I clung to my cousin Alexandre's hand as Papa stepped between the count and me.

"I don't care if she meant to pronounce some magic over it and increase its length threefold!" He leaned around Papa to glare at me as he yelled.

"She's just a child. She didn't know what she was doing."

"What she did just cost you two thousand livres."

"Two thousand! I could buy a second estate with that!"

"That's the exact amount it took to buy the cuffs. But…" He looked at Papa in a way that made him seem older than his years. "Perhaps I ought to charge you more. When I purchased it, such laces from Flanders were common. Now, all lace is forbidden. It would take twice as much to buy the same length today. If you dared to."

I held my breath. No one ever dared Papa to do anything.

"I don't have two thousand livres."

"I don't want two thousand. I want four thousand."

Alexandre was tugging me toward the door. I didn't want to go. "Come."

"*Non!*"

Alexandre bent and picked me up. He had never done that before. He had rarely ever touched me. Though he had never been anything but gentle and kind and good, there was something about him that precluded any contact.

Papa had put a hand to the count's arm. "I don't have the money. Please. You must understand. I could sell all I own, and still I could not pay you." He swiped at the beads of sweat that had sprung into relief upon his forehead.

I beat at Alexandre with my fists, but he would not let me go.

"Yes, well, it's too bad you took part in Chalais's conspiracy against the King's chief minister."

Papa swayed as if the floor had suddenly tilted.

"I know the Duchess of Chevreuse. She was the Marquis of Chalais's lover. If you're going to involve yourself in further conspiracies, may I suggest you choose your companions more wisely? If she who helps make the plans does not bother to guard them…? Did you truly think the King would not take offense? Or Richelieu himself would not be troubled?"

Papa was trembling. "I'd thought no one…I had hoped—"

"Truly, it would indeed be too bad if you were brought to the King's attention. The duchess has fled the country… Chalais is dead…there would be only you to answer for their sins. And make no mistake; Richelieu continues to search for conspirators. That's why I try always to avoid such plots— they're so easily scuttled."

What was a conspiracy? And why should the King himself care? It did not take long for me, a girl who never failed to satisfy her curiosity, to find the answers to all of those questions. And less time still for those answers to change all of our lives.

. CHAPTER 6 .

The Count of Montreau

CHÂTEAU OF ERONVILLE
THE PROVINCE OF ORLÉANAIS, FRANCE

WHAT I WANTED WAS LACE: THE PERFECT, IRRESISTible bribe. That I needed it at all was a humiliation, predicated upon the whim of a tyrannical old man who was grieved beyond measure that he must call himself my father.

I closed my eyes against the headache building at the bridge of my nose.

If only he hadn't commanded us all to the countryside. If we had been at court, then I might not have aggravated him so easily. But in such close quarters, where he was daily confronted with the fact that I was his son, how could I have expected him to treat me with anything other than contempt? He'd surpassed even himself that morning when he stormed into my chambers and placed my entire future in jeopardy.

He hadn't bothered to announce his presence. He'd thrown open the shutters, bathing the room in ungodly light. One lamentable thing had led to another, and soon we were doing what we had always done. He was yelling; I was pretending not to listen, infusing my indifference with a tincture of ennui.

"My son?" The venom in my father's voice had matched the look on his face. Things always finished badly when he referred to me in that tone. "My *son*?!"

But it was even worse when he pronounced it like that, as if I were some grand disappointment to him in his old age.

"I gave you one of my titles, but I'll be damned if I give you another! There is nothing I can do about the happenstance of your birth, but I will not live to see you destroy my good name."

I clasped my hands behind my back. "There are other options..." I could think of several, though only one had any true appeal.

"What? What was it you said?"

My mistake. He was not yet so old that he was deaf. I lifted my shoulders. Took a deep breath. Bowed my head in a way I hoped would convey all of those sentiments I did not feel: obedience, filiality, humility. "I said, 'Please, sir. What are my options?'"

"Options? Options!" His face was contorted with rage.

"My options. If you please."

"There are no options. Not anymore. I've told you before: you must turn your back on your despicable ways, marry, and produce an heir. Had you done it, I might have considered leaving you all of those things to which your birth entitles you."

He had said those things before. But this was the first time he had placed himself in danger of paroxysms to make his point.

"So then...you say I must marry?"

"I said you must produce an heir."

"There are some things only God himself can provide." It was true, though, I was not yet so aged I could not expect to sire a son...should the situation ever permit itself.

"I wish you had fallen to your knees and begged for a miracle."

"I don't see why it should matter so much."

"Because I have had enough of your disgraceful and

42

contemptible ways. And"—his cheeks flushed even darker—
"your stepmother is breeding and—" He frowned. "I'm drawing up papers to have my marriage to your mother annulled."

"You...what?" *What! What was it the bastard had said?*

"I should never have married her. She lured me into it,
and then she turned on me. I can't say I wasn't warned. She
was my half-sister..." His voice had petered out, and his eyes
glazed over. I could only assume he was lost in memories we
both tried not to revive but had never managed to forget.

"You can't just—!"

"I refuse to speak to you of this again."

"You would risk my validity as your heir on the birth of
a son? What if it's a g—?"

"It will be a son. It can be nothing else. I won't accept
anything else!"

The fool. Was he so certain of Providence's favor that he
would deliberately tempt Fate?

"Soon, you will find yourself my bastard, and then you'll
have to take your vices somewhere else." In one last burst of
rage, he spun on a heel and left my chambers.

I stood there for a moment. Long enough to be sure he
had, in truth, gone. And then I released all the air corked up
inside my lungs.

A snicker erupted from my bed.

I turned my back on the door and addressed the bed.
"Come. You heard him. We should fall to our knees and
beg for a miracle."

Remy emerged from the bedclothes where he had been
hiding. He pushed the bed-curtain aside with a sweep of his
arm, surveying the detritus of the previous evening's enter-
tainments. "Do you think he noticed?"

Noticed? The upturned gilded chair? The collection of
drinking glasses? The flurry of feathers that had fallen about

43

the room? Or the pile of discarded gowns in the corner? How could he have failed to notice those excesses any more than Remy could have failed to note my inadequacies? The spirit, as they said, was willing. It was my damnable flesh that had, of late, become so flaccid…and so weak. "Noticed you? When I was standing in front of him quite naked?"

"You don't think he noticed."

Oh, he had noticed. But he had refrained from directly commenting upon my proclivities. He always did, for he preferred as much as possible not to acknowledge them. He was too much a gentleman for that. And I was too much a gentleman to let Remy know. Mother always said "better the foot slip than the tongue." And I had always tried to follow her decrees.

Some time later that morning, after Remy had gone out hunting and I had taken myself back to bed with a book, a knock sounded at the door. My manservant announced the visitor. "Physician Bresson."

My headache increased. I had no complaints but the normal kind. To which he would no doubt respond with his normal cure. It was thought an enema was the best way to treat the symptoms that had increasingly begun to plague me.

"And how are we this day, my lord?"

I pulled the covers up under my chin. Bresson was one for poking and prodding at the most inconvenient of places. I did not relish his visits, though I hoped fervently for a cure. "*We* are fine."

"No pains in the head?"

Bon. Maybe I was not completely, unequivocally fine. "A few."

"No pains in the bending of the arms or the legs?"

"Some."

"And you have only your usual complaints?"

Usual? They were *un*usual and not welcome, which was the reason I had complained. But I nodded.

"I can see…?" He gestured toward my nether regions. He wanted me to turn back the covers and lie in a state where he could observe me like some prized pig. "You have had no more sores down…there?"

"*Non.*"

"Not even one?"

"Absolutely not."

Bresson frowned. "It is very important you tell me the precise truth."

I smiled. "The truth is I am so very thankful for your conscientious care."

"Well." He turned from the bed and fumbled with his instruments while I turned over. "I would not wish for you to be syphilitic."

Neither would I.

ༀ

Once the physician had gone, I had my servant dress me. I went down to the hall, only to discover the meal was nearly over. I was late. I took my stepmother's hand up in mine as I passed by her chair, and pressed a kiss onto it.

"Good afternoon." She smiled up at me.

"Still in your morning coat?" My father's tone was not benign.

"I was so involved in my affairs I had no time to change." He looked a question at me.

I busied myself with my food, refusing to respond.

"I hope I made myself clear earlier."

"Quite."

"*Bon.* You must see there are things that need to be arranged. For posterity's sake…" As he tried to delicately refer to the spawn my stepmother was breeding, a high color sprouted on his cheeks. How endearing. He cleared his throat. "…some things are necessary."

∽

As I waited for Remy to return from his hunt, I decided to take a turn in my stepmother's garden. The air had chilled with autumn's coming, but there were still blooms bursting forth everywhere. Over on the bench beneath the shade of a tree was Gabrielle herself. She looked like some overfed cow. And she was trying, without success, to stand.

I walked over and offered her my arm.

She nearly pulled me down on top of her with the heft of her extra weight. "*Merci*, Julien."

"It is my very great honor, *ma biche*, to be counted upon to assist you."

"You see, it's for this reason exactly you should find the taking of a wife so easy!" How grand she must seem to herself: married and a marquise at the age of twenty. And how generously she bestowed the wisdom gained from all of her life's experience upon one who'd already seen nearly twice her years. She dimpled. "You could charm a nun from her convent."

"If I had to charm anyone into my bed, don't you think a monastery more suitable to my tastes?"

She laughed. That was something my father would never have done.

"Why does no one ever believe me when I speak the truth?"

"Because we want so much to believe the state of your soul matches your angelic looks." She frowned as she stood there, trying to regain her breath. "You must know I have nothing to do with this plan to disinherit you."

"He wasn't serious." He couldn't be serious. If he were serious, then I might as well kill myself now to save my many creditors the trouble. Though my debts were great, everyone at court knew my eventual inheritance would be greater still.

If I were but there!

Nothing could be gained here in the countryside but a virulent cough. For all my father waxed rhapsodic about them, there was nothing noble about our peasant countrymen. About their cows and their hayseed. I would give all the fresh air in Orléanais for Madame Sainctot's salon in Paris, though it be fogged with tobacco smoke, soaked with the scents of a dozen different perfumes, and underscored by a mad melody played on a relentless harpsichord. Give me a place where every word was calibrated for amusement and spoken with wit…instead of this moldering château where words were wasted on topics as mundane as the latest calvings and the rising level of the miller's stream.

I yearned for my gaming tables.

Draughts, *hoc*, or *hasard*. I wasn't as particular as some. To risk all on the roll of a die or the turn of a card. God! That took true courage. *That* was an exercise in daring! These country bourgeoisie didn't understand. If you had to gamble with the wringing of hands or the constant wiping of the brow, then why gamble at all?

It had nothing to do with money. It had everything to do with the nature of the man. To stare Fate in the eye and dare her to slap you? That took nerve. To respond as stoically in the winning as one did in losing? That required true nobility. My father had earned his on the battlefield. I had found mine in the tumble of dice and the dealing of cards.

Unfortunately, noblesse required that eventually one repay

his debts…or at least not leave that possibility in doubt. If my father spoke too loudly of his desire to change heirs, then I, too, might be reduced to the wringing of hands.

I took a turn around the path with Gabrielle. She needed exercise; I needed not to be in the vicinity of my father. It was difficult to hide from him, out here in the country, if one was not impassioned, as was Remy, by falcons or riding or the hunt. But at the end of our circuit, as we turned back toward the château, I spied a figure watching us from the head of the garden. "There's my father. He's scowling at me. Again."

"He has only your best interests in mind."

"He has his own best interests in mind. He always has."

"He wants so much to be proud of you."

Proud of me? When had he ever been proud of me? He was proud of his hunting dogs; he was pleased with his new wife; he was delighted with the year's harvest. But he had never, not once, entertained any synonymous sentiment regarding me. I bowed at my father's approach. Released my stepmother from my arm.

She moved forward with all the grace of a lumbering ox.

"My dear." He offered her his arm. She took it and walked off without a backward glance.

One could not be particular about companions when there was so little company to be had.

Gabrielle and I were thrown together once more the next day. She was picking at her needlework in the petit salon, while I was pretending to read. I wished she hadn't chosen to work her design in taupe and saffron. Those colors each made the other look more insipid.

A sudden rattling came from outside, followed by howls from the hunting dogs.

I went to the window and peered down into the court-yard. "Who is this come to visit?"

"Hmm?" She lifted her gaze from her work.

"There's a carriage. A man of the church, by the looks of it." The coach was carved from ebony and gleamed with gold. The windows were hung with crimson curtains.

"I expect it's probably Cardinal St. Florent."

What reason would the cardinal have to visit? He gener-ally preferred to perch in grander places than this.

"He's come about the arrangements for the annulment."

I shut up my book with a vehemence that surprised even me. "There will be no more talk of annulments! I already told you he wasn't serious. You wouldn't know this, but he's been spouting threats like that one for years."

She fastened her gaze upon me. "I don't think it's a threat this time."

"You don't know my father."

"Perhaps not as well as you do, but he did make a special request for the babe's baptism…" She held up her needle-work, and before my eyes appeared the coat of arms of the Marquis of Eronville. A shield upon which ten blazing suns, reflecting the presumed glory of our King, surrounded a lion rampant. It was a coat of arms reserved for the Marquis of Eronville alone. And that was my title. At least, it should be.

I lingered in the salon until I heard the cardinal leave my father's chambers. I caught him as he was descending the front steps toward his carriage. When he offered up a plump, gout-swollen hand, I kissed his ring.

"You must know, Your Eminence, that age has begun to show itself in my father's mind. You must not think he's serious about these plans of his."

He pursed his lips as he withdrew his hand from mine. "What plans?"

"Come now." The man had never liked me. A sentiment perhaps born of the fascination that glittered in his eyes whenever he looked at me. I tried out a smile, just to see what might happen. Many times, in my experience, a throw of dice could change everything. "You cannot take his demands for an annulment seriously…"

He cleared his throat as he continued down the steps. "Everyone knows he and your mother were unsuited. The match was doomed from the start. It's a simple case of consanguinity."

"And yet nobody stopped it at the time."

His harrumph was dampened by the sheer magnitude of his collar. It was made from the finest linen and edged with a band of exquisite lace. Lace in the style I once had. But lace had been deemed illegal. No lace could be worn in the kingdom of France. Of course, in Cardinal Richelieu's eyes, there were the common sort of nobles and clergy, and then there were the favored few. Those who could break the rules and keep their fortunes, and their heads, intact. Cardinal St. Florent clearly wanted to be one of those… though I suspected he had not yet climbed quite as high as he hoped.

"You can see how it might be an inconvenience for me to be denied my inheritance at this point in my life."

"Yes." His gaze took my measure from tip to toe. "I've seen a thing or two."

"Considering how much the Marquis of Eronville will leave to his heir, and considering this new babe of his will never know how great a debt of gratitude he owes you… might it not be wise to side with one who does?"

"Wise?"

"Profitable, even…?"

"I've never had anything against profit…which is why I'm so inclined to agree with your father's point of view." His smile was perfunctory as he moved to step into the carriage.

Apparently, my father had thought of everything. "So he's offered you money, then."

The cardinal turned, his brow raised.

My gaze fell once more upon that splendid collar, and then shifted to the avaricious gleam in his eyes. I made another gamble. "What does a man like you need with money? What you need is power. Influence. You need something that will let all the court know you are a man to be reckoned with."

"Well…I like to think that…" He proffered a modest shrug.

I leaned close. "What you need, Your Eminence, is *more lace.*"

"Lace?" His gaze narrowed as he looked at me. "Lace is forbidden."

"Tut, tut. As are all manner of things one can confess to a priest and then receive an indulgence for." I leaned even closer. "Indulgence." I whispered the word. "A privilege only the pious can hope to obtain. And lace is an indulgence only a very privileged few can even find anymore." I reached out to touch the lace that trimmed his collar. "I can get you what you want. I can find you something better than this."

His gaze touched my lips and then crept up to my eyes. "You disgust me."

"Tell God whatever you think he will believe, but between the two of us, let there be nothing but truth. The truth is that if you deny my father's request, I will get you the finest length of lace you have ever seen. Courtiers will envy you, and Richelieu himself will wonder why he hasn't thought to take you into his council before. Think of it. You could be the owner of the finest length of lace in France. And all you have to do is agree with God himself, with me as supporting evidence in favor of your decision. My father was married to my mother. It's so simple, Your Eminence. How could you be expected to rule in any other way?"

He pulled his gloves onto his hands. Squinted up into his waiting carriage. "I hear the nuns up in Lendelmolen make the finest lace in Flanders."

I took his gloved hand in mine and pressed it to my lips. "I've heard that very same thing."

. CHAPTER 7 .

Alexandre Lefort

Château of Souboscq
The province of Gascogne, France

ACCURSED, DAMNABLE LACE!

How was it a flimsy confection of thread could have turned into such a weighty burden?

I stood behind a parapet on the roof of the château, surveying the fields of Souboscq, a great rage building within me. All I saw before me, all that grew in the fields that rolled beyond my sight, down into the valley, enriched the Leforts no longer. All of our care and worries, all of the peasants' hard labor would fill not our own coffers, but those of the Count of Montreau. It had been thus for ten years. There was little solace that there was not very much in those fields to be seen. The crops, again, had mostly withered and died before the harvest.

Damn the count and his pernicious lace!

We hadn't wanted him to lodge with us, Lisette's father and I, those many years ago. His reputation as a libertine had preceded him, even so far as our small corner of the kingdom. But we hadn't the grounds to refuse him. He was from a family both old and noble, and his father was one of the King's most loyal supporters. He ought to have been no different from the dozens of nobles who had stopped at Souboscq on their way through the countryside. It would have been the very definition of ungraciousness to have turned him away.

And so we had suffered his airs and his affectations. We had suffered the attentions he paid to the companion he had brought along with him. We were suffering from him still. As many times as I had told Lisette what had happened was not her fault, she had refused to believe me. As many times as her father had tried to draw her close, she had refused him the solace of her touch.

But she had been right in her claims of culpability.

And she was also dreadfully wrong.

She had destroyed the lace, but she had not been responsible for the count's extortion. And it was not she who had persuaded her father to take part in the Marquis of Chalais's conspiracy to assassinate the King's chief minister, Richelieu. In our great naiveté of ten years before, the plot had seemed destined to succeed.

If only it had not failed!

If it had worked, then nobles like my cousin the viscount, Lisette's father, would have maintained some control within the kingdom. As it was, the failure of the plot had allowed Richelieu to strip all power from the nobility and then tax them for his trouble. And the cardinal had spies everywhere. Had we known of them then as we knew of them now, my cousin would never have been tempted to join such folly.

He was neither noble enough nor powerful enough to depend upon the King's mercy. The Queen and the King's own brother had been privy to Chalais's plans...and yet they had been able to reconcile with both the King and the cardinal. 'Twas only those without power and influence who had been executed for their part in the plot. If Richelieu ever discovered my cousin's involvement, there was no doubt he would share the unlucky conspirators' fate: a dishonorable death in prison or the horror of an executioner's block.

It was not safe even to think an untoward thought about the cardinal.

Yet not all of the estate's woes were the fault of the count. These poor harvests had taken a toll, as had the King's policies of taxation and my cousin's unwillingness to let the peasants suffer from the King's levies. Though the Count of Montreau came every year for payment on his lace, and though he seemed to squeeze it from us one hard-won coin at a time, as long as we were not required to forfeit the land, there was hope that one day we would reap harvests sufficient to pay the debt.

As my cousin's heir, I clung to that hope.

I was not, by birth, a Lefort. I was a Girard. I would not inherit my cousin's title, but as his closest kin, I was inheritor of the estate. In taking his name as my own, in becoming Alexandre Lefort, I guaranteed I would never again be known as the son of one of the King's most celebrated warriors. At one time, that might have been a boon, but my father had been struck down in his prime by leprosy. A disease so terrible and shameful no one could avoid being tainted by proximity. The Viscount of Souboscq's heir had every opportunity open to him; the leprous warrior's son had none.

I put a hand to the dagger I wore at my waist. My father's dagger. With Souboscq's fields so stunted and withered, it might prove my only legacy. I fingered the jewels set into its hasp. The dagger was cruciform in shape, and its short, slender blade was designed to finish off the mortally wounded, to offer a sort of mercy to those not expected to survive. There had only ever been one other like it.

Find its match, fiston. *Therein lies your destiny.*

Those were the words my father had babbled toward the end of his life. That I had been able to decipher them at all had been a miracle, for the disease had eaten away at his lips as well as his tongue. Those words had often been in my thoughts of late, but they were a cryptic and useless legacy. To admit to the dagger's ownership, I would have to admit also to my paternity. Find its match? I only hoped it would never find me.

The estate was my only chance at respectability.

But not only for myself did I despise the Count of Montreau. It was for Lisette's sake, as well. All that was carefree and innocent and childlike had left the girl that night when she was seven. And nothing but misery had come to replace it. She was compliant to a fault, never questioning, never contradicting. She only ever did exactly as she was bid, and then she retreated. She was ever and always retreating, as if she could not believe any would want her present. More than extorting the viscount's money, the Count of Montreau had extracted my cousin's heart.

The viscount of Souboscq had always been modest and unpretentious, preferring the simple pleasures of his country estate to all of the pomp at court. He had never been comfortable with the subtle repartee or obsequious gallantries upon which reputations rose and fell in the King's inner circle. That he should be impoverished to pay for another's extravagance was unjust. But whenever I chafed at the count's unreasonable demands, my cousin only paled and said, "Better to meet with misfortune than to meet with Richelieu's executioner."

Had I foreseen the disrepair the estate would fall into, I might have married for a generous dowry and saved us all. But back then, just five years ago at the age of twenty, I had too much of the leper's son left in me and too little of the viscount's heir. I didn't understand how problems that seemed so enormous could be solved through genteel means in salons or at the altars of churches. I had also nursed an impossible, yet undying, hope. I had measured all the maids of my acquaintance by the standard of my cousin, Lisette. And I had foresworn them all for the possibility of winning her love. Now, at the age of twenty-five, when the viscount desperately needed the money a dowry could bring, it was too late to reconsider. The promise of a fortune, which might have attracted a bride, had withered with the crops. Though I suspect nothing would have pleased the viscount more, the flower of love I had hoped would bloom between Lisette and I had never blossomed.

And so we lived together in uneasy proximity. The three of us nursing the flame of a single hope: that the Count of Montreau would die. And soon. Whenever I visited the estate's chapel, I knelt on the *prie-dieu* and made an earnest petition for his immediate death, even though I had no reason to think God would listen to my prayers.

I gave one last glance at those rounded hills, which looked for all the world like a cluster of grapes emerging from the cradle of the earth. Imagined the brooks and streams that splayed across the land like fingers, their muddy depths glinting silver and gold. The land must be saved. Souboscq was the only home I had ever had.

If we had to pay the count by selling off what few treasures we still had, we would do it. But I would not—could not—allow the selling of the land.

"*Bonne anniversaire, ma biche.*" The viscount fairly sung the words as Lisette walked toward the table at dinner. He gestured furiously toward the door, and a retinue of servants advanced toward him. Though our fields had withered, the hills still provided. Wild dove was served alongside a tart that was surely stuffed with mushrooms. And there was a confit of pears and a conserve of apples.

Lisette looked startled, as if she had forgotten it was her own birthday. Her cheeks reddened as she looked around. "*Non*, Papa." I derived the words from the movement of her lips, not from the sound of her voice. She shrunk from the table toward the shadows, as if she could not bear to be remarked upon.

"Please, *ma chérie*. There is so little to celebrate these days. You must grant me this one pleasure."

I pulled a chair out for her.

She bowed her head for the briefest moment, and then she raised it and looked at me.

I nodded.

Her gown may have been turned to hide the wear on its fabric, and the hems of her skirts might have been frayed, but she lowered herself into the chair as gracefully as any duchess as I pushed it toward the table.

The viscount rose and put a hand into his coat's pocket. "I have something I wish to give you."

She made as if to rise. "No, Papa. Please. No gifts."

"Ah! But it is not from me. This gift is one I have been keeping for some years. It's a present from your mother."

He passed a small ebony box across the table toward her.

When she did not move to take it, I picked it up and placed it before her.

"*Merci*, Alexandre."

He settled back into his chair, as if watching her open the box was an event not to be missed. "It's your mother's chain of pearls. She wore them on the day of our marriage, and she never looked more beautiful. Try them on."

Regret and pleasure warred in her eyes. She opened the

lid and reached inside. When her hand came out, it was clutching a string of beautifully matched pearls. She gazed at them for a long moment before placing them onto the table. And even then she did not relinquish them completely. She drew a finger across first one glowing orb and then another. Moved to cup her hand around them and then stopped and placed it into her lap. She shook her head. "You must give these to the count, Papa. To pay down our debt."

"No!" His voice echoed in that vaulted chamber like a clap of thunder. We both fell back before it. "I will not allow the memory of your mother to be profaned by that vile and detestable man."

Her hand closed about them. "Then I shall give them to him."

"You will do no such thing!" His jowls trembled as fire lit his cheeks. "I would throw them into the well myself before I would watch you give them to him." But as he looked at his daughter, his face softened, and he put a hand out to cover hers. "I appreciate all you have sacrificed these years past, *ma chérie*. I know how much this debt has cost you. But these...I have saved these for you. Please, receive them."

"Cost *me*? But I...I can't..." She bolted from the table, leaving behind an astonished father gaping in dismay.

✑

I sought her where I had always been able to find her: at the top of a ridge from which the estate spilled down and spread out toward the wood below. The mists, clinging to the lowest of dales beneath us, wound like a river through the valley, making islands of even the highest hills.

"It's not safe to be about like this, at night's fall." A bat flitted past us, and a wolf howled as if to help persuade her of the sense in my argument.

"It's the most beautiful time of day." There was wistfulness to her tone. She nodded toward the gathered mists. "It looks like a pathway to heaven."

It did. The mists trailed out toward the gilt-edged horizon, where they seemed to vault up into the sky.

"I used to think if I could be here at just the right moment, and if I could jump far enough to make it to that mist, then I could walk up into heaven and visit *Maman*."

We watched in silence as the mist seemed to stir itself, to gather and thicken. It reached out to grasp at the forest. And then, it started to rise.

I slid a glance toward her. "Did you ever do it? Did you ever jump?"

Her lips curved in a sad, self-mocking smile. "I tried. But I could not jump far enough…and I was never quick enough." She voiced the words with the profoundest regret.

We stayed there watching until the sun blazed out in one last protest. It touched the mist, singeing holes in its fabric, and the white vapor was soon consumed in a purple smoke. A cloud crossed Lisette's face, and the glow that had seemed to light her from within dissipated.

I held out my hand to her, palm up, the chain of pearls curled into a mound within it. "You forgot these."

She did not even look at them. "If you insist upon giving them to me, I shall sell them."

"Your father saved them. For *you*."

Her eyes, gone dusky with twilight's falling, sought mine. "I don't deserve them. My father has sacrificed everything for me. And my mother…I've tried to reach her since she died, since I was four years old, and I could never do it. But even if I could, even if I could walk that mist straight up into heaven, why would she want to see me?"

"She would have wanted you to have these."

"You aren't listening to me! I've destroyed everything she once loved. Better to give them to the count and try to preserve what's left."

"You cannot think that."

"What else can I think?"

"That this is not a judgment of your worth. It's an indictment of his!"

"Why can't you just see me as I am? Why do you have to be so kind...and so...so *good*?" That last she accused me of as if it were one sin too many.

God grant she would never discover just how wretched I was. I seized her hand and tried to press the pearls into them. "Because I care for you too much to let you pretend anything different." Care! Care was contemptible. Care was cowardly. I wanted more than fondness and friendship. I put my other hand atop hers. "Don't you know? I love you." A miserable and unwanted confession, perhaps, but it was true.

Tearing her hand from my grip, she took a step back. "You love me! God, why—?" Her appeal was directed toward heaven. But then her face seemed to crumple, and she looked at me. "I loved *you*. I love you still! But my love is a curse. Why can't you just *see* that? How could you gain anything but pain from loving me?" There was a note of regret in her whispered words, though it was masked by despair.

I didn't hope to gain anything. I never meant to press my suit at all. I wanted only that she would shed that mantle of guilt she kept fastened about her shoulders. But my wish was as hopeless as her trying to walk on the evening's mist. We were but mortals, and we were bound, the both of us it seemed, to fail at what our hearts wanted most.

My confession must have meant nothing; she moved to leave.

"When did you stop trying to jump?" I raised my voice to reach her ears.

She shot me a look over her shoulder. "I did not say I had."

I was desperate she stay. To lose her to the twilight and her mists would have been one loss too many to bear. "But what would you say if you reached her? And why would you do it? Why would you give yourself to such a useless, hopeless task?" Even as child she must have known she would not succeed.

"Because she knew me before." Before: before the count and his lace had come. "She knew me, and she had no reason not to love me. I just want someone…" Her words trailed off as she took up her skirts and ran into the fast-falling gloom.

I could finish her thought. I knew it as my own. I just wanted someone to love me as I was. Regardless of anything I had done or failed to do. I wanted to know that at some time, at some point, I had been worthy of someone's love.

I rose the next morning when I heard the maid knocking about, opening the shutters to the day. I pulled on my hose and breeches and opened the door, expecting to find a bucket of water waiting for me.

It was not there.

Putting on a shirt and tucking it into my breeches, I went down to find the maid. She was stirring the ashes in the hearth.

"I need some water."

She turned and then straightened, putting a fist to her hip.

Now I knew the reason for my missing bucket: this maid was new to Souboscq.

"Why?"

"Now." The old maid had always placed a bucket outside my chamber door. I couldn't wait any longer for it. My skin was already crawling, itching with an urgency that had set my heart to pounding and my fingers to scratching. Already I had nearly torn a hole in my shirt, trying to dig through it to my skin. I had to get away from my skin. "And be quick about it!"

She clomped from the room, muttering beneath her breath, though she was back a few minutes later, lugging a bucket. Water sloshed onto her skirts with every step.

I took the bucket back to my chamber and stripped off my shirt, breeches, and hose. I took up a brush and squatted on the floor. Examined my arms, my legs. Scooped up a handful of water and cupped it to my chest. Once. Twice. Took up the brush and scrubbed myself nearly raw, trying to exorcise all the terrible memories.

"You'll catch your death."

I looked up to find the maid staring at me from the door. "*Dégage!*" I might have shut the door on her, blocking her view, but my task was too important. And, more than that, it was almost complete. I turned my back toward her, took up the brush, and began to scrub once more. I closed my eyes as I scoured my cheeks and forehead, and I could see *him* reflected in my memories.

My father.

I saw him once more sitting in his cave beside the River Saleys in Béarn, wrapped in rags. I saw myself there, as a boy, cringing at the horror of seeing my father's skin melt from his bones. Watching the leprosy consume his fingers and toes, his nose and his ears. The disease stole both his voice and his sight. I hadn't come within ten feet of him all those years of my childhood, though I slept each night just outside the entrance to that cave. And each morning, after I had begged bread for our day's meals, I ran down to the stream and scrubbed at my skin with a stick. Sloughed off even the possibility of that wasting disease, shedding it into the river. Letting the water carry it away.

Hurry, hurry, hurry!

Before the disease could corrupt me. Before it could take root and spread forth its destructive tendrils.

I scrubbed behind my ears, beneath my fingernails, between my toes. I had done so each morning for years, examining my skin for lesions and then scrubbing at my flesh. Sometimes…sometimes I was too zealous. It could take days for the wounds to heal. And when I smelled a particularly ripe chèvre cheese or passed a herd of goats, it could take days for my nostrils to rid themselves of the scent. Of the odor that smelled like rotting flesh.

I was marked—I was tormented—by memories.

My father had wasted away over the years, in both mind and body, and then one morning, he simply failed to stir at all. It was the summer of my twelfth year.

"Papa?"

I poked him with a stick. Poked him again. Harder and harder, until the sharp tip broke right through his disease-eaten skin. I pulled it out and then flung it away.

"Papa!"

I found another stick and used it to draw the cowl off his face. I hadn't seen him, not clearly, in over a year. He'd taken the habit of keeping his face shadowed beneath the folds of black cloth. Had I seen him before that morning, I might have believed him already dead. Worms could not have corrupted his flesh as thoroughly as the disease had done. Surely they would not have devoured it with such complete ruthlessness.

His eyes were not closed. The lids had been eaten away long before, consigning him to blindness soon thereafter.

But there was dullness to them that morning I could credit to nothing but death.

Where could I bury a man who had already, long ago, been declared dead by the village priest?

And how could a boy inter a man he was not supposed to touch?

I solved the problem by using a fallen branch to roll him farther back into the cave, and then I walled him in behind a fortress of stones. It took me the whole day to haul them up from the river. But by the time I was done, no man or beast would ever be able to reach him. Yet the goatlike odor of his decaying flesh haunted me. It seeped out of the cave in the spaces between the rocks. I spent the next day fortifying the walls I had constructed the day before. Someone must have spied me at my work, from the far side of the river. Before the sun had abandoned the day, a voice hailed me from the forest. "Is he gone, then?"

I climbed up the wall I had built and shoved a last stone into its place. Slid back down, shredding my hands in the doing of it. "He's dead."

"Come into town." It was the sheriff standing there holding onto the reins of his horse.

I considered the invitation. "You mean…I can go back to the house?"

"*Non.* It's been occupied."

"Not by me. Nor my father."

"It's no longer his. He was declared dead, lad. Remember?"

And me along with him. By the priest. "What would I do there? In town?"

"Beg. Just the way you've been doing."

I looked at the cave I had just finished sealing. Looked back at the man who was standing there at the edge of the wood in his fine clothes and handsome hat. Town. There was nothing there for me. Nothing but disapproving wives and their surly husbands. Little girls who screamed in terror whenever they saw me, and boys who spat on me and kicked at me whenever they were given the chance. There was nothing worse than being a leper…but being a leper's son was close. "I'll stay here."

The man lifted his hat, scratching at his head. "What will you do?"

Did it matter?

"Do you have any kin?"

I shrugged. "My father had a cousin. In Gascogne."

"Does he have a name?"

"The viscount of something or other." My father had always shaken his head when he said it. Always wondered why the good fortune of his cousin Henri couldn't have been shared by the rest of the family. "Henri. His name is Henri."

"If you decide to come into town, you can sleep by the church, as long as you don't mind the cemetery. There's a big, sheltering tree there."

I'd already been sleeping beside the dead for seven years. He could offer me nothing more than I already had.

I stayed outside that cave, continuing to live there for at least another month. That's where the viscount of Souboscq and his men had found me: living outside a blocked-up cave, dressed in the rags I called my clothes. I heard them coming long before I saw them—horses' feet battering the earth, the leather of their saddles creaking. He and his retinue rode right up to me. "Are you Nicolas Girard's son?"

"I am."

"Then I'm your cousin. Of a sort."

I looked at him.

He looked at me.

"Where's Nicolas?"

I gestured behind me to the cave.

His gaze traveled the distance from me to the cave. Then it traveled back. "We shall leave him there in peace. Now then. You're to come home with me. We can't have a cousin of the Leforts living in the forest as if he's no better than a beggar."

No better than a beggar.

It had never occurred to me that I was better than anything at all. It took six years under the viscount's tutelage before I considered myself truly a part of his family, even though he never treated me otherwise. And even then, it had seemed as if I was acting. As if, at any moment, someone might come and tear the mask of respectability from my face and recognize me for the leper's son.

The day Lisette's father led my horse into the courtyard of his château at Souboscq, I slipped from the horse's back, touching the sand-colored earth of Gascogne for the very first time. Lisette had run into the courtyard. A little bit of a girl of the age of four, all bouncing curls and excited squeals. Her father caught her up in an embrace. He had kissed her and then turned, introducing her to me.

She grabbed him about the neck, whispering in a voice much too loud not to carry. "Does he have a name?"

"His name is Alexandre. He's your cousin."

"I've never had a cousin before." She wriggled from his grasp, slid from his arms, and ran toward me.

I put up my hands, more to keep her from touching me than to catch her. But she ran right through them, threw herself into my arms, and kissed me on the cheek.

She kissed me.

I had never been touched before. Not that I could remember. Everyone was afraid to touch the leper's son. But she kissed me on the cheek. And it made me feel as if everything would be all right. As if *I* would be all right. Right there, in the middle of the yard, she had redeemed me.

. CHAPTER 8 .

Katharina Martens

LENDELMOLEN, FLANDERS

I N THE MORNING, AFTER PRAYERS AND AFTER THE
taking of bread, we washed.

We washed our faces and our hands. Scrubbed at them:
forehands, palms, fingertips. Especially our fingertips. We
washed three times a day. Three times a day to protect the
lace from ourselves. To keep it from being corrupted.

We held them up to Sister for inspection.

Mathild was stopped.

The Sister frowned. Spoke two words: *Chilblains. Go.*

I grimaced at the pronouncement. It would not do to
have an ulcer rupture all over the lace.

Mathild left my side and soon disappeared down the hall
in the direction of the infirmary. I had been there only
once. It was a room filled with warmth and all manner of
good smells, but it was not a room I wanted to visit often.
Too many visits there and soon, one did not return. There
had been many over the years who had not come back:
Elizabeth, Aleit, Johanna. Beatrix, Jacquemine, and Martina.
I did not know what had happened to them.

Their names had never been spoken, but their absence had
been noted. And with each disappearance, there always fell
a sort of…dread.

The rest of us left the shelter of the abbey and walked

through the wind and rain, water sloshing into our clogs along the way.

Once inside, we passed the cows and the pigs. Secure in their pens on the ground level, they munched on hay and slops. We climbed the tall, narrow steps to the loft, elbows pointed toward the soiled, daub walls in case of stumbling. We were forbidden to touch anything with our hands. Least not until we sat with our pillows and put our bobbins to work.

I could touch my lace but once, and that was during the creation of it. The completion of each twist and each cross meant the stitch was mine no longer. The smallest speck of dust could mark it. The slightest smear of dirt could stain it. At all costs, I had to save it from myself. Yet for the time I worked on it, while I created it, the lace was mine. It was mine until it spilled over the edge of my pillow and disappeared into the silk pouch where it was collected.

As we ascended that steep stair, the odor of our animal neighbors grew…but so did the warmth of the air. Without them we might have frozen to death on our benches as we worked. There could be no fire in the fireplace. Ever. A fire produced smoke and ashes, and a hint of either would soil the lace. Far better to risk chilblains, lung fever, or worse than to risk a single ash from one sole fire.

We worked all morning as the sun's light crept through the tall, narrow windows. I could feel it warm my face. Our hands kept their own rhythm, bobbins clicking. Our clogs scraped the floor now and then as we wriggled our toes to try to keep them warm. Across the room, I could hear Sister chant a rhyme for the children, for those learning what it meant to be a lace maker, those who still sat on a bench without hunching over a pillow. But soon…soon…they would know. And soon they would become entranced by

the dance of the bobbin, enslaved by the emerging pattern
of lace.

❧

Needle pin, needle pin
Stitch upon stitch,
Work the old lady out of the ditch
If she is not out as soon as I
A rap on the knuckles will come by and by
A horse to carry my lady about
Must not look off till twenty are out.

❧

I set my own dance to the rhythm of the chant, but I went
about it twice as quickly.

After a while, Sister walked over to me. I felt tension pull
at the lace as I heard her draw it forth from its silk pouch.
"Lovely."

Oh, there was such joy to be had in the pronouncement
of Sister's one word. Lovely. It would live in my memory
forever. It was the highest compliment I had ever been paid.

"When will it be done? Two weeks? Three, perhaps?"

I straightened. Or tried to. "…three. Weeks." My voice it
seemed had gone rusty from disuse.

She nodded.

My heart thrilled. I could feel it thumping in my throat.
She had spoken to me. And I had a second reason for hap-
piness this day. Today, my sister would walk the four hours
from Kortrijk to come and visit.

I worked as quickly as I could until the noon meal. When
Sister clapped, I noted in my memory the place in my pattern

and then rose from the lace and followed the others down the stairs. This time, we could put our hands to the walls. It mattered not if we soiled them on the way to the refectory. They would only get dirtied with food. After, we would wash them once more before we returned to our work.

We ate quickly, as was expected in the ten minutes provided. It had been difficult to learn to eat so swiftly when I had first come, but a hollow stomach is an effective teacher. Far better to spend our time washing. Once washed, our hands were inspected. I looked for Mathild, thinking she might join us, but she did not.

Perhaps tomorrow.

Back at the workshop, I worked through one petal. Then a second. A third. And then it was time to begin my deceit. I raised my hand.

"*Ja?*"

I inclined my head toward the stairs.

"Go."

I arranged my bobbins to mark my place before rising and laying my pillow on the bench. I descended the stairs, hands out. Without others in front of me, it was difficult to know where the stairs were. It would not do to stumble to my knees.

Hands could be washed.

Aprons could not… least not so easily.

I peered out the door, though in truth, if someone was watching from the abbey, I would not have known it. Swiftly, I walked toward the privy house. And then, once I had reached its door, I walked beyond it, behind it, and lowered my head to a gap in the stones.

"Heilwich? Are you there?"

There was only silence. And then some shouting. That woman accusing Pieter of making a mess of things again.

"Heilwich?"

Nothing.

I waited.

"Heilwich?"

The woman had done with her shouting. A door scraped. A dog barked. But no steps came near across the cobbles. No cough sounded to let me know she was there. I waited some moments more, standing in the rain, and then I walked around to the front of the privy house and washed my hands with water from a pail. But before I returned to the workshop, I bent to the gap again and spoke her name one time more.

"Heilwich?"

"*Ja.*"

"You are there!"

"Is it not Tuesday? And do I not always come on Tuesday?"

"Thank you. For coming."

"Here. Take this." A hunk of bread pressed against my nose. I inhaled its moist, yeasty scent for a moment, and then I stood and pulled out my prize.

"And there's an egg pushed up inside it."

"Thank you!"

"You're the thanking-est girl I've ever known. Just eat it."

"I am." Or I would when I discovered where the egg was. I probed at the bread with my fingers then held it up to my nose to see it better.

"Let me have a look at you, then."

I bent once more and pressed my face to the gap.

"I want to see more than just your eye. Stand away."

"But then I can't see you." And seeing her face was one of my greatest treasures. It enlivened the words she spoke to me. I recalled them together, her words and her face, in the days between her visits.

"For shame. Of course you can."

I could see a shadow where I presumed her face to be, but I could not truly see her, not when I stood away. Not clearly enough to distinguish her features.

"Can't you?"

"I can tell you're there."

"And what color are my sleeves?"

"They blend…with the color of the stones." There now, when she moved, I could see them.

"With the stones? For shame, they do not! Eat now and leave me to think a minute."

I ate. And with pleasure. The last egg I had eaten was the one she had brought me the week before. During her weekly clandestine visits, I always told her I had no wish for anything, having eaten so recently, but in truth, I discovered I could. When she pushed her bundles through the wall for me, my stomach never failed to cramp with hunger.

"Why haven't you told me your eyes have gotten worse? Stand away and let me see you from the side."

Though I ate, I did as I was bid.

"You look shorter than last I saw you. Stand up straight."

I lifted my shoulders and uncoiled my spine.

"I meant straight. As a pin."

"I am."

"You're bent as a shepherd's crook."

I was? But I was standing as straight as I could.

"Come here. Come toward me. Put your eye to the gap."

I swallowed the last of the egg, wiping the yolky crumbs from my fingertips onto the bread. I set my face to the hole.

"I have to get you out. No more delays. I spoke to the Reverend Mother last month, and I've saved one coin more since then. Perhaps this time—"

"*Nee!*"

"You're hunched as a grandmother...and you've almost gone blind."

"*Nee*. Please. Don't speak to them. Don't say anything."

"Why not? I've been saving money for years to buy you back. And with that extra coin...perhaps that will be enough if I promise to return with the rest later..."

"Don't. Please don't."

"And why not?"

"Because. Because...I'm in the middle of a length, and I must finish it. I have to finish it."

"If you don't finish it, I've no doubt they will find another who will."

"*Nee*. They won't."

"It's not you who has to finish it. It's the abbey."

"It's my length."

"Truly, Katharina, the buyer will care nothing for your name. He will never know it."

"But..."

"If I don't take you out, they'll push you out."

"*Nee*. They won't."

"They will. They have. I see what's left of you poor lace makers all over the city, doing...vile things, Katharina. Vile things. Things that cannot be forgiven."

"Which lace makers?"

"Which of them? All of them! What do you think will happen to you when you can no longer work? When you can't see to thread a needle?"

"Bobbin."

"Needle, bobbin, it doesn't matter which. And they don't care, either. They care nothing about you!"

"They do. I'm the best lace maker they have."

"And their best lace maker has almost gone blind. Can't you see the work is destroying you?"

"But it isn't." It couldn't. How could I be destroyed by something I loved?

"I will speak to her. Today. And I'll see if I can't have you out by Sunday."

"*Nee!* Please. Please. Let me just…let me finish the lace. Three weeks. Please." And perhaps by then she would have forgotten her threat.

"Well…you don't think they'll notice?"

"They haven't noticed yet."

"Then…be off with you. Before they come looking."

"Thank you."

"I'll see you next week. And I'll ask the nuns in three weeks. Once I've had the chance to come by more money."

I turned from the wall and left her, washed my hands once more, and ascended the stairs. But this time, as I took up my work, I found no pleasure in the dance. Only duty and dull repetition. Petal after petal, flower after flower, scroll after scroll. There was nothing magical about a length of lace. There was no story in its pattern. There was only thread.

Yards and yards of thread.

❧

The next morning started much like the one before. We assembled after breakfast, hands washed, held up for inspection. Again Mathild was separated from us and sent to the infirmary. A rustle of unease rippled through us.

One time more. Perhaps two. How long would it be before she too vanished?

We assembled together and then walked to the workshop. But halfway through the morning, Mathild appeared. She sat down beside me and took up her work.

"I have lost my place."

The sound of a whisper, a voice not belonging to Sister, was so extraordinary, I did not know at first from where it had come. I looked up. Around.

I felt the slightest pressure at my elbow. "Help me."

I worked on, considering what to do. Mathild's hands were moving. I could see the blur of them, and I could hear her bobbins. To help her, to talk to her, would bring the wrath of Sister down upon my head.

And my back. And my buttocks.

I trembled at the thought.

"Please."

She was working. I could hear that she was, so how could she have lost her place? And if she had, if she did need help, then why did she not ask Sister?

Nee. There could be nothing good gained from answering her plea.

But once again, that voice entered into my thoughts. "Help me."

Her voice echoed in my head, her words creating a pattern.

I have lost my place.

Help me.

Help.

Please.

Those words created a design of lace disrupted, unfinished. A lace no one would wear.

But…how could she have lost her place?

It was with Mathild I had come into the abbey. It was with Mathild I had learned the patterns at Sister's knee. Mathild and I, who slept side by side, pallets pushed together for warmth. Mathild and I, the best—the oldest—girls in the workshop.

And it was then I began to wonder.

Where *had* Elizabeth gone? And Jacquemine? And Beatrix? What had happened to all those girls, the older girls who had been making lace and fulfilling commissions when we had first begun? And how was it every one of the girls who had come before us had disappeared?

Where had they gone?

I had the feeling that, hidden beneath the confusion of my thoughts, was a pattern. I had only to wait, to watch, to determine what it was.

But still, that left Mathild and her plea.

She had lost her place.

Perhaps, if I could feel her threads, I might be able to find it for her.

I pressed against her elbow.

Heard a sharp intake of breath.

I patted the bench between us with a hand.

She placed her hand atop mine.

I grabbed it and pulled it toward my pillow while reaching for her pillow with my other hand. In the doing of it, I was careful not to uncoil myself and sit upright. Not to move my shoulders or my head. I prayed she would be as careful as I.

I sat there for some several seconds, her pillow on my lap, expecting to be punished. But then I heard Sister's voice start up a chant for the younger children, and I knew we would not be discovered.

Mathild must have known it, too, for she sighed.

I bent over her pillow, nose to her pins, trying to feel where she had stopped. It was a pattern like my own, though not as wide. It seemed as if…*nee*. I turned the pillow around. Began anew. It seemed as if she had stopped in the middle of…a leaf? A petal? Sliding my hand along the length, I felt the pattern contained within its thread. She had stopped in the middle of a petal. And it seemed as if…I fingered the stitches she had completed. And then, I pressed her elbow.

She reached out toward my lap, but her hand did not find the pillow.

Quickly, I pushed her fingers down to her work.

She took her pillow from me as I felt for my own. "You are..." I paused. My voice had come out raspy and raw. I tried once more. "The middle of the petal. Five stitches. Then turn."

If she thanked me, I did not hear it. But if I could not hear it, then neither could Sister.

CHAPTER 9

Heilwich Martens

KORTRIJK, FLANDERS

ON WEDNESDAY I WAS LATE TO HERRY STUER'S. IF I hadn't known it before, I could tell by the way his pallet reeked of stale piss. I glowered at the girl who looked after him. "You could change it a time or two."

She flounced away from me toward the door. "And taint my hands with the scent of it?" With a flash of her skirts, she was gone.

Marguerite was her name. And it was only because our blessed Lord had once cared for such as she that I did not speak my mind.

Whore.

With some pushing and pulling, I rolled Herry off to one side and then swept the fouled straw out the door. I left it in just such a place that Marguerite would have to tread upon it when she returned.

"If she's to have a few coins for the keeping of you, pardon my saying, the least she could do is remember you while you're yet living."

He said nothing. He hadn't, not since that night a month ago when he'd been felled by apoplexy in one of the rooms above the inn. He'd been wrapped in the arms of the young Marie. Old Herry had always been one for the pretty girls. He'd come sniffing around my own skirts a time or two back fifteen years ago or so. And from the sights I'd seen during my care of him, I was sorry I had not been more willing.

I tore away the blanket from Marguerite's own pallet and took half her straw to make a new one for Herry.

"The least she could do is share some of what's yours with you."

I rolled him onto the clean pallet. He blinked.

Kind eyes he had. Kind eyes he'd always had.

I stooped down and pressed a hand to his cheek.

He blinked once more.

"*Ach*, Herry."

A tear bloomed at the edge of his eye.

I knelt and brushed it away with the hem of my apron. "And what would the guildsmen say if they knew old Herry Stuer was a man for crying?" I shook Marguerite's blanket. Once. Twice. Let it settle itself down across Herry. "I won't tell a soul."

Poor man. When had old Herry ever harmed anyone? What had he done to deserve an end like this?

"You know, that girl did ask for the looking after of you." Though anyone with any sense could guess she had asked to care for him only after his guild had made known the amount of money they would provide for his care. Old Herry still had his wits about him. I knew it by his eyes. He might not be able to move or talk, but he could see. And hear.

I wasn't quick enough to catch the next tear before it leaked onto his cheek. It crept down to his neck, leaving a trail in the grime that covered his skin. I rose, and finding no rag, took the edge of Marguerite's other shift and dipped it into a bucket of water. "Just let me get the look of you." I scrubbed at the sides of his mouth where drivel had made a crust and then worked beneath his chin where the remnants of a pottage had collected in his whiskers. "You were always one for a neat shave and a clean shirt. 'There's nothing like the sight of Herry Stuer on a Guild Day,' that's what I used say." I dipped the shift back into the water and wrung it nearly dry. "I did. And that's a fact." It could do no harm to let the man know how much I had fancied him. Even if he had been older. He'd had such a way about him. If only he hadn't fancied everybody else. Such a fine, good man. "Shall I give you a shave, then?"

I would. I did. There was time enough for it. If Marguerite returned before I was done, it would be a miracle to rival the virgin birth. There was only Father Jacqmotte who awaited me, and with his head in his books this day and his thoughts on the eternal, I doubt he knew I had gone anywhere at all.

Such a fine thing to see Herry's face revealed. And I have to think it did him some good, as well. I lay a hand to his cheek, just because I could. Who was there to stop me? And who but Herry would ever know of my foolishness? So soft was his cheek. But gaunt. And gaunter by the day. He was not long for this world. But he probably knew it as well as I, so there was no point in dwelling upon it. Death would claim us all soon enough.

I patted his hand and then took it up in my own. Of course, I had to curl his fingers round mine, but there was a nice heft to it as it lay in my palm.

"*Ach,* two fools are what we are. You for lingering. And me for dawdling." As I said it, I shed a tear for the man with nothing left but his wits, and the woman with nothing left but her work. I sat there beside him, holding his hand, until I heard Marguerite coming toward the door.

The devil himself would have heard Marguerite coming, accompanied as she was by some man or another. All shrieks of mirth and howls of laughter, they were.

I gave Herry his hand back and tucked it underneath the

blanket I'd settled atop him. For certain it would stay there for the night.

I opened the door when I heard the straw's rustle and Marguerite's curse. "You might have pushed this all to the side!"

Hiding a smile beneath a hand, I did push it aside with the toe of my clog as I brushed past her. "And you might give him a look over in the middle of the night. To see if he wants for anything."

"And if he did, could he tell me?"

"You've only to look at him. He'd tell you. With his eyes."

She sneered and then shut the door in my face.

CHAPTER 10

Denis Boulanger

THE BORDER OF FRANCE AND FLANDERS

ONE MONTH, THE LIEUTENANT SAID HE'D GIVE ME. BUT I still hadn't found any lace.

Once, though, I had been close. I'd stopped a man as he stepped into the line. There was something about his eyes. Something in the way they shifted back and forth as he looked around. There was only the shack and the lieutenant and myself to look at. It seemed strange to me he should be so interested in the goings-on about him. Especially when everyone else concerned themselves with the tips of their own shoes.

I'd asked him to remove his cloak.

There was nothing hidden inside it.

I'd asked him to remove his coat.

There was nothing in there, either.

I might have stopped right there, but it seemed to me if he had nothing to hide, he would have said so.

I asked to look in his pack. He had a purse in there and a shirt and what looked like a very fine loaf of bread. "Is it any good?"

He looked up at me. "What?"

"Is it good? It looks as if it is."

"It's…very nice."

My father was an excellent baker. Anyone in Signy-sur-vaux would have said so. It wasn't easy to make a good loaf of bread. That's why I'd joined the army.

He coughed. "May I go?"

"What?"

"Have you finished?"

Had I? I didn't think so. "Might I have some?"

"Some…?"

"Some of your bread."

"My bread."

Even if there were no lace hidden inside, I had a sudden longing for a good piece of bread. He was no destitute peasant; there were no children staring hungrily at this loaf. I thought—I hoped—he could spare just one bite.

He broke off the heel and handed it to me.

It was very good. Quite good, in fact, though not quite so fine as the bread my father made. I waved the man into the line and stepped back to survey the crowds.

I wondered that day and the next and the one after it whether I ought to have left Signy at all. There were benefits to being a baker.

A hot oven to warm the home. Bread without end for the children.

There had been ten of us at my father's house. A brood of brothers and sisters. And there had been cousins, as well. My family had flowed along with the river from Signy-sur-vaux out to l'Abbaye and even unto Dommery.

Why had I ever left the place?

I'd had bread in abundance and a fire that had rarely ever gone out…though in the summer, with the fires roaring, I might as well have lived in the pit of hell.

My father had never understood why I could not be content. "You want to be the only Boulanger who makes no bread?" That's what he'd asked me when I told him I was leaving for the army.

And that's when I'd had to tell him the truth. "It's not

THE RUINS OF LACE

what I want to do," I'd said. I didn't mind the fires in the winter. Or the fall or the spring. I liked the smell of bread rising. I didn't even mind kneading it. I just didn't want to become known as the man who made bread.

He'd thrown up his flour-drenched hands, loosing a fine, dusty cloud that settled upon his shoulders as he spoke. "What does that have to do with anything? You're a Boulanger! And *boulangers* make bread."

It had everything to do with it in my opinion. That's why I'd joined the army. Once he'd gotten used to the idea, my father had claimed it as his own. And when I was posted to the border, he'd told everyone in town I would soon make my fortune catching smugglers.

And I might have. Had I caught any of them.

So how was I supposed to write him and tell him I'd failed? Again. At something that was supposed to be so simple to do? I couldn't decide which would be worse: working for the lieutenant who expected so very much, or working for my father who was content with so very little.

CHAPTER II

The Dog

RURAL FLANDERS

HUNGER HAD GNAWED A HOLE RIGHT THROUGH MY belly and come out on the other side. I knew it, because I did not hunger anymore. Neither did I sleep. Neither did I hear.

I did nothing.

I was nothing.

There was nothing.

Nothing but the box.

I woke, though I had not been sleeping. I woke to the scent of something sweet. Something clean. I was out of the box, and the bad master was in front of me. I could see his feet.

"Drink."

In front of his feet was a bowl.

"Drink, Chiant!"

I wanted to drink from it, but I couldn't get my head to move.

He reached out, grabbed one of my ears, and jerked on it to lift my head. Then he slid the bowl beneath my chin with his foot and let go my ear.

My head fell into the bowl.

"Drink!"

I wished I could drink. I opened my mouth enough to let my tongue fall out. The liquid was sweet, but I could manage only one lick.

"Do I have to feed you myself?"

He grabbed my head, hooked a finger between my jaws, and forced them open. Then he took up the bowl and poured it down my throat.

I could not swallow fast enough, and most of it ran down my muzzle to my paws.

"*Emmerdeur!*"

Kicking the bowl away, he shoved me back into the box and sealed it up. I licked my paws where the liquid had spilled, and I did not stop until I had consumed it all. After a while, I began to hear the birds again. And the squirrels. And soon, I felt my strength returning.

With the bowl had come a memory. The sweetness of the liquid had served as a reminder. I remembered everything now. That bowl would be followed by another. And another. And finally, I would be freed.

I turned onto my side, rolled into myself, and at long last, I slept. I dreamt the memory of a hushed whisper and a hand that stroked my fur. Moncherargent.

Moncher, Moncher, Moncher.

❦

When I woke, it was to the sound of footsteps approaching my box.

I curled into a ball and hid my nose beneath my paws.

A nail pulled through wood, and then a wall came off my box.

I blinked at the sudden invasion of light. Slunk back into a shadow.

Something struck the top of the box.

I flung myself against the back wall.

"Come out!" The box shuddered.

I curled back up into a ball.

"Chiant! I give you something to drink. That's all. See? Here."

I heard the sound of something sliding along the ground and lifted my face so I could see. It was a bowl. I raised my nose and took a sniff.

It was a bowl of something sweet.

I raised an ear.

Listened.

"Are you coming out?"

I let my ear drop, pressing it tight against my head.

The bad master's face appeared in front of the bowl. "Drink, damn you!"

He shoved the bowl toward me with his foot.

The smell of it flooded my nostrils and brought hunger creeping back into my belly. I put forward one foot, stepping out from the shadow.

"*Oui*. That's it. Drink." His face disappeared.

I waited a moment to make sure it would not return. Then I stepped forward. Raised my nose. Sniffed.

The bad master was nearby. I could smell the sour scent of him. I took another sniff. He was not too near. Perhaps if I drank quickly…I put my head into the bowl and lapped it up as fast as I could. But I was too slow.

The wall hit me on the snout as it came down.

And as I pulled back away from the bowl, as I retreated into the box to the safety of darkness, the wall was pounded back into place. The next time he came, I would be ready. The next time, I would not cower in the box. I would not creep out to drink. The next time he came, I would jump right over the bowl, take to the forest, and run straight to my other master. That is what I would do.

I would do everything right this time.

And I would never be sent away again.

∞

I woke to the sound of a door opening. I raised an ear.

It was the door to the house.

I crouched. Tensed.

The wall came off my box, and a bowl was placed in front of me.

Ignoring it, I made ready my escape.

But then...

My nose picked up the scent of the liquid...so sweet. I could not keep hunger from rallying inside me.

No. All I had to do was run. I would run and run and run and not stop until I came to the good master's house. And he would feed me all I wanted and just a little bit more.

I looked out beyond the bowl to the forest. It waited for me.

The wind blew a breeze into my box, and it brought with it the scent of the bowl. It smelled so good.

Perhaps...just a little sip. Just one.

I crept forward, looking at the bowl.

Just one sip. What could it hurt?

I put my head out of the box. I looked around, but I could not see the master. I could smell him, I could hear him breathing, but I could not see him.

Just one sip.

One quick sip, and then I would run. I would run so fast he would not catch me.

I lowered my snout to the bowl and thrust out my tongue for a quick sip. It tasted so good. And as it went down my throat, it warmed everything inside. Just one sip more. What harm could it do?

I stuck my snout down deeper into the bowl...let my tongue linger in the liquid.

What was I doing!

Quickly, I lapped up another sip. And then another. And one sip more.

The wall caught my paw as it came crashing down.

I drew it out from underneath the wood with a yelp. By the time I had finished licking it, finished tending to it, I was trapped.

Again.

༄

I slept. But I did not dream of cream. I dreamed a memory, one of whips and muzzles.

In my dreams, the bad master carried me into his house.

I hated being in his house. It smelled stale and sour. But being in his house meant the time was near. It meant my wounds would be treated, and my belly would be given food.

All I had to do before being freed was endure one thing more.

In my dream, I whined at the memory of that one thing.

The bad master laid me on a pile of straw, but he kept hold of my feet, wrapping a cord about them and pulling it tight. Then he took a pair of shears and started to work on my fur. Beneath the bite of the blades, it fell from my skin in clumps.

After he finished clipping me, he drew a pot of water from the fire and dipped a piece of cloth into it. Then he rubbed it over what was left of my fur.

Even in my dream, I was thirsty. I leaned my head over and tried to lick up the water.

He cuffed me on the nose.

"It's for cleaning, not for drinking. You will have enough to drink, more than enough, when you get to my cousin's." The master finished cleaning me, and then he took up a razor. Like always, it got caught on my skin.

93

I yelped, turning to try to lick at it.

"*Connard!* Stop moving!" He tried once more.

Again the razor bit into me.

"*Chiard!* You're bleeding all over!"

He dropped the razor and stalked to a cupboard. Came back with a bottle, which he raised to his lips.

I was still thirsty. I licked my nose. I wished he would let me have a drink from his bottle.

"Perhaps I should give you some too, Chiant. To send you faster through the forest?" He laughed. "*Non.* This drink is too good for you." He took another sip and then set the bottle down. When he picked up the razor, it went better that time.

"Here, Chiant." He tossed a blanket over me. I curled into myself beneath it, trying to hide from what I knew was coming.

He used it to dry my skin, turning me this way and that beneath it. After he uncovered me, he unwound the cord that bound my feet and set me on a table. And then he placed a piece of fabric across my back.

"Silk. How do you like that? Nothing but the best for the best. That's what we're paid for."

I liked this part of the dream. The fabric was soft against my bare skin, and it kept me warm.

"So. What do you think of that?" He held out a long length of a white web. I could see the fire's light through it.

I stood, completely still, as he wound it around my body. To move even one muscle would mean...I whined at the thought of what he would do to me as a nightmare began to nibble at the edges of my dream.

"Don't even think about it, Chiant!"

Around and around and around the web went. And then another piece of fabric was placed atop it. The next part was the worst. I cowered as I saw him pick up the hide.

"Come, Chiant. Don't you wish to see your brother?"

I wanted to back away from him, but I wouldn't. I couldn't.

The first time he'd done this to me, I had squatted on the table with the web wound around my body, and I had pissed into it just for spite.

He had pulled out the nails from one of my back paws. Only the thought of fires and laps and cream had pushed me through the forest that night to the good master's house.

I heard myself whine, but though I tried to rouse myself from the dream, I couldn't.

This part was the worst. It brought back memories of a time when my brother and I wrestled in front of the fire at the good master's house. Memories of a time when we slept entwined, his head resting on my belly. *Legrand* he was called. He was bigger than me. But somehow, whenever we played, he always ended up on the bottom.

He always let me win…until *that* day.

Until the day when the bad master came and took him into the good master's barn.

I followed, because I did not know then how my life was to be. I did not have any knowledge of switches or boxes, of hunger or thirst. I only knew sleep was for dreams and life was for play. I followed to see what new game there might be.

But I followed too late.

By the time I reached the barn, the bad master had already plunged the knife into Legrand's throat. His blood had already spilled out upon the ground, and his tongue hung, motionless, from his mouth.

The smell, that odor of un-life, had filled my nose and stilled my legs. I could not breathe. I could not move. I could do nothing but watch.

I watched as the bad master shoved a hook through Legrand's leg and hung him from the ceiling. I watched as all Legrand's blood drained out into a pail. I watched as the bad master took a knife and began to separate Legrand's skin from his body. I heard the tear of skin from flesh, the rasping of knife against bone. And I watched him peel the fur back from my brother's body in one big piece.

And then he turned, and he came at me, just like he was doing now. "And now, Chiant, it is you who are Legrand." He said those words that day just the same way he said them in my dream.

I cowered at the horror of it, but I dared not move. If only I could close up my nose. If only the scent of Legrand's hide were not mixed with the odor of death.

The master came at me from behind.

Even in my dream I closed my eyes, for I did not wish to see what I could not help but feel.

He lifted first one back leg, then the other, threading them through Legrand's hide and pulling it up over my back the way I'd seen the good master pull on his clothes. He pulled Legrand all the way up to my neck.

I shrunk from the feel of him. From the scent of him.

Coming forward, he lifted my front foot, tugging it through the place where Legrand's front leg used to go. Then he did the same with the other.

I was bound up with, I was shrouded in, Legrand. The weight of him, the feel of him set me to shivering. The memory of him made me whine.

"Hello, Legrand. It has been a long time since we see you! Ey—no crying, Chiant. He was such a good brother to grow so big for you. Such a good brother to let you borrow his coat." He put his hands around my padded body, picked me up, and set me on the ground.

I woke with a bark. And then I sat there in the dark of the box, and I shivered.

CHAPTER 12

Lisette Lefort

Château of Souboscq
The province of Gascogne, France

THE COUNT OF MONTREAU RUMBLED INTO OUR courtyard one afternoon at the beginning of October. His carriage raised a cloud of dust that rained down upon the outbuildings and the courtyard.

Though he retained his striking beauty, he seemed to have grown thinner. He possessed a feral grace that reminded me of the fox that lived in the wood lining the estate. There was both refinement and menace in each of his steps. And his clothes served only to heighten that impression. Even veiled by the settling cloud of dust, the colors shone. I knew, from regrettable experience, they were made from only the finest materials. They would have put my own gown to shame three years ago when it had been new.

As the count disappeared into the château, Alexandre came toward the barn, as if he knew where I was hiding. His gaze raked the gloom as he stood at the threshold. Between us, a ray of light had pierced the stone walls, slashing through the darkness. In its shimmer, dust floated in the musty air, glistening like gold.

I clung, even more desperately, to my shadow.

"I know you're here, Lisette."

He always seemed to know where to find me.

"If you wish to remain veiled by shadows, you should not wear so pale a color."

I looked down at my worn and faded brocade that glowed even in the near absence of light. "It's the only gown I have." Least the only one that did not require me to pull in my shoulders, tighten my fraying laces, and flatten my bosom to don it. It was a difficult task to maintain the outer aspect of a viscount's daughter, when that viscount's monies had been so drastically reduced.

But worse than that, in my deepest heart I desired all of those things I had made certain we would never have. All of those things we had possessed when *Maman* had still been living. I craved the silks and the jewels and all of the comforts I had been born to. All of the luxuries we had sold to repay our debt. Was that not fruitless and vain? Perhaps it was the thorn in my flesh: to be always aware of what I might have been. Of what I might have had.

An eternal penance.

That's why I so often walked the ridge of an evening. There was beauty enough in the hill and in those mists for the taking. Though it often made me wonder what my mother would think of me now.

I tried to be like her; I tried to be good. I tried to ask for nothing more than what was needed. And most of all, I tried to damp my desires. 'Twas my impulses that had betrayed me. Everyone thought me kind and meek and unfailingly mild. I hoped it was only I who knew the truth.

Alexandre's eyes had darkened as he looked at me. "You should have trunks filled with gowns. And slippers in abundance."

It brought to mind the words he had spoken at dusk on the hillside, and an uncharacteristic blush burned my cheeks. Perhaps I should have. But it was my own fault I would never possess them. I considered burrowing my bare feet into the straw, but he could not see them from where he was standing. What did it matter in any case? I saved my slippers for only the most special of occasions. There were precious few of those to be had anymore.

"Come out from there."

"So the count can gloat over all his coercion has cost us?"

"No. Because you are worth ten thousand of him. It isn't right that his presence should deprive us of your own. How else could we bear his visit otherwise?"

The perfect gentleman. That's what Alexandre had always been. He always smelled so clean, like the sunshine or the wind. And his flatteries somehow always seemed to sound like unimpeachable truth. I allowed myself a smile. And a hint of my old spirit. "If I come, it's only because you're the one doing the asking."

"And if I ask, it's a selfish request, since it would benefit me the most."

As I departed my refuge, I brushed the dust and cobwebs from my skirts, shook the straw from my feet, and pushed back the curls that had sprung free from their restraining riband. I stepped into that errant ray of light, and the world went bright for a brief moment. Then I plunged back into the gloom.

I eyed Alexandre as I began to brush past him.

As a child, I always used to kiss him for his attentions in spite of his holding himself away from me. I had taken particular pleasure in doing those things I was not supposed to do.

Such an impulsive, spoiled, and petted creature I was!

Though I had imagined kissing him a thousand times since his confession, I held myself apart from him now. This impulse I would control. Alexandre could still marry well. If he put his mind to it, he might find an heiress far from here who knew nothing of Souboscq or our decline in fortunes. If he couldn't save us, he might yet be able to save himself. He reached out a hand and brushed my cheek with his fingers.

Pressing my back to the timbers of the doorframe, I slipped past him, hand to my cheek, as I added one item more to the list of those things I would not let myself desire.

☙

I loved the home of my birth. I always had, with its red tiled roofs and rounded towers, nestled in the heart of Gascogne. Though it had been a place of plenty, those in the King's circle would have scoffed at those things we considered luxuries. Though nothing about the château was fashionable, everything in it was familial. From the sturdy, dark walnut furniture to the tapestries that had decorated the walls with scenes of the peasantry. From the blackened mantels above the fireplaces to the timeworn stone floors. But the presence of the count seemed somehow to have offended. It was all closed doors and dark corridors. What had, in the past, seemed so expansive and familiar, now seemed to have shut itself away.

At the hour of supper, I descended into the hall as the count was conversing with Father.

"We so enjoy our time here and always look forward to your *generous* hospitality." The count's companion, who stood beside him, snickered.

Father's face went red, and Alexandre's hand moved toward the hilt of the dagger he kept hidden beneath his coat. As many times as I had begged, as a child, to see it, he had always refused me that honor.

I stepped in front of them both to address the count,

100

curtseying. "Please, my lord. Won't you join us at the table?" No good would come from words spoken in anger. There was nothing to be gained by hostility. I tried to hide my bare feet beneath my skirts, though the shortness of the hems and the new, longer length of my legs did not allow for it. But just the same, I lifted my chin in honor of my father's title.

The count bowed toward me with a twist of his lips. "As you wish."

The only thing I wished him was far from Souboscq…and a gruesome death on the road back to whatever hell it was from which he had come.

Supper was eaten in relative silence, save a belch or two from the count's companion. The food did not reflect our decline. We had thrown ourselves upon the mercy of Providence. The stream could always be counted upon to yield a trout or two, and the orchard its apples and pears and noisettes. It was after the cheese had been served that Father began to speak. "I must tell you plainly, my lord, we have no money. The crops last year withered in the earth from drought, and this year's harvest was also poor."

The count waved his knife in the air, as if to banish my father's words. "Have no worries. I have not come, this year, for gold."

Father and Alexandre exchanged a glance. Father raised a brow. "No gold?"

"No, my dear fellow. I've come to settle the debt."

Astonishment must have gripped us all, for Alexandre dropped his spoon, and Father's brows nearly disappeared into his hair, while a wild sort of elation threatened to bubble from my throat.

"I've no concern for gold, you see, for I've come to be repaid in lace."

Alexandre collected his spoon and then placed it carefully

upon his plate. "The arrangement, I believe, was for us to repay you as we are able."

"No. The arrangement was that you would pay me for my loss, and I would keep your role in Chalais's conspiracy to kill Cardinal Richelieu to myself. That was the arrangement. Unfortunately, however, I need the lace now."

"You will be paid as we are able to pay you." Alexandre repeated the words as if the count hadn't quite comprehended them.

"Oh! I see. You misunderstood me. How can I put this plainly? I no longer want money. I no longer need it. What I need is what I don't have. The lace."

"We don't...we don't have any lace." My father seemed to be choosing his words with some delicacy, as if that might placate the count. "The King has forbidden the wearing of lace."

"I see how it might seem that way, with his edict and all of that nonsense, but the thing about kings is they so rarely say what they mean. You can hardly depend upon them at all. He said no lace, but everyone knows the lace he doesn't see won't disturb him. He's very reasonable that way, you know. Or perhaps...I suppose you don't know. Having taken part in that regrettable plot."

Father's brows had now reappeared, hurtling toward his nose. "I...I don't understand—"

"*Lace*. It's the lace I have need of now. Gold is no longer of any use to me."

"But I...we...I do not have your lace! It's for that reason I have repaid you these many years."

"Ah! Tsk, tsk. There now, you have not spoken honestly. It's for your abominable folly in joining that doomed conspiracy against Richelieu all those years ago you have paid me. We might as well be frank, you and I, since it seems we're to be bound together for a while longer."

A sweat had broken out upon Father's brow. "I have no lace."

"Yes. I know. That's what caused all this trouble from the first. I suppose you'll have to send to Flanders for some."

"To—? But…it's forbidden! Lace has been forbidden by the King himself."

"True. But you are a clever fellow. I'm sure you'll think of some way around it."

The count's companion smirked as he listened.

"To be caught with lace is to be subject to a six-thousand-livres fine. And exile. And the confiscation of estates."

The count raised a finger. "Only if you are caught."

"But…I can't…I don't know…I don't even know how much it would cost…" Father had gone pale as he spoke. "And I've already paid you so much…"

The count smiled as if his extortion had not cost us nearly everything we owned. "I can see my simple, reasonable request has taken you by surprise. Perhaps I should have stated my requirements more delicately." He sniffed. "I've no doubt a night's sleep will be…illuminating…for I'm convinced you'll come to the same conclusion I have. It is my belief you have no other option." He touched a cloth to his lips, nodded at his companion, and then stood. "*Belles rêves.*"

Father and Alexandre talked long into the night. I lit a precious taper for them. When it had burned to a stub, sparking and sputtering in a pool of its own wax, I lit a second.

"We must refuse him." Alexandre had not taken long to reach this conclusion. That he clung to it for so many hours was admirable. That he insisted upon repeating it often was less so.

Father sighed and ran a trembling hand through his thinning hair. "As I have already said, we cannot refuse him."

Alexandre took to his feet and followed an already well-trod path in front of the hearth. "I say we must refuse him, only because we cannot honor his request." His voice had risen by that time, as well.

"We must. You know how Cardinal Richelieu is! He acts as the King himself. He has spies everywhere, and if the count breathed even a word of my involvement with the conspiracy, he would take my head in a minute. Just like the Marquis of Chalais's. If he took a marquis's head, what would he do with me? A viscount. What would be left for you? And who would care for Lisette?"

I sunk deeper into my corner, pressing myself against the cold stone of the wall as he said my name and as Alexandre's gaze swung toward me. It must have taken great control on both their parts not to have thrown my mistake up in my face. It was no one's fault but mine that the count had demanded from them such an impossible thing.

Father continued with a sigh. "We must face the facts. The count can ask me for anything he wants, and I have no choice but to give it to him." He shook his head when Alexandre tried to speak. "I am simply stating what's true. If we sell the estate, then—"

"No!" The word escaped my lips before I could think to stop it. They must not sell the estate. The estate was all that was left. As long as Father held the lands, then there was hope. With the estates as his promised inheritance, Alexandre might still marry. The weather might change— next autumn might bring a more generous harvest. And who knew when the count would die? We might, all of us, find relief sooner than we thought. But without the lands, we would be nothing at all.

Father's face seemed to crumple in upon itself as he turned toward me.

I stepped farther back into the shadow.

"*Ma chérie*...I do not have many choices. My past does not allow me that luxury."

"Please...don't do it." Then I would be responsible for his complete and total destruction. I stepped toward the light of the taper. Toward him. "Please don't."

Alexandre joined me in beseeching him. "You must not. He has no right to demand it!"

Father tried to smile. "Sometimes the past has the power to devour the future. If only I had known then what would be required of me now...but perhaps there is still some hope. If we can get a high enough price for the land, then perhaps we can keep the château..."

"But...it's not fair!" There was no use trying to hide the tears that seeped from my eyes. I had come so near him by that time, when he reached for me, his hand found my cheek. He cupped it there, just as he had done so many times before when I was a child. I wished, how I wished, I could be the daughter he needed. In spite of the slow deterioration of our circumstances, he had insisted I be trained in singing and dance and the playing of the lute. Somewhere he had found the money. He wanted me to have the same advantages *Grand-père* had given *Maman*. He'd always claimed me to be the picture of her person, but why couldn't he realize I could never match her soul?

Against all reason, he kept planning for my future. He kept asking me my opinion of this count's son or that duke's nephew. As if I still had the chance to marry and become some great lord's companion. In truth, I had never wanted a great lord, and without a dowry I would never have one now. But my dreams, as well as his plans, were dead.

I had only ever wanted to be the woman with a cool, gentle touch. I longed to speak in melodies and have hands that danced along to the rhythm of my words. To laugh without care and to offer grace without stopping to calculate the cost.

I wanted to be like my mother. I wanted to be worthy of my father's pride.

But I had wanted overmuch.

I had insisted on playing with a pair of lavish lace cuffs instead of contenting myself with memories. I had longed for the love and admiration of Alexandre instead of accepting the consequence of my sins. It seemed I was destined always to want more than I could have.

And in the wanting, I had forfeited everything.

My hand found his as I knelt before him, weeping. "It's all my fault."

"No, *mon trésor*. Never. The fault is mine. I should never have taken part in such schemes. And I should not have sheltered so abominable a young man as the count. If only I had turned him away from our door that night...told him to pass on to Mont-de-Marsan."

His hand lingered a moment more on my cheek, a moment longer than I deserved, and then he dropped it with a sigh, turning toward Alexandre. "You can see, dear cousin, there is nothing else to do."

Was there nothing I could do? Nothing I could give in order that my father be allowed to retain the estates?

The count wanted lace? Would that I knew how to make some, but I did not. I could do nothing. Nothing of worth or real value. What use was there now for lute playing or singing?

There was a deep, profound, and abiding anguish that

dulled Father's eyes the next morning as he bid farewell to the count.

"I will have my lace, then." The man didn't even phrase the words as a question.

"You will have your lace." Father's speech was stiff, as if it caused him great pain even to speak.

The count smiled, a wolfish baring of teeth. "How generous you are. To a fault one might say. If you would allow me a suggestion…?"

Father inclined his head.

"One can always count on the abbey at Lendelmolen to make a lovely length of lace at a price worth the effort." He presented a letter.

Father took it with a shaking hand. "The abbey at Lendelmolen."

"Yes. And I think six yards would suffice. Six yards of their loveliest lace."

Alexandre stepped forward, one hand at his dagger, the other balled into a fist. "You scoundrel! The length you lost was only three yards. You said so yourself."

He blinked. "Did I? Well…I must have been mistaken."

"Six yards will cost the viscount everything."

"And if I tell the King about his secret activities, it will cost him one thing more!"

My hopes died within me. The estate would have to be sold. Better then to cease being the one thing that had always caused those I loved the most harm. Better to throw myself upon the mercy of a stranger. Then Father would be released from the debt, and Alexandre would be free to marry. "Take me. For pity's sake!"

The count regarded me through a narrowed gaze.

I found myself falling at his feet. "Take me, and be done with it."

"No!" Alexandre's strangled cry and lunge made me grab at the count's feet. If he would just take me in exchange for payment, then all would be right. But the boots I had grasped shook off my hands and then took a deliberate step away from me.

All was lost.

"Take you?"

I lifted my head, meeting a gaze from eyes so dark they reflected nothing at all. "Please. Take me instead. Instead of the lace. Take me and consider the debt paid."

He stretched out a hand toward me.

Gathering my skirts about me, I sprang for it, grabbing at the certain freedom it would bring my father.

He seized it and pulled me to standing. "Yes, I will take you. I'll take you for safekeeping, for I have an idea that assuring your safety will assure I get what I want." He put an arm about my shoulders and turned me to face my father and Alexandre. "Don't you?"

Shoving me before him into the carriage, he paused as he ascended behind me, turning to address my father. "I will take your daughter with me, since she has so kindly offered herself, but only as a guarantee. I shall expect that length of lace directly…if you ever hope to see her again."

But…what? I had no other wish than to reach out for my papa's arms. But I could not do it; the coachman had already put a whip to the horses. I scrambled toward the window, only to fall back as the carriage lurched forward.

The count's companion laughed at me.

Trying once more, I reached for the window and pulled myself up to it. It was only then, as I saw something very much like despair stamped upon Father's and Alexandre's faces, I began to consider that I might have done the wrong thing.

. CHAPTER 13 .

The Count of Montreau

ALONG THE ROAD TO THE CHÂTEAU OF ERONVILLE

I LEANED FORWARD, TOWARD THE OPPOSITE BENCH of the carriage, and lifted the girl's chin with a finger. "Let's see what we have here."

Her gaze met mine.

"I must say I approve of your spirit. Your willingness to sacrifice…but I find myself inquiring as to whether you actually expected me to accept your kind offer as it was stated—your admirable self in exchange for your father's debt and his unfortunate secret." I pulled the gloves off my hands and then handed them to Remy.

Her cheeks went flush.

"You did?" I could not save myself from laughing at her. "Why, my dear girl, then you understand nothing about me at all!"

She pressed her back against the cushioned seat, putting herself out of reach of me…although Remy was sliding looks at her from underneath his lashes.

"What I am to do with you?"

She was rather pretty in a provincial sort of way. All golden ringlets and fair complexion. Though the girl's attire was shamefully ill fitting, her figure might have attracted the glances of many of the men at court. She was the kind of girl my mother would have called correct...the kind of girl my mother had once called me.

There ought to be something I could do with her.

Remy leaned over and whispered into my ear.

I frowned as I tried to hide my revulsion. "Perhaps she's to your taste, but she's not to mine." I did not care what he did with her. I could hardly demand fidelity in my lover when I could not always service his needs myself. Ignoring him, I addressed myself to her. "There must be some use that you can be put to. What is it that you do?"

She blinked.

"Are you dumb as well as daft?"

"I am not." Something sparked in her eyes.

"Then speak on your behalf. If you do not wish to be used by the chevalier of Fontenay"—I inclined my chin toward Remy—"then you must be prepared to offer some other sort of amusement."

She looked at Remy as if in horror, face blanched white. "Amusement...?"

I hoped she was not one of those girls who fainted at the slightest of provocations. "You're the daughter of a viscount. I could hardly hire you out as a common servant, and my own requirements are adequately met, so what other good can you do me?"

"I can...I can read. And sing. I'm quite useful in the making of unguents and cures."

"My father has a wife for all of those."

"Excuse me, my lord. Your father?"

"It's to his estate we are returning." What I would not give to make it mine!

"I can play the lute, and I can dance."

"I don't dance. At least not with girls."

Beside me, Remy snorted.

I turned to him. "If you cannot be kind, then you must not say anything at all."

He gave me a sardonic grin. "I beg your pardon."

The girl's color had rallied, and she was no longer breathing quite so shallowly. "I've been trained to marry. To serve as a companion to persons of the *noble* class." The look she shot at Remy was filled with poison.

Bred to marry, trained to be the perfect companion, as all fine ladies should be. Perhaps I *could* find a use for her.

∾

After the passage of four hours within the close confines of the carriage, the fact that the girl had thrust herself upon me began to grate. I did not want her. I had a horror of girls. What I wanted was lace. And I had tried my best to obtain some.

Journeying the byways of the kingdom to Souboscq had not been my original plan. I counted on the viscount's money; it financed my gambling, sometimes, for the better part of a year. I would have much preferred to have kept that source of funds unencumbered.

I started my quest for lace at court.

Over a month before, the morning after Cardinal St. Florent's visit, I roused Remy from my bed and made him find a servant to pack up the trunk.

"Whatever for?"

"For posterity's sake. Both mine and yours."

Though he scowled and muttered bitterly at having to face the day at such an early hour, he did my bidding. He always did my bidding. I had bought him his title, I had settled his debts, and I kept him in money when I could. I also shared my bed with him.

I made my excuses to the marquis, which he countered with his tiresome and familiar bluster. "Court? To do what?"

Collect the funds to buy the lace to guard the fortune he was so set upon denying me. "We've been here since your marquise discovered she was breeding. If you will not represent our interests at court, someone must, or you risk returning to find you have no interests left to protect."

He opened his mouth in what seemed certain to be a protest, but then he shut it up with a frown.

How could he protest the truth? When new intrigues at court seemed to be birthed with the rising of the sun each day, it was far better to be present than to risk being implicated in one. These were trying times. The King was embattled with the Spaniards to the west and in the north, and with the Hapsburgs to the east and in the south. With the King's brother intriguing against him, and the Queen Mother instigating rebellions from her exile in the Spanish Netherlands, it took only a whisper to link one to the wrong side. Indeed, it was difficult to find any right side of late.

At least the King was favorably disposed toward my father. And the Queen had made Gabrielle a favorite. My stepmother's blue eyes generally sparked with merriment, and her rosy cheeks betrayed the high spirits that never failed to amuse Her Majesty.

Though I would pay my respects to the King, I would try my best to keep myself far from the Queen. Her Spanish sensibilities could not allow her to approve of me, and becoming known at her court had the disadvantage of becoming suspect in the eyes of the King.

Though His Majesty liked my father, I knew my kind weren't his favorite. He preferred men like Remy, who enthused over hunting and horses. And he was not one to approve of the flaunting of wealth. His only passion seemed to be for working himself into an ill health.

And taking part in a ballet now and then.

Taking leave of my father with a bow, I pulled on my gloves, threw out the edges of my cloak, and adjusted the pleats. Then I cocked my hat at just the right angle: the one that cast a shadow over my eyes. When I joined Remy, who had aided in preparing the carriage, bits of straw and manure still clung to his boots. Though I'd bought him the title of chevalier, his breeding had a tendency to betray him at the most unfortunate of times. His father had been equerry to the King, and he could not seem to master his fascination for all things equine.

I, on the other hand, had difficulty tolerating the beasts. Their stench had ruined a pair of my breeches on more than one occasion. And their hair had the habit of working itself into even the most intimate of garments.

I pushed aside my cloak to mount the carriage and then straightened it once inside.

Remy sprawled onto the seat beside me, planting one of his boot-clad feet on the cushioned bench across from us. I removed it with a tap of my walking stick.

Unfortunately, I lost the carriage at Madame Sainctot's the first night back in Paris. It was unavoidable. I'd been dealt a bad hand, and my concentration had been inhibited. At least I hadn't bet my brass pocket pistol. Losing that would have been the worst of sartorial sins.

Remy had been playing at a different table on the far side of the room. Above the clink of drinking glasses and the murmur of conversations, I had heard him laugh. There had been a certain timbre to it. And a telltale glimmer in his eye.

They were the laugh and the glimmer that used to belong to me.

As I watched him, he flipped the ruffled edge of his sleeve away from his wrist with a graceful twirl and reached out his hand to collect the chips with his long, elegant fingers. And then something on the far side of the room caught his attention.

I leaned past the Marquis d'Armont, to try to detect who or what it was, but I was not fast enough.

Damn him!

He wasn't offering his charms to anyone in particular. Not yet. And not overtly. He was being subtle. Too subtle for anyone to think of casting glances at me, to begin laughing at me. Not for the first time did I curse my sex and my inability to command it.

The Duke of Mirebeau's son winked at me as he laid down his cards. "Don't worry. I'll put the carriage to good use for you."

"Thank you ever so much." I tossed my cards into the middle of the table.

"A fine carriage like that. You might want it back someday."

I wanted it back right then, for I didn't envy a trip through the countryside on horseback.

"Let's call your carriage a down payment on that pile of gold you owe me. Your father's old. He's bound to die soon. If we can make an arrangement for payment of your debt in full, I might one day consider returning the coach."

"You're a saint."

He canted a smile at me.

"Are you playing this hand, then, Montreau, or would you rather flirt?" The Marquis d'Armont was beginning to deal.

"With you?" I gave him what I hoped was a look of disdain. "I think not. I've a certain standard to uphold."

At a ribald pun on the word "standard" and a gesture too crude to be repeated, the table broke into laughter.

I slid my card back toward the marquis. "I find I've developed a sudden taste for company more refined than you." I rose from my chair and bowed.

"And we've developed a taste for more of your fabled fortune. Don't go! Don't be a villein. You ought to share with those less fortunate. It's good for the soul."

"I have it on good authority, gentlemen, I have no soul worth saving." I took up my walking stick, tucking it beneath my arm as I toured the room. What was wrong with me? I was here to win a fortune, and I couldn't even concentrate on my cards.

Four short days later, we rode from Paris toward Souboscq, traveling in a rented coach. It was more to remove Remy from the court's temptations than because I had lost all my money. I had, in fact, retained some of it. Enough to last our journey. But my appetite for the game had disappeared. Though I had once risen to the challenge of cards and dice with the zeal of a warrior, this time I had not even been able to acquit myself as a nobleman.

I had taken up the habit of visiting the viscount of Souboscq at this time of year. The roads were generally in good repair, the weather was pleasant, and I could stop in at my own crumbling estate at Montreau on the way. If my father didn't attach so much sentiment to the title, and if it weren't for the fact it was the only thing he had ever given me, I might have well sold it. It didn't do to be associated with Poitou and its renegade politics, or its heretic religion.

As we traveled, we passed field after field shorn of grain.

God, how I envied the peasants their crops! One good harvest could bring them a small fortune. I had no such luxury. Had I owned a field, I could not have worked it. I could have collected rents from it, but I could not have actually sold any of its fruit, nor could I have lent a hand to their labors. Not if I wanted to retain my nobility. Gambling was the only honorable way to make and dispense fortunes. Though could farming not be considered gambling of a sort? I wondered as we passed by those fields, who offered the better odds: God or man?

God had been none too kind to me. Much better to trust in the insatiable greed of Cardinal St. Florent. But to turn him to my side, I needed lace.

If I'd had those cuffs the Lefort girl had spoiled, I would have given them to the cardinal already. That would have solved all my problems. But I didn't have anything at all, really. My finery was borrowed on my father's good name, and every livre I had wrung from the viscount of Souboscq had gone to keep me in cards.

Only now the whole consequence of my father's death had been placed into question.

But the cardinal was a creature quite like me. If I offered him something more than what my father could—and how could a length of lace fail to be more?—then he would respond in an entirely predictable way. My failures at gambling and my desperate need for lace are what had led me to Souboscq in Gascogne.

⁂

Somewhere along the road back to Poitiers, the girl stopped glaring at me and fell asleep. So did Remy. I nudged him awake. "Don't you know some countess or other in Berry?"

"The Countess of Bardelles…and the Duchess of Tillay."

"The girl needs some presentable clothes and some slippers."

"You're going to keep her, after all, then?"

I scowled at the desire that lit his eyes. "Not for that."

His face fell.

"If you're unhappy with me, you only need say so…"

"No! No, I'm quite content."

Was he? Truly?

"As far as the countess and duchess…I haven't seen either of the women for some time, and I don't know if they'll be amenable to my charms."

His charms. They were quite considerable, and they had always worked on me. I reached over to adjust the lie of his cravat, rearranging its ribbons. "Do only what you must."

A several days' stay in Berry yielded a stylish wardrobe. From the Countess of Bardelles we acquired a gorgeous basque and gown in blue Turkey velvet, decorated with gilt spangles. It was given to us with slippers to match. Two days later, from the Duchess of Tillay, we received a lovely green satin gown with its sleeves pinned back to reveal a gold-embroidered lining.

Remy tossed the satin beside me onto the bed we were sharing. It gleamed like a living thing atop the counterpane of gold-embroidered, claret-colored damask.

I resisted the urge to stroke the gown's length, though I knew from damnable experience how the silk would feel against my legs. How the skirts would rustle when I walked. And how elegant the slippers would look on my feet. I rolled over onto an elbow and poked at them with my book instead. "And how did you manage these?"

"I told the duchess you required them."

I raised a brow. "Indeed."

"Do not blame me if she received the impression it was *you* who would be wearing them."

I shrugged, though I wanted to shudder. I'd had enough of such games as a boy to ever want to don a gown again. Least that is what I told myself. My mother had wanted a girl, and it had fallen upon my shoulders to ease her disappointment. The day my father first recognized me as his son was the last day he had ever looked upon me with any sort of pride.

It had taken the longest time to get over caring.

∞

The skirts were too long, and the sleeves, meant to sit just off the shoulder, were cut too broadly for the girl. They kept sliding down her arms. But they were an improvement upon her provincial attire, nonetheless. Once I coaxed a maid to dress her hair, she looked fit for the royal court itself. With her hair cut in a stylish fringe and the sides pulled back to expose her ringlets, she looked every bit the noble companion I wanted her to be. As the carriage passed into Orléanais and wound its way to my father's estate, I made my wishes known to her.

"We will arrive this day at the Château of Eronville, the seat of the marquis."

She nodded, though she looked upon me still with great suspicion.

"My stepmother is breeding. The babe is soon to be born. Until your father can obtain my lace, you will serve as the marquise's companion. She can be quite pleasant..." When she wasn't trying to disinherit me. "I'm sure you'll find the company diverting."

As the girl sat back against the cushions, some of the tension seemed to leave her shoulders.

"You'll find if you please me, there will be no reason to

118

have to please the chevalier of Fontenay." I could not control Remy's vices or his fascination with women, but if, from time to time, I had let him indulge in such vagaries, then he had remained a more or less faithful companion. As long as he had kept his dalliances from my sight, I had not worried overmuch about them. But now, I could not stop thinking of our time in Paris. And I could not rid myself of the feeling he was mine no longer.

The girl's eyes blinked wide as the color drained from her face. Her gaze bounced from Remy to me. "You mistake me, my lord, for the common sort."

"No. You mistake me for the honorable sort. I assure you my intentions range somewhat farther than your obvious good breeding allows."

"You...you threaten me?"

"Not if you play the role you've been given. I'm merely offering you some advice. Respect my wishes, and there will be no need for any unpleasantness."

Remy took himself into the stables when we reached my father's château. The girl descended the carriage on my arm. The marquis soon appeared at our arrival, my stepmother toddling out behind him.

The marquis was so astonished at the girl's appearance he not only forgot to chastise me for taking—and losing—the carriage, but he also failed even to note the girl's name. He leaned close as ever he'd come to me as we walked together into the château. "Who did you say she was?"

"The viscount of Souboscq's daughter."

"Daughter! Then she's not yet married?" He put a hand to my arm, which stopped our progress. When I turned to look at him, I was met with a doleful and despairing expression. "I thought I had made my position plain. I have given you too many chances already, Julien, and you have failed me with them all. It's too late. I cannot undo what has been done. I've already consulted with Cardinal St. Florent about the annulment."

He thought my interest lay in the girl? "Do not worry yourself. I simply stopped in at Souboscq after I visited Montreau. I knew your wife was bereft of company, having secluded herself from court. I did not see why two such solitary souls should not find solace in each other. If the girl serves no other use than as an amusing companion to the marquise, then I shall find myself satisfied with my decision."

The marquis was looking at me as if he suspected me of something. "There is much joy to be found in marriage... even if it is too late for me to change my plans."

He was deceiving himself. I had no doubt but that my stepmother would soon make him just as wretched as my own mother had.

My stepmother, however, nursed no reservations about the girl's sudden appearance. She clapped her hands. "How kind you are, Julien! How generous you are to think of me." She held out a hand toward the girl. "You and I shall be the best of friends!"

CHAPTER 14

Alexandre Lefort

CHÂTEAU OF SOUBOSCQ
THE PROVINCE OF GASCOGNE, FRANCE

ARE YOU LISTENING, *FISTON?*"

Fiston. My father had called me *fiston.* Roused from my thoughts, I did not know where I would find myself: back in the forests of Béarn with my father or in the Château of Souboscq with the viscount. "Pardon me, Cousin." If ever clarity of thought and purpose were needed, this was the time. But…

He folded trembling hands atop the table where he was sitting. "Do you think you can do it?"

Could I? My cousin's lack of choices had ensured I had none. I had no choice but to do whatever was necessary to avoid being caught while I smuggled lace into France.

"You will have to be discreet."

I was the soul of discretion. None had ever guessed I had once been an urchin and a thief. Nor had any ever accused me of being a murderer. I had left that life far behind me, and now I was being asked to return to it. Everything within me cried out against it.

But the voice of Lisette cried louder still.

I could not blot the image of her face from my mind. Nor the sudden and terrible grief I had experienced since her absence. It was complete and overwhelming. Become a thief for her? A smuggler? I would descend even into the depths

of hell if I had to. There was nothing left to lose now. "I
will do it."

I would do anything.

♊

The estate was sold to a man who had always coveted its
abundance of fields and its enviable situation overlooking the
river. He was short and stout with a well-trimmed beard that
pointed toward his ample girth. But the golden embroidery
of his coat was overly ornate. The great floppy hat he wore
was far too large for his head. He was a man who went to the
greatest and most obvious of lengths to boost his reputation
to vaunted heights. Though he was one of the province's
tax administrators, there was nothing noble about him save
the robes he had purchased to go along with the position.
He had bought what others had, at one time, been born to.
At least people like my father, one of old King Henri's finest
warriors, might have aspired to *noblesse d'epée*, a nobility
gained in the fires of war and tested in the heat of battle. But
the only test this provincial official had ever undertaken was
to check the doneness of his meat or the fitness of his purse.

Someone, somewhere, ought to have laughed at me. How
earnestly I was defending a whole level of society of which I
had never truly been a member!

The man took me aside after my cousin had given him
the keys. "My daughter always pined for you, young Lefort.
Good thing I always told her to look to our interests elsewhere. Had I let her marry you, where would she be now?"
He stepped close enough that I could smell the garlic he
must have eaten for dinner the day before. "The truth of it
is, I've a chance at a position in the King's own household."

Had he *let* her marry me? He flattered himself to think I

122

would even one day have asked for her hand. But there was nothing to be gained now in vexing him. "I'm sure she will soon find a man well suited to your position."

He chuckled, a hand to his belly. "I hope those pretty manners of yours will keep you warm and fed."

The man bowed to the viscount. "A title without lands, and lands without a title. I wonder which one of us it is who's gotten the best of our arrangement?" His laugh left little question as to which of us he thought it was.

The official had given my cousin gold for the humiliation. We counted it as we sat in the house of the town's physician. We had prevailed upon the man to offer the viscount lodging while I journeyed to Flanders to obtain the count's lace. The viscount separated out one lone coin and pocketed it, and then he deposited the rest into a leather pouch and handed it to me.

I hesitated in placing the purse into my pocket. "You should keep more for yourself." If anything happened to me on my journey to buy the lace, I wanted him to have some sort of hedge against penury.

"The one thing I need is the one thing it seems I cannot have. Least not until after your return." His eyes were tired. His voice had gone old.

Lisette. She was the only thing that had ever brought light into his eyes and laughter to his voice. I wanted her, too. I hid the coins in a gusset of my doublet. "I shall return just as swiftly as I can."

He closed his eyes, nodding. Then he opened them and looked up at me, a warning in his gaze. He had me bring him a coffer he'd carried from Souboscq. From it he pulled a pair of pistols and pushed them across the table toward me. "Guard yourself. There are so many dangers...so many bandits on the roads these days..."

I took them, though I feared far more than highwaymen. I feared those who had the power to toss me back into the life from which the viscount had taken me. I feared the reach of the King's men and the power of Cardinal Richelieu. They could fine me six thousand livres, which I did not have. They could confiscate the viscount's title, and they could exile us all from the kingdom...if they did not execute my cousin first.

I had earned a fair bit as a child by gambling. Even now, far removed from those days, I felt a sad confidence in giving myself no better than even odds. "That money will keep you, then? Until I return?"

"Don't worry yourself about me." He reached out and clamped a trembling hand around my forearm. "The next time I see you, you will be with Lisette."

I could only nod and hope Fate would be kind. That I would, in fact, be seeing him again, and that I would be able to retrieve Lisette from the count.

"Perhaps while you're gone I should write a letter to the Marquis of Eronville to tell him what his son has done to us."

I gripped his hand in my own, kneeling beside him. "And give him reason to turn you over to the cardinal? You must say nothing! The count cannot harm her. Whatever his reasons, he needs the lace too much. The best way to guarantee her safety is to leave her exactly where she is."

It took five days of hard riding to reach Flanders. Once I crossed the border, I went on to the city of Kortrijk. After securing a room at a lodging house, I opened the count's letter.

What could be said about a man whose writing flowed in an even, measured script? Who began each line at the same point along the right edge of the paper and ended at the same point along the left? I would have thought such a man rational, reasonable. A man of self-restraint. But this writing didn't match what I knew of him. He of frivolous taste and a deficit of virtue. But there now at the bottom: that absurdly large, scrawling signature. Here was evidence of such a man.

In any case, I could not detest him more than I already did. I read past all of his pleasantries until I found the information that mattered.

✍

The item can be attained through the abbey in Lendelmolen. You will contact Arne De Grote, a purveyor of liquors. His store is located on Leiestraat near the market in Kortrijk. He will arrange transport of the item into France.

✍

I set out north for the abbey the next morning and was soon glazed with rain. Though at first I traveled through hills, those quickly flattened. A road had been raised across the flat plain of Flanders. It wound between marsh and pond, marsh and field, marsh and ditch. This was a land wrung from the sea, and yet its earth still had not dried. It oozed water in a dozen different ways, and the hooves of cows and sheep constantly trampled dirt that had thrust itself from the sludge back into the mire.

The air was scented with salt, earth, and manure. Myriad windmills churned the mist with their enormous sails.

125

They spun restlessly, almost silently, giving out only a faint *phhwoof-phhwoof* when I passed close enough to hear it.

It ought to have been an easy ride, but the horse struggled to keep its feet on the slippery clay. What might have taken two hours took four. And by the time I arrived, the rain had soaked through my hose, wetting my skin. I looked less like the nobleman I had nearly become and more like the urchin I had once been.

After the prosperous bustle of the city of Kortrijk, the humble town of Lendelmolen looked as miserable as I felt. Its houses were little more than rain-shedding hovels, its aspect colorless and rude. Even arriving as I was in the middle of the day in the rain, I might have been entertained by any number of prostitutes. As I declined their offers, I dodged a fish seller shouting his wares, and a woman shrieking at her son. It was with great relief that I spied what had to be the abbey's roofline over the top of a high stone wall. I followed the wall until I saw a gate. Nearby several unprincipled-looking men had gathered. At my approach, one of them broke from the others and came toward me. "Are you staying in town then, stranger?"

In this part of the old French county my language was still spoken, but I had difficulty understanding his accent. And wanting to tell no man my business, I tried to ignore him.

"Tell me where you're staying." He jogged alongside me. "I can get you a lace maker. One just turned out of the abbey. She's practically still a virgin."

One of the other men jeered. "If you can wait a few days, I'll get you a real virgin. My cousin works in there." He nodded toward the gate. "Says there's bound to be one put out before long."

"I've not come for that." I tried to direct my horse around the man, but he stepped into my path.

He leered. "But you could stay for that, now, couldn't you?"

I dug my heels into the horse. He pushed forward, knocking the man in the shoulder.

"Here now! There's no need to be rude about it. If you don't want her, we'll sell her up to Brussels or Amsterdam. But why let those city folks have all the fun?"

I dismounted quickly and pulled at the bell.

The nun who opened the gate looked in every direction but mine.

"I am here to see about some lace."

She nodded, her protruding eyes grave as her chin disappeared into her wimple. She opened the gate to me.

I followed her to an arcaded building.

She stopped me at the door with a raised hand. "Sister Margriet will show you to the treasury."

A second nun stepped from the arcade and led me onward.

A snapping fire and glowing candles lit the treasury. Vividly colored tapestries decorated the walls, and finely woven carpets lay on the floor. Souboscq had once been similarly ornamented. I had not realized how much I missed those luxuries until now. I presented my purse to a nun who was seated behind a large counting table. She nodded at me as she took it.

"I would like a length of your finest lace. Six yards."

She raised a brow, though she did not stop unfastening the thong from the pouch. She poured the money onto the table and counted it. Once she had separated the coins into piles by weight, she consulted an accounts book. "Six yards...our best lace maker is at work on a piece of some length just now. It should take her only two more weeks, perhaps a few days more than that, to complete it."

"Two weeks! But I had hoped—" How naïve my hopes seemed now. How naïve they must always have been. "I had hoped I could collect it now."

"Now?" She said it with no little disapproval, as if doubting I had all my wits about me.

"I had hoped…"

"It is not possible. It will take at least two weeks more."

At least two. I would have to count on three, then. Add a week for the return journey, and it would be a month before I could rescue Lisette from the count.

✺

The liquor merchant's shop was located on Leiestraat just as the count had said. I entered the store and addressed myself to the clerk working the counter. "I am here to see Arne De Grote about arranging transport for a length of lace. Across the border."

The store's lone customer had halted in his steps. Now he turned toward me.

The clerk's cheeks flamed and then went ashen. "You have the wrong De Grote."

"De Grote, purveyor of liquors? On Leiestraat near the market?"

The clerk was waving his hands as if he didn't want anything to do with me. "These foreigners! They come to the city, and they cannot even properly speak the language. They don't know what they're saying!" The clerk was mocking me, but he was making a mess of what had been a relatively tidy counter.

"De Grote smuggles lace?" the customer inquired.

"Smuggle lace? Why would he? Doesn't he have a fine business already? He sells only the best of liquors!"

The man frowned, shrugged, and then left the store without making a purchase.

The clerk waved me toward the counter. "Hush! Do you want him to hear you?"

"Who?"

"De Grote!" The clerk nearly yelled the name, face flushed once more.

I blinked. Who could understand these people? I straightened myself to my full height, stiffened my shoulders, and glared at him. "Yes. I suppose I *would* like him to hear me. I came to speak to him, after all."

"Then keep your mouth shut."

"It's not forbidden to speak of Flemish lace in Flanders."

"But no good can come from talking about it when there are mercenaries who haunt the city looking for smugglers!" The words came out in a hiss.

I felt my own face blanch. I could not afford to be apprehended. I must not forget that no matter the status of lace on this side of the border, King Louis had outlawed such trafficking. The King brooked no defiance and, above all, he was just. If I were caught, he would not care about my circumstances or Lisette's plight. "Where is he, then?"

"In the back."

"May I...?"

The clerk gestured in that direction with a vicious sweep of his chin.

∽

After stepping around casks and bottles in varying shapes and sizes, I knocked on the only door I could find.

"What is it?" The question was asked in none too kind a voice. "Klaas? Is that you?"

"It's not Klaas."

There was a momentary scrape of wood against wood, the sound of a heavy footfall, and then the door was wrenched open. "If it's not Klaas, who is it?" A man stood there, glaring at me from russet-colored eyes. Lace frothed beneath a precisely trimmed beard. Lace cuffs showed beneath the sleeves of a fine brocade doublet.

"Is it…De Grote?"

"*Nee*. It is not De Grote, because I am De Grote. It's you."

Feeling more than a little foolish, I nodded. "I am Alexandre Lefort."

"And who are you, Alexandre Lefort? What do you want?" The words were almost a whisper.

"I've been told to speak to you about a…commission."

His face relaxed. He smiled. Swept his arm wide in a gesture for me to enter. "Then please, come in."

"He asked for you up front, De Grote." The voice came from behind me: the clerk's voice. "He asked about…you know…"

De Grote looked from the clerk back to me. "About what?"

"About…" The clerk mouthed the word "lace."

De Grote turned to me. "You said the word?"

I nodded.

"Did anyone hear him?"

The clerk shrugged in a helpless sort of way. "Otto Stroobants."

"Quickly—have him followed. See he goes home without getting me into any trouble along the way." The orders were given in a hiss.

The clerk turned to go, but De Grote stopped him. "Does he buy much?"

The clerk turned back. "Who?"

"Stroobants."

The clerk inclined his head. "A couple of bottles every month or two."

De Grote folded his hands atop his froth of lace. Sighed. Shook his head. "Well. If there's any trouble, if I have to do anything with him, it won't cost us much in business." He waved the clerk away, pulled me by the arm into the room, and shut the door. "About the lace." He took a seat behind a counting table.

"I saw the abbess at the abbey in Lendelmolen just this morning."

"And?"

"She said it would take two weeks, at least, for my lace to be finished."

"Good. Fine. When it's finished, bring it to me. I'll have one of my dog runners get it across the border for you."

"*Dog* runners?"

"I've a terror of the beasts myself, but I've never lost a length. I'll need your money now, though, in order to do it."

I pulled the purse from my coat and placed it into his hand.

He hefted it and then sent me a quizzical glance. After tugging the string loose with a finger, he poured the coins onto the table. "It's not enough."

"Some for now, to guarantee your services. Some for later, once the work is completed." I had divided my remaining money among two pouches.

"That's not the way I conduct my business. If you want me to help you, then you give me the money—all of it—now."

I don't know why I should have been surprised the count had suggested doing business with someone so similar to himself. Heeding the lessons learned from bitter experience, I decided not to ignore my instincts. Sweeping the coins back into the purse, I resisted an urge to blot away the cold sweat that had formed above my lip. I wrapped the thong around the pouch, knotting it once. Twice for good measure. "Unfortunately, this is not the way I conduct my business." I nodded and then turned on my heel and moved toward the door with the insouciance of the urchin boy

I once had been, he who didn't care what others thought about him or what they might do.

I was expecting to be called back at any moment, but I reached the door without eliciting one word from the man. So I stopped.

Nothing.

Put a hand to the doorknob.

Nothing.

Turned it.

Nothing, nothing, nothing. Damn, damn, and damn! I'd been so sure he would acquiesce. What was I going to do now? De Grote was my only contact in this city, and it was quite clear I couldn't hope to smuggle the lace across the border by myself. If he wouldn't take my commission then…? I opened the door. Stepped through it.

Nothing.

All was lost.

"Wait." The word was spoken with a sigh of resignation.

I nearly stumbled in my relief. But I did not turn. It would have been disastrous to seem too eager. That was something I was beginning to remember from my child-hood: people always responded not to obvious hunger or to need, but to strength. "What?" I threw a glance at him over my shoulder.

"Come back, come back. I'm sure we can work some-thing out."

"I will give you a quarter of the sum now. And the rest when the lace is completed."

"And what if you never end up paying for it in full?"

I smiled. "I am an honorable man. I deal in honorable

ways." I removed some of the coins from my purse and tossed them onto the table.

De Grote gave me a long look. "Why don't you tell me where it is you are staying? In case I need to send word to you." He was looking at me just a bit too benignly.

"I don't know exactly. Not yet."

"Where are you staying right now?"

Right now? My best protection during my youth had been that no one knew exactly where to find me...until the night when the village priest did. To keep myself from shuddering, I shrugged, fixing to my face the look of a gentleman who is finished speaking with one deemed inferior. "Nowhere. The place I found has far too many fleas. I plan to move tonight."

"Too many fleas? I don't know that you'll find any place with less. But there's an inn on Ramen at the very end. It's run by a good man. That's where you should stay."

"On Ramen."

"*Ja.* Turns into Stovestraat."

I nodded and determined to avoid Ramen in the future. De Grote reminded me too much of the priest of my youth. I didn't want to be anywhere this man could find me.

While I had been inside the shop, the rain had become finer, filtering into a mist. I tugged my hat tighter down around my ears and gathered the tips of my cloak's collar up toward my chin. Passersby had done the same. Most of them. We walked the streets, wraiths of a kind, made more ghostly by the weather.

As I passed an alley, a hiss made me turn.

In that dim and uncertain light, I could not see into it clearly. As I stood there squinting, someone pushed me from behind, causing me to stumble toward the darkness. Obeying my rapidly reviving instincts, I pulled my dagger from my belt. I tried to free myself from the confines of my cloak, but a man had somehow got round me, and he kicked the weapon from my hand.

It dropped into a puddle as I was assaulted from the front and the back.

Though I anticipated where every blow would be placed, and though I tried to defend myself against them, I was always too late. My movements were too slow. Eventually, I could only stand there, like some stupid beast, head swaying, peering at my attackers through vision gone red with blood.

A blow to the gut finally felled me. When I sunk to my knees, gasping for breath, a hand grasped the collar of my cloak, pulling me to standing. Another hand snaked inside my doublet and pulled the purse from my gusset. "De Grote says he'll take the rest of the money now."

De Grote? "But—"

"Be a good lad, and don't go crying to the sheriff."

One of them bent and fished the dagger from the puddle, pushing it into his belt with a sneer at me. "He'll like this, De Grote will. He favors fancy things."

Bloodied and beaten, I lay there, ear in a puddle, watching as people splashed by out on the street. A mist gathered on my eyelashes and made the world go grey at the edges.

It took a sniff and a nip from a passing dog to rouse me from my stupor. I waved him off and cried out as pain pricked holes in my vision. The dog gave a bark and then trotted away into the street.

As I pushed up on an elbow, my shoulder seemed to collapse beneath the weight. I bit off a cry and gingerly rolled to my knees. From there, I slowly gained my feet, pausing now and then to keep hold of my senses.

Staggering, I groped for my hat, but it looked as if it had been stomped into the mud by a horse and then shit upon for good measure. I left it there in the sludge.

⁓

When I got to the inn, they would not countenance my presence. The mistress of that place stood, arms crossed over her chest, as I staggered into the hall. "We don't serve your type here."

"You already are." A swollen lip and slit cheek made tough work of speaking. I licked my lips and tried again. "I'm a guest here. Came last night. Lefort, Alexandre Lefort. I was given a room up the stairs."

The mistress pierced me with her narrow-eyed gaze. "Dirc!" She called the name over her shoulder without hardly turning her head.

A man turned from serving one of the tables.

"You recognize this scoundrel?"

He looked me over. "*Nee.*"

She tossed the corner of her apron toward me as if she could not be bothered to touch me herself. "Out with you, then."

"But I'm the... I'm an heir. To the viscount of Souboscq!"

They both exploded with laughter. "Viscount! It's a wonder you even know how to pronounce it. Out with you, now. Be off."

"But I—"

"Out!"

If I'd had my dagger, I would have dared her to mock me. But if I had pulled it out, I'm sure she would have accused me of stealing it. As I lurched through the hall toward the door, I caught a reflection of my face in the glass hanging on the wall. My cloak sat askew my shoulders. One eye was blacked, and the other had almost swollen shut. There was a gash on my cheek, and muck clung to my hair.

∽

I set my cloak straight as I left the inn. Using the pump in the courtyard, I cleaned the dirt from my hair and the blood and filth from my hands and arms, scrubbing at them with my nails. Angry, bulbous welts soon rose on my skin, but I did not care.

Clean at last, I went into the stables, intent upon retrieving my horse. But when I moved to take him, the stable hand blocked my way.

"The likes of you has no business in here."

"This horse belongs to me."

He began to laugh. "To you! As if you're some kind of gentleman. You haven't even got a hat for your head!"

"I've been accosted by a band of rogues." And my entire body ached damnably. Shouldn't it be obvious I'd been waylaid?

"A band of rogues! Maybe that's what I should tell my wife next time I stop by the tavern on my way home. A band of rogues..."

"I shall take my horse and be gone from here if you would just move out of the way."

"I'll move just as soon as you pay for its board."

I couldn't. Every coin I'd brought with me had been stolen, and those few things I'd left in the room were as good as gone. But he didn't have to know that. If I just acted like the gentleman I'd become, I was certain the man would do as I asked. I tried to straighten and square my shoulders, but that piercing pain returned. I winced. "I'll pay you. Just as soon as I recover what was stolen from me. In the meantime, you can mark the account to the viscount of Souboscq. I promise the debt will be honored." Just as soon as I could manage it.

He had been speaking conversationally, but he suddenly lunged toward a stall and took up a pitchfork that was leaning against the door. He brandished it at me. "You can have your horse when you pay for it."

"I told you, I've been robbed!"

"Of what? Your fleas? Or your lice? I can believe you're French, but I never seen a gentleman so pitiful as you. Get out!" He thrust the pitchfork toward me.

I left the place, cursing as I went. It was just like the Flemish, those sanctimonious and self-righteous people, to disrespect nobility. In any other country, those ruffians would have been detained and my claims believed. Expecting to find sympathy if not respect of the law from the city's officials, I went to the sheriff to file a complaint.

"De Grote?" He looked at me, brow raised, in seeming amazement. "*Arne* De Grote?"

"The very same."

"He can't have."

Now it was I who looked at him, brow raised. "He did."

"He's an upright member of the city council, and he's having a chapel constructed at the church in his wife's honor."

Honor? The man had none!

"And you say he accosted you?"

"No. I say he sent his men to accost me. They stole my purse and the coin inside it. A substantial number of them."

"I'll have to know why you were walking the streets with such great wealth."

Ah. My reply would require great care. To admit to my reasons would be to identify myself as a smuggler. "I was sent here to conduct business for my cousin, the viscount of Souboscq."

"Nothing good can come from a man walking around with a fortune in his purse. Of course you were robbed!"

"Yes. Of course I was robbed. That's what I'm saying." Couldn't these Flemish understand anything? "I was robbed by Arne De Grote."

"That's impossible. He hardly ever even raises his voice."

"What's impossible is your insisting it's impossible!"

"If you're a gentleman, then show yourself as such."

Show myself—!

"You haven't even a hat to your head."

"It was lost in the fight, and I—"

"Ah! The fight. So you admit it, then. You picked a fight with some men of Kortrijk, and you can't stomach the fact that you lost."

I took a deep breath, which had the unfortunate effect of causing my ribs great pain. "I came to make a complaint and ask for help in recovering my purse."

"Why are you here in Kortrijk?"

"I am on business for the viscount of Souboscq."

"And your business is with…?"

"Arne De Grote."

He leaned back in his chair and crossed his arms, hiding his thumbs in his armpits. "I see. You came here to do business with Arne De Grote, and now you accuse him of waylaying you."

"Yes!"

"And why would he do that?"

"Because…" I realized I had very nearly walked into a trap of my own making. To admit to the sheriff I had contracted with De Grote to smuggle lace out of the country was to turn myself into a criminal. I wondered how many men, just like me, had lost their gold to that man. If I admitted to my reasons, then I might as well have simply handed the lace to the mercenaries who haunted the borders, trying to confiscate it. "Because he is a dishonorable man."

"He supplies the armory with gunpowder, he pays for extra masses to be said on behalf of the poor, and he provides the city's orphanage with food. I would very much like to meet an honorable man!"

I could see I would find no understanding here, so I nodded and turned to leave.

"Monsieur Lefort?"

I paused. "Yes?"

"I would be very careful around Arne De Grote if I were you."

The boy I was at twelve would not have needed the warning. And he would not have allowed himself to be ambushed in a fight. He would have walked through the streets with his head up, regardless of the rain, so he could see the danger that lay before him. That boy would have noted there was something amiss about men who did not turn up their cloaks against the weather.

That boy would not have been pummeled as I had been.

There was nothing of the gentleman left about me now. The man had become the boy once more.

"Be careful of Arne De Grote." I was tired of being careful! I had acted with all the restraint and reserve my cousin had taught me, all of the care I once promised God, and it had gotten me nothing. I was without funds, without friends, and without means. I had no lodging, and I had no food.

❧

I slept that night in an alley protected by overhanging buildings and then quit the city the next day. I had no doubt my attempts at begging had been thwarted by the way I looked. No one seemed to believe me the gentleman I claimed to be. Perhaps in the countryside, the peasants would be more discerning. Perhaps they would look beyond my wounds and the shabby state of my clothes and would offer the food and lodging I sought.

Two weeks.

Then I could collect my lace, show myself to De Grote, and make him abide by the terms of our agreement. I would retrieve my father's dagger, by means just or foul. And I would also regain my horse.

As I walked along, shoulders to my ears, back bent against the wind and rain, I imagined doing those very things. In truth, it gave me much more satisfaction to imagine forcing De Grote to give up what he'd stolen than it did to imagine he would surrender them without a fight.

My path lay in the direction of Lendelmolen. As night fell, I came upon one of those windmills that stood sentry along a canal. Its silhouette loomed in the falling night. Slipping in through the unlocked door, I hoped to find a bag of grain from which to skim a handful or two, but it seemed I was in the wrong countryside. The mill dealt in water, not grain.

Stepping out, securing the door behind me, I struck on through the night. Hunger soon drove me to the doorstep of another windmill. This one belonged to a miller, though there were no bags of grain from which to pilfer. I chased the mice from the milling machine and scraped together the meal that dusted the floorboards. Then I lowered myself to the floor, taking great pains not to disturb my injured shoulder. There, I settled in to sleep.

Throughout the night, the giant sails creaked, and the gears groaned. In the darkness around me, vermin scratched and scurried. It put me in mind of the nights I had passed in the forests of Béarn. Here, at least, I was not being rained upon. And the mush and grit in my mouth reminded me, when I was wont to complain, that I had eaten.

I was awakened before dawn by the sails. They strained against their moorings, the wind battering the canvas. The entire structure moaned and seemed to sway as if pleading for release. There was no use trying to sleep and no value in nursing an empty stomach. I took to the road, stepping into the mist, listening to the gulls splash about in the water. I reached the next town at first light.

There was no work, no sympathy, no food for me there, according to the owner of the tavern. I left to save him the trouble of tossing me out, stumbling through the door and then down the road. The next town ought not to have been too much farther, but with each step I took on those miry clay roads, I seemed to slip two steps backward. If I did not find both food and shelter, an insistent voice within me told me I would soon die. I hadn't the strength to argue with it, but neither could I acquiesce. Lisette's life depended upon the delivery of the lace. And so did the viscount's fate.

So when I heard a cart splashing in and out of the puddles I had just trudged through, I turned to face it. And when the man driving the oxen hailed me, I did not move. I would force this man to be my savior.

"Hey—get off the way." He waved toward the side of the road.

"I need…" I needed everything.

He halted his mud-streaked cart several paces from me. "You look like you've found trouble, friend."

Trouble had found me. I gripped my elbow, trying to keep my shoulder from moving, hoping to spare myself that piercing pain. "I need food. I'm willing to work for it."

He tipped up his hat and took a look at me. "What are you good at, then?"

Good at? "Stealing things. And being stolen from."

A rumble of hearty laughter erupted from him. "At least you're honest. For a thief." He looked me over and then nodded. "So what's to assure me you're not set on stealing from me?"

"I'm reformed."

He gave me a long look beneath his brow. "I doubt it."

I gave him an even longer look. And then I decided to tell the truth. "I'm here on business. Only the man I'm to do that business with robbed me."

He chewed on the inside of his cheek as he listened to me speak. "This business you're conducting…?"

"Is none of yours."

He held up his hands as if to fend off a blow. "No need to take offense. Where are you headed?"

"Lendelmolen." Eventually.

"I'm going past. Toward the sea."

I didn't care if he was headed to Spain, as long as he wouldn't leave me stranded on the road. "I shall be done with my business in two weeks' time and headed home…" No. Not home. Souboscq was home to some other man now. It would never be my home again. "Until then, however…?" He would either help me or he would not.

"I have a farm, and I could use some help repairing a dike, though I won't pay you for it."

I hadn't hoped for payment. "Bed? And board?"

"If you earn it. Reginhard Deroeck never cheated any man."

"I'll earn it."

"But first—" He reached out and clapped one of his hands to my shoulder.

I nearly fainted from the pain.

His other hand grabbed my elbow, and then he gave a sharp tug to my arm. With his grunt, my scream, and a loud popping sound, my shoulder came right. "I suppose I should thank you…" I lost consciousness to the sound of his belly-shaking laughter.

I awakened in the cart and found myself sharing the space with a cage of chickens and a pile of turnips. When we lurched to a stop, the man Reginhard helped me to standing. Then he pulled me over to a small hut from which ushered a spindly thread of smoke and the tantalizing smell of what I hoped would be supper.

He pushed open the door to reveal the homely scene of a family lit by a glowing fire. Two small children played with a top at one end of the sole room while two other older children aided a woman cooking at the fire.

The woman straightened as we stepped into the place.

"That's Gertrud. And this…" The man gestured to me as he hung his cap on a hook and shrugged off his cloak. "This is…a Frenchman."

"Alexandre." It didn't matter that I was a Lefort. In these circumstances, I might as well have been a Girard.

"He's to help me with repairing the dike."

She cast a glance toward me and then went back to stirring a kettle that hung over the fire.

"I told him he could have a corner to sleep in."

She deigned to give me a longer look this time, as if I merited further inspection. After she was done, she turned toward the man. "I'll give him some straw, as well, if he'll plug that hole in the roof."

The man raised a brow at me.

I nodded

"He'll do it."

"Fine. That's fine." She took a bowl from a sideboard and ladled something into it from the kettle. Then she set the bowl in the middle of the board, which sat in the center of the room. One of the two girls helping her pulled some bread from the fire and swept the ashes from it. The other had busied herself with carrying the smallest of the children toward the table.

The man spoke a blessing and then broke the bread. The woman divided it among the family and then gave me the hard, ash-stained end. Once everyone else had dipped their bread into the bowl, it was pushed down to me. I sopped up the remainder and ate it, then followed it with several sips from a jug of beer. There being no cloth, I wiped my fingers on the hem of my doublet.

Afterward, the woman nodded toward a ladder I might have had trouble climbing in the best of conditions. "You'll find the hole up there, in the loft."

I wish I could say I made quick work of the task, but climbing the ladder seemed to wrench every aching bone in my body, and examining the hole in the loft's dim light didn't make the work easy. Once I found the hole, I didn't know what to do about it. My experience had to do with forest living and stone-walled châteaux.

"Fallen on hard times, has he?" The woman's voice carried up to the loft through the sizeable gaps between the floorboards.

"*Nee.* I rather think he's trying to come up in the world, to advance himself."

I poked at the hole glumly. The man had got it right: I was a fellow who had been hoping to advance himself. Now I was just a fellow who was hoping to survive.

It felt as if the hole had been made from the slipping of a tile. Reaching up past the roof into the rain, I pulled the tile back into place, sending a stream of water down my arm and dampening my shirt in the process. I finished the work from the inside, by thrusting my fist at the tile and using that jarring motion to close the final gap.

The woman fulfilled her promise. As I bedded down for the night, I fluffed up my straw, settled my cloak about my shoulders, and then closed my eyes. When sleep came, it brought with it a desperate longing for Lisette, who could mock me with a teasing glance and then redeem me with a single touch. Were she to see me now, she would know without doubt I was not worthy of redemption.

Due to the interminable rains, it took a full two weeks to mend the farmer's dike. By the end of the first day's work, I began to suspect the sun never shone on this miserable place. We wrestled mud into the cart to transport it to the banks of the canal, only to pack it into the dike and watch it slide away, down into the waters with the constant, dripping rains.

There was no work we did that the rain did not undo. I fell onto my corner of straw each night, exhausted both in body and in spirit, filled with a sense of complete and utter defeat. Each new day saw us starting again to repair the same washed-out place. "How is it that you stay here?" I asked the question one especially frustrating afternoon, when thunder rumbled in the distance and the sky was more parsimonious than usual with its light.

Sweat and rain comingled, so when I paused to wipe my brow, I could not say whether I was swiping away evidence of my own spent efforts or the heavens'. Rivulets of the stuff had turned my locks into channels, directing streams of water down my brow to either side of my nose. These streams ran down into the canal waters that pooled and eddied around my thighs. The more I labored, the greater I added to my own discomfort. "How do you do it?" I could not imagine one more hour, one more day trying so strenuously to delay the inevitable advance of water toward the family's hut.

The man sent me a bleak look. "Don't you mean to ask why?"

I didn't have the energy to shrug, and the phrasing of the question mattered little to me. The how and the why were not so very different things when my hands were coated in layers of muck and I had been standing, for hours, in water that surpassed my knees.

"I tell you, Frenchman, there is nowhere else to go."

Nowhere else to go.

That, I could understand. What would compel a man to fight God and nature, to wrestle with mud and rain, to wrest from the sea land that was never meant to be seen? Only the fact that there was no other choice. If he wished to survive at all, he must do the impossible, must spend his life doing the unbearable. He must try through any means, be they useless or futile, to bring reason to such insanity.

There was nowhere else to go, therefore a living must be stolen from the sea.

I could find no greater logic, and I could imagine no better answer. Things must be as they were simply because that's the way they are. And so, standing in that murky canal, with rain pouring down upon my head, I laughed as I had never laughed before. I laughed until I wept, my tears mixing with my sweat and with the rain. It all streamed down my face and joined the water, which did not care from where it had come, and only added, in the end, to my work.

There was nowhere else to go.

How exactly right that my journey had ended here. There was nothing in the world for me now except this one thing. This one task: to finish repairing an irreparable dike. And after that, to deliver a length of lace to the Count of Montreau. And after that? There was no inheritance; there was no château; there was no home.

But I would do what I had to, simply because I must.

The load of mud we had just packed into the dike slid down the embankment and was swept away by the canal.

There was no way to come clean after such work. The water from the well was nearly as muddied as the ground itself. And yet I knelt in front of it every evening, trying to rid myself of the day's mire. The farmer regarded me silently that first evening and then left me to my own devices after that.

By the fourth night, I had rubbed all the hair off my arms, and my skin had gone red from my efforts. The fifth night I'd borrowed a knife to clean my fingernails. The tip had gouged furrows beneath the nails, which subsequent days of work had filled in with dirt.

By the end of that first week, I had given myself an even more thorough scrubbing, for I had determined to visit the abbey to inquire after my lace. I nearly flayed my own skin in the doing of it. While trying to excavate the dirt from beneath my nails, I'd pried one of them entirely off my finger. And there was an ooze that issued from the places where I had scrubbed the top layer from my skin.

"Stop this foolishness!" I looked up from examining the damage to find the farmer's wife staring down at me. "What are you trying to get shed of? It's only the remnants of God's good earth." She gestured to the lesions I was trying to scrub clean. "Are you too good for God? Is that it?"

Too good for God?

"You're only harming yourself. And besides, you can only be as clean as you are."

For the first time in memory, I felt shame on account of my washing. I'd always known it had marked me as odd, but I had also figured it had left me purer than the others around me. It had left me clean. But here, washing was as useless a task as trying to mend the dike. I would find myself just as dirty the next day. And quite soon, in fact, I would run out of skin.

I poured water into my hand and then splashed it onto my face. Rubbed it into the beard so new it itched. I looked a proper Dutchman now. Not even Lisette would recognize me. "The Flemish are known for being clean, are they not?"

"*Ja.*" She nodded. "But even we can see where good sense lets off and madness begins. You keep yourself so clean you've begun to grow ill from it." She circled a finger above her ear as she spoke.

If the leprosy were going to take me, wouldn't it already have done so? If any were going to discover my paternity, wouldn't they have already done it by now?

"Clean your face, clean your hands. Wash your clothes once in a while, and be done with it. You can't be rid of it all. Not this time of year. And besides, you're frightening the children."

I leaned to look around her skirts and saw the children peering from the door.

You can't be rid of it all.

Was that what I had been trying to do? Rid myself of all traces of my father? Shed this skin of mine to hide the truth of my past? To be someone I was not?

Perhaps she was right. Perhaps I could only be as clean as I was.

CHAPTER 15

Katharina Martens

LENDELMOLEN, FLANDERS

ONE DAY AS WE SAT UPON THE BENCHES, SIDE BY SIDE, I heard a rustling from Mathild. She cried out as I heard her bobbins hit the floor.

The unthinkable had happened!

She had dropped her pillow. All of her work would have to be discarded now. Though every precaution was taken to keep the workshop clean, it was inconceivable that the lace could have survived its contact with the floor. I could have wept from the injustice of it all. That such a beautiful creation should be cast aside.

"What's that?" I heard Sister tapping across the floor, and I clutched at my own pillow so I wouldn't be accused of having lost mine, as well.

"Mathild?"

Mathild pressed herself against me.

"Go!"

Mathild rose, but as she tried to leave, she must have stumbled, for she fell to the floor.

"Help me." For the first time, I heard her speak without whispering. I heard her words fully. Clearly. But her voice was dead. It had no life.

"Get up!"

"I can't."

"Now!"

"I can't. My clogs—the threads!"

"You're making a mess of it. Of everything."

She had gotten to her knees, right below my feet, I could tell by the way her shoulder bumped into my own knee. She was weeping. "I can't...I can't see."

"Come." The shape of Sister leaned over and grabbed Mathild's arm, pulling her from the floor. She tugged so hard, Mathild stepped right out of her clogs. I knew it because I heard the shuffle of bare feet against the floor. Sister kept on walking toward the stairs. But then she paused. "Katharina."

I raised my head toward the sound of her voice.

"Watch. Keep watch."

I nodded, though I knew I could see no better than Mathild. I opened my mouth to speak, but I knew not what to say. And so I said nothing. And the work continued around me as always. In spite of the mess on the floor. In spite of the emptied pair of clogs.

When Sister returned, she took up Mathild's pillow and set it on the bench beside me. Soon another girl, a younger girl, came over from across the room to take her place.

Mathild didn't join us for prayers, and she didn't join us for supper. When I fell onto my pallet that night, that same new girl from the workshop was there in Mathild's place.

I climbed the stairs the next day as the last of the girls, the oldest of the lace makers. I wondered then, what might happen to me.

And what had happened to Mathild.

Had she joined the shouting voices beyond the abbey wall?

And was it true what Heilwich had said? Did the girls who left the workshop turn their efforts to vile things?

What vile things? Did they make messes and defy orders and make people late?

I could not imagine such a life. But more than that, I could not imagine a life without lace. My sister had said she would see me freed. But freed from what? If I did not make lace, then what would I do?

I could not see. Not everything. Not most things. What would I do out in the middle of a city filled with shouting people? What *could* I do?

I began to know a certain anxiety. It disrupted my work and turned the dancing of the bobbins into lurching as my fingers faltered. And so, I determined not to think upon it. Not to imagine the world outside the wall. Why should I?

I loved lace.

Lace was my life. It was the reason for my existence.

What else had I been created to do? If God in his mercy had granted me life, then surely it was to do this. To create exquisite, beautiful lace was my duty, my sacred trust. That's what the nuns had told me.

That's what I believed.

And so why would God rob me of this one task? The only task I could perform, the only reason for which I was created? Surely he would not do such a thing. I loved lace.

Mathild had not.

It was not so much her failure to make the lace that had betrayed her. It was her failure to love it. For how could the memory of that which you loved desert you? Even with the coming of perpetual darkness, how could those patterns fail to illumine the way?

But throughout that day, as I fumbled with my bobbins and resorted to checking the count of my stitches with my fingers, I realized I was no longer an aid but an obstacle to what I created. It could no longer be made with me…and it could certainly not be created without me.

The dance was nearly done.

In that moment, I realized my great sin. Pride. Vanity. It was not my love of lace that had enabled me to do great work, it was very great pride that had deceived me. I was no better than Mathild, no better than any lace maker in the workshop. I was just more vain. But I smiled as I bent closer to my work. Perhaps, there was yet a certain humility in my vanity. I did not need to be known. It was enough that the lace had a chance to leave, had a chance to live and be loved. *Nee*. It did not matter. Not to me. No one had to know my name.

The three weeks Heilwich had given me were almost up. She spoke as she shoved a loaf of bread through the wall for me. "I know I promised to get you out, but I haven't got the money just yet. Not all of it."

"I'm almost done with the lace."

"Almost done?" Heilwich yelled the words at me. "But I'm not ready for you to be done! You can't be done."

"They don't know I'm almost done. I haven't told them yet." I didn't want to be parted from the lace. I hoped God would forgive me.

"Good. Good! Don't tell them. You can't tell them until I have the money."

"But they're going to know. They'll check soon, and I won't be able to hide it."

"When?"

"On Saturday. They check on Saturdays." Unless we told them before that. "For certain by then I'll be finished."

"Saturday! I don't know if I can get the money by Saturday. And in any case, I can't be here on a Saturday. Father Jacqmotte would never let me come. Not with all the preparations to be done for Sunday. It takes me half the day to get here and then back. But…what will happen when they find out you've finished?"

"They'll give me another pattern."

"Then start on the new pattern."

"I don't know if I'll be able to."

"Why not!"

"Because…" I hated it when Heilwich yelled at me. This was all her doing, anyway. All of this deceiving and hiding things. "If it's not a pattern I've made before, I won't know how to do it. I have to be able to see the pattern to work it."

"For certain you do." Her voice had softened.

"I don't know what to do."

"Here's what you don't do. Don't leave the abbey."

"But how do I stay?"

"If they don't check until Saturdays, then you're safe until this Saturday. When will they give you the new pattern?"

"On Monday."

"Then you have to pretend until then. Can you do that? Can you pretend you're doing what you're supposed to?"

If I pretended, then I wouldn't be doing what I was supposed to, would I? "I don't know…"

"Maybe…can you just…do it slower?"

"Why?"

"So they won't throw you out of the abbey! Least not until I can come and get you out myself."

"They wouldn't do that. Sister wouldn't do that. Not to me."

Her hand came through the wall and grabbed at my own. "Just promise me. Promise you'll do it."

"Fine. I'll try."

"Don't try, Katharina. Do. You must do this for me. For you."

"I...will."

"You can't let them know until Saturday, understand?"

"I guess—"

"This is important, Katharina! Until Saturday. Whatever you do, you can't let them know about your eyes."

"I won't. I won't tell."

༄

Don't work so fast.

But how could I do my work to the best of my ability unless I worked as quickly as I could? Wasn't that being slothful? And wouldn't Sister notice? She had trusted me to finish the lace, and now Heilwich wanted me to be late.

I tried to do as Heilwich said. I truly did. But I couldn't. Not once the bobbins began their dance. Even as artlessly as I now moved them, they insisted upon keeping their own rhythm. And it was only as we headed down the stairs of an evening that I remembered my promise to my sister.

I did remember.

I just hadn't done it in time. For not two days later, I created the last of the petals and felt the last of the scrolls form underneath my fingers. I was done. The sheer exhilaration of it prickled my scalp. I was done. Done! But...what would happen now?

I set my bobbins to dancing, forming a pattern that was no pattern. They looped and dipped and twisted without creating anything at all. I needed time to think. I stayed up all night trying to decide what to do. But I had no choices. Not really. I was done with the lace. But there were still five more days before Heilwich's visit.

CHAPTER 16

Heilwich Martens

KORTRIJK, FLANDERS

HOW WAS I GOING TO SAVE KATHARINA? I HAD only a week. Less than a week if her secret was discovered on Monday. That night, after I returned to Kortrijk and after I had banked the fire in the kitchen, I sat down on my pallet and counted the money I had saved.

The coins had not grown in number since I had showed them to the Reverend Mother. I had added one to them, but then I had given one to that urchin, Pieter.

I felt a desperate panic. Which was followed by the impulse to pray the rosary. But what good would that do? How could that save Katharina?

What I needed was money.

More of it than I had.

But what could I do? How could I come by more?

I supposed…I could do what I had done for the other coins.

Sighing, I covered my head with my apron and then pressed my forehead to my knees. Had it truly come to this? To helping De Grote? After I had told him, once and forever, I would never work for him again?

My hands began to tremble as I thought on it. About how terrible it had been that first time, digging up the coffin Father Jacqmotte had buried just the morning before and opening it to hide a length of lace inside.

At least De Grote hadn't hacked up any of that body. Sometimes he ordered a corpse's chest be cut out so lace could be rolled up and placed there instead. But that first time, he'd only lifted the dead man's arm and tucked the lace inside his coat.

Such a horrible, horrible night.

The char girl caught me not once that next morning, but twice, staring into the fire at nothing at all. And when I went outside to go to market, I found I carried not my basket, but my broom. And I was gripping it with the same fingers that had helped to dig up a coffin.

I had turned around and taken the broom back to the kitchen, and then I'd sat down on a stool in the cellar and peered at my fingers in the dim light.

Opened them.

Closed them.

Tried not to remember what they felt when they had touched the dead man's coat. That feeling ate at me. It soured me. And right there in the cellar, I fell to my knees and retched. Again and again and again. I retched until I tasted only bile. And yet again until there was nothing left but a guilty conscience and a wicked soul.

If only I had been able go to confession.

But I never would. How could I confess to…to…doing what I had done? What words could I use? What could I possibly say to induce a priest to pronounce forgiveness?

I let someone else prepare Father's meal that afternoon. He wouldn't have wanted to take the food from my hand. Not if he had known.

I deserved no mercy from God. Not after that.

Dómine, non sum dignus, ut intres sub tectum meum. Lord, I am not worthy that thou shouldst enter under my roof. Forgiveness was too great a gift for a soul like mine.

Oh! I did not wish to do it. I did not want to go to De Grote again.

Besides, he must have found others to do the work I had done. There must be dozens like me in the city. I imagined there was one of me at each of the parish churches. There had to be. Lace was that important.

I did not want to do it. Not after I had promised myself I wouldn't.

But De Grote might be my only choice. Blind as Katharina was, she'd be no match for those men who loitered by the abbey's gate. They'd snatch her, and bed her, and what could be done then?

I made my rounds the next day, taking soup to the aged, rags to the poor, and medicines to the infirm. I cast a careful eye about as I walked. If I had to do it, if I had to go to De Grote, it would be nice to know there was a body ready to fall into a coffin. If I decided to do it, whom could I count upon to die?

There was Annen, the weaver's wife. She would drop a babe any day now, and her last two had died ere they'd had a chance to breathe.

"Annen Moens!"

"Heilwich." She put a hand to her back and stretched in a way that reminded me of a sapling. "How is Father Jacqmotte?"

"Same as always. But how are you?"

She took a great breath of air into her cheeks and then blew it out in a huff. "Sick unto death of breeding."

"But it's to come soon?"

She smiled. Or perhaps it was a grimace. "Any day."

"Make sure you send someone to fetch me." Just in case. Just in case I decided to go to De Grote.

159

She nodded.

I continued on to the Lievens's. They had a daughter in poor health, and the week's wet weather was sure to have set her back. Knocking once on the door, I lifted the latch and pushed through.

Elen Lievens came at me, smiling, hands extended. "Look at our Zoete!"

I looked.

"It's a miracle, isn't it?"

Truly miraculous. The girl who for so long had lingered abed was bent over the fires, stirring a kettle as if she never intended to stop. As I gazed upon her, she lifted her head. "It was the borage."

"The what?"

"The borage conserve you brought last week. The jar you said was blessed by Father Jacqmotte."

Just because I had said it didn't mean it had been true. Father Jacqmotte was too busy to bless every jar and vial I waved in front of his nose. If anyone had done any blessing, it had been me. I'd sprinkled some holy water on it while I'd been cleaning in his office. "I'm so...glad."

"Aren't we all?" Elen left my side and went to press a kiss to her daughter's forehead.

I left soon after.

I argued with myself the length of the street. But I came to no other conclusion than this: I did not want to go to De Grote. But I might just have to.

CHAPTER 17

Denis Boulanger

THE BORDER OF FRANCE AND FLANDERS

*I*F I ONLY KNEW WHICH PEOPLE SMUGGLED LACE across the border, then I would stop them.

Men and women. Children and dogs. The very young and the very old. That was who the lieutenant said I should look for. Well…there they were, all of them, in the crowd standing before me, waiting to cross the border. Where was it the lieutenant said lace was hidden?

Loaves of bread.

I looked the crowd over once, twice, before I spotted a woman carrying a loaf of bread beneath her arm. As she saw me look at her, she covered the bread with her cloak.

I gestured her over.

Her brow furrowed as she put a hand to her chest.

I nodded.

Her cheeks paled, but she detached herself from the line. Several children followed, like goslings, behind her.

"I need to examine your bread."

"Please, sir. It's all we have."

"I'm sorry, but I have to." I took the loaf between my hands and tore it into two pieces. No lace there. But maybe…a piece of lace could be very small, couldn't it? And it didn't have to hide in the middle, did it?

I tore each section apart and then tore each of those

sections in two again. As I divided the bread into smaller and smaller pieces, one of them fell into the mud at our feet. "I'm sorry! I mean…I am…truly." The bread had been torn into pieces so small it was obvious there could be nothing hidden inside. I moved to give them all back to the woman, but as I did, one of the children jostled me, and they slid from my hands into the mud.

The children stared at me with piteous eyes. One of them began to cry.

"Don't—please—"

The woman had knelt in the mire and was picking up the pieces, brushing the mud from them with trembling hands as she sent dark looks up at me.

"I'm sorry. Here. Let me help." I picked up the rest of the pieces and handed them to her. She placed them into a kind of sling she formed with the tail of her cloak.

When I rose, the lieutenant was standing right beside me. "Found any lace yet?"

"*Non, chef.*"

"Well. You'll have to try harder, then." He nodded toward the side of the shack where an old man was standing, propped up by a crutch. "They're hollow sometimes."

"Hollow…?"

"The crutches."

"Oh. Oh!"

I approached the old man and held out my hand.

He fumbled in his coat pocket and then pulled out a document.

"*Non.* I mean—I need to see your crutch."

"My crutch?"

I nodded.

He leaned against the wall, puzzlement etching his brow, but he handed the crutch to me.

I glanced back toward the lieutenant. He put his fists together and wrenched them apart, as if he were breaking something.

Ah! Now I understood. I put one end of the crutch to the ground and then came down on it hard with my foot. It cracked but didn't quite break clean. I gave it another stomp.

"My crutch!" The old man had come away from the wall and attached himself to me, trying to pull me away from the crutch, though he couldn't quite manage it.

I fished it out of the mud and looked at the broken ends. Nothing but splinters. I examined the piece that fit under the arm. Nothing there, either. It was just a crutch after all.

"What have you done?"

"I'm sorry."

"What am I supposed to do now?" He was looking down at his foot, which was wrapped in a rag. A very dirty, very bloody, very holey old rag.

"I don't know. I'm very sorry...I—"

"How am I supposed to walk?"

I backed away from the man, apologized once more, and then went to look for the lieutenant. I found him, finally, on the other side of the line. He was looking at me, and he was laughing.

"A word of advice, Denis Boulanger." He linked his arm with mine. "Come with me. Let me show you a trick." As he walked us to the front of the line, all the people grew silent. He marched us up to a hunchbacked old woman who was leaning on a cane.

I had a bad feeling. At the very bottom of my stomach.

"All you have to do is—" He grabbed the cane away from her without warning. Her hands flew up as she gave a cry and landed face-first in the muck. "See there? That's the trick. The smugglers won't fall. They're only pretending to be crippled or lame. They've still got their balance. Those who fall? Well…they're not the ones. This old hag isn't one of those we're looking for."

"But—"

"That's how it's done."

The woman was churning in the mud like a windmill. The harder she tried to free herself, the more she seemed to swim in the filth. And now the crowd was laughing at her.

"If that's the way it's done, then I don't want to do it."

"Don't be a fool." He had already started up the steps to his shack. "You've work to do! Lace to confiscate. Besides… it's all in fun."

I might have held out a hand toward the old woman, but I felt too guilty. And then someone in the crowd hissed at me. At least, I think they did. Shamed, I ran to catch up with the lieutenant. As I jogged up the steps, cartridge box slapping at my side, I thought of those poor children. Of the man I'd left without a crutch. Of that old woman having nothing but clothes soiled by mud to show for her encounter with me. Finally, I caught up with him. "I'd rather have my orders."

"Your orders?"

I squared my shoulders. "*Oui, chef.*" If the job entailed torturing the good citizens of France—and Flanders—then I didn't want to do it. I'd rather do…anything else.

"Fine, then." The lieutenant strode before me into the room and came out with my orders in hand. He shoved them into my chest so hard I nearly fell off the step as I grabbed at them. "You know what your problem is?"

"*Non, chef.*"

"You've no imagination."

No imagination. I saluted and turned to leave.

"Last chance, Denis Boulanger. That's your last chance to become a real soldier. Don't squander it."

∽

I left the lieutenant and walked down the steps. Held up the orders so I could read them.

Signy-sur-vaux. I was being sent to guard a gunpowder manufactory.

I felt heat rise to my cheeks; my heart sounded as if it were beating in my ears. I was being sent to Signy-sur-vaux? Not many people even knew that village existed. Still fewer even knew its location, nestled as it was to the east against a bend in the river Vaux. Signy-sur-vaux was in the exact center of nowhere at all. It was a pimple on a flea's ass.

Pimple on a flea's ass.

That was one of my father's favorite phrases. My father in Signy-sur-vaux, the village where I was from. The village where I had been born and had lived until just six months ago. How was I going to explain to my father I had been sent straight back home? It had taken me a year to convince him I wasn't meant to follow in his trade. Now, I would have to tell him I wasn't good enough to be a soldier, either.

No imagination?

The lieutenant was wrong. I could imagine exactly what my father would say. Every word. Every gesture. Every look.

Signy-sur-vaux.

The lieutenant might as well have sent me to purgatory.

I spat at the shack then watched as it splatted against a board and rolled over itself all the way to the ground. I spat again. Then I turned to watch the border.

A farmer was leaving Flanders for France. Was he smuggling lace? He didn't look the type. I heard him speak. Not his words, I was too far away. But I heard the sound. It was guttural. Flemish, then. And the Flemish didn't smuggle the lace in. Not according to the lieutenant. The French did.

It was all so confusing. Why didn't people just do what they were told? Why did they have to lie and cheat and steal? And smuggle? What was wrong with obeying the King's law?

The guard pointed to a chest that was sitting in the cart. The man shrugged. Said something. The guard climbed onto the cart and gestured for the farmer to open the chest. Once the clasp had been unfastened and the top lifted, the guard began to empty it. A sheaf of papers. A silver cup. A packet of what turned out to be seed.

A purse.

The Spanish guard seized it. He loosed the strings and emptied it onto the straw that lined the bottom of the cart. Stared at the coins that fell out, and then dove at one.

Two.

Three.

Bastards. That's what those Spaniards were. The Flemish I'd come to know were nice enough, in spite of what the lieutenant thought. It wasn't their fault they were ruled by Spain.

The guard jumped down from the cart and then dropped the three coins into his own purse. They were probably French, coins that were forbidden in the Spanish Netherlands, but coins a man might need if he were to journey to France…where Spanish coin was forbidden.

What a mad world this had become. How was the man supposed to do business in France if he had no French money?

I spit again.

I shoved off from the wall as the man walked toward me, toward the lieutenant's shack. With the smell of herring and the sound of the sawing of bread coming from the shack, I knew he'd be waiting a while. The lieutenant relished his morning meal.

. CHAPTER 18 .

The Dog
RURAL FLANDERS

*I*T HAD HAPPENED, JUST AS I HAD DREAMED IT would. I had been muzzled, lace had been wrapped around my body, and now I was dressed in Legrand.

I was almost free.

"Run fast, Chiant. Run hard." My bad master opened the door before me, shoving a foot beneath my behind.

I sat down hard upon it.

There was something out there. I could smell it. Something lurking in the forest just beyond the path.

The master lifted his boot so swiftly it plunged me out into the dirt beyond the doorstep, onto my nose. "Run! *Vas-y!*"

I took one step forward. Stopped. Lifted an ear. Took a listen…and…yes. Just there. By that big tree. Under the hoot of the owls there was a cough. A whispered word.

"What do you wait for? Go!"

I took another step forward. Lifted an ear. Heard…talking. Footsteps. People advancing through the night. I whined.

"So now you do not wish to leave me? Now, with the most expensive lace you have ever carried? I should have beat you more! I should have fed you less!" His foot glanced off the tip of my nose.

I had not seen it coming! I yelped.

Cries came from the forest, and then the shadow of something emerged from the trees. Two shadows. Two men. "Stop!"

The bad master picked me up. "*C'est foutu!*" He began to withdraw back into the house, but then he stopped. Set me down. "Run, Chiant. Run like a brook. Make it to France. Go!" He pushed me away with a shove.

"The dog—stop him!"

The shadows separated, one running toward me, the other toward the bad master.

"Stop!"

"What do you need, friend?" The master spoke even as he kicked at me. "I am but a poor farmer."

I stumbled away, beyond the reach of his foot.

"You're a smuggler!"

I cowered. I could not see the color of his clothes, but his intent was unmistakable. I had been freed. I would not be taken. I would not be put back into the box.

"Where is your dog?"

"What dog?"

"Find the dog!"

"Where is he?" The shadow man held up a long gun and pointed it at the bad master's chest.

"I do not know what you—"

"The dog!"

"I have no dog."

The shadow coming toward me walked on past. I slunk away, my belly close to the ground.

"There! Along the edge of the house!"

"Run, Chiant!" The master started toward me.

I would not be taken. I sped away from the side of the house, taking one last look over my shoulder as I did it.

A flash of light erupted in the darkness. It was followed by a great roar.

I barked.

The bad master lurched and then fell to the ground, hands outstretched toward me.

I paused. Lifted an ear.

Heard one long, soft sigh fall from his lips. It was not followed by another.

But now...I lifted my nose...the scent of blood. The odor of death. I whined. It was everywhere, that scent. Behind me, before me, on top of me.

"Here, *chiot*. Nice dog. Good dog."

I shifted my gaze from the bad master to the shadow men. They were creeping toward me, hands reaching...and in the dim light of the moon, their hats glinted.

I would not be taken.

I would not be returned.

I would not go back in the box.

With one last look at the bad master, I turned and ran.

༄

He's dead. He's dead. He's dead.

If the bad master was dead, then I could not be returned. No matter what I did, no matter what offense I committed, I would not be brought back. I could not be brought back. But I would be careful just the same. I ran past trees. Splashed through the brook. Scrambled up a hill.

He's dead. He's dead. He's dead.

I paused for a moment, panting. I was hungry. I was thirsty. I was losing my strength. I could feel it seeping out of my legs.

I crouched for a moment.

Tugged at Legrand's hide with my teeth.

No. There was no way to get rid of it. The sooner I made it to the good master's, the sooner it would be removed.

I would be fed all I wanted and just a little bit more. My wounds would be tended. There would be cream and a lap and a fire. And a gentle hand stroking my skin.

I pushed to my feet. Stumbled over a gnarled tree root.

On I ran. Up and down. Over and around.

And then I paused.

Lifted an ear. Took a listen. Lifted my nose. Took a smell.

There was something at the edge of the forest this night.

Something different.

I took another sniff.

Something…strange.

But finally, at last, I saw light blinking through the trees. The forest had thinned, and the ground had flattened. But before I put out a paw and stepped away from the trees, I paused once more.

Took a listen.

I heard nothing.

Took a sniff. But…that smell.

Strange.

I walked into the clearing. A horse whinnied. A pig snorted. But…I paused.

Lifted an ear to listen.

Everything…waited. I could feel it.

Waited and watched.

I started off again. More slowly this time. Ten steps more, and I would be at the kind master's. I saw his outline against the open door. He was waving at me.

I ran to meet him.

"*Non! Non!* Run. Run away! Do not come this way. Go back! Go home!"

I skidded to a halt as two shadows appeared from the walls of the house. They were wearing shimmering clothes. And glinting hats.

I stopped. Barked.

"Run. Run away!"

The shadows closed in on my master. "We arrest you for smuggling, in the name of the King."

I took a step nearer.

My master broke free. Ran at me.

"Run. Get away!"

A light blazed from the shadow, and my master fell to the ground at my feet.

Slowly, slowly, he stretched out a hand.

"Moncher. Moncher...*Mon cher argent*..."

I put my nose beneath his hand and pushed it up to my muzzle so he could stroke it.

"*Mon cher*..."

He was...I pulled my snout from his hand. Lifted my nose to sniff. Held up an ear to listen. There was no sound coming from the master. And no scent but that of blood. He was dead.

I lifted my head and howled. And then I howled some more.

"Get that dog. Shoot him if you have to."

"And risk the lace?"

"Just do it."

As the shadow men advanced, I abandoned my master, ran back through the clearing and into the forest.

He's dead. He's dead. He's dead.

He's dead. He's dead. He's dead.

They're dead. They're dead. They're dead.

I ran back toward the hills.

Paused.

Collapsed.

And it was only then I stopped to listen.

I heard...a rustling in the forest. Twigs snapping. A panting that was not me.

I paused to sniff.

I smelled again that strange smell. It was following me. I did not know what to do, and so I crawled to the roots of a tree, settled myself between them, and put my head down on my paws.

They're dead.

I closed my eyes.

No food, no drink.

No fire, no gentle hands.

No lap.

No soft whispering of my name.

No more Chiant… but no more Moncher.

I whined. Once. Twice.

And then I smelled that scent again. That scent that smelled of…nothing. It was not an animal. There was no musk or staleness to it. But it was not a person. There was no sourness, no odor. It was…it was…an empty space in the air.

I lifted my head. Sniffed.

Lifted an ear. Listened. The snapping of twigs had come closer.

I sniffed again. That smell of nothing had cut a wider swath in the air. But what did it matter? There was no food waiting for me. I curled myself into a ball and hid my nose beneath my paws.

The thing in the forest had crept quite near.

"*Chiot*." It was said in the barest of whispers.

I raised my head. Looked out toward the forest and into the eyes of a man. He was crouched before me against the trunk of the tree.

"Come here."

As I watched, a hand stretched out toward me.

I recoiled.

"Come here, *chiot*. Come here…*please!*"

He was not wearing the shimmering clothes. He did not wear a glinting hat.

"Come here. What do you want? Are you hungry? I will get you food...just...just stay. Stay right there." He stood and put a hand inside his clothes. When he withdrew it, he held it out toward me.

I raised my head. Held my nose high to take a sniff.

Food.

"Come here." He waved it at me. Set it within the hollow of his hand and held it out. "It's for you. Come here, *chiot.* Come here, *mon cher.*"

Moncher? He knew my name! I leaped to my feet and closed the distance between us.

CHAPTER 19

Lisette Lefort

Château of Eronville
The province of Orléanais, France

*I*T HAD BEEN NEARLY THREE WEEKS SINCE I HAD COME to the Château of Eronville. The province of Orléanais was gentler and milder than my native Gascogne. There were streams here, and hills, but they were of the softer, less pronounced variety. The land ascended less abruptly; the streams ran more slowly. Though I missed Souboscq's sand-colored stone and the red tiles of the roof, the Château of Eronville was charming. It must once have served a defensive purpose, for it was comprised of a collection of towers, though the arrow slits had long since been replaced by paned windows. The drawbridge spanned an admirably deep, dry moat in which a herd of goats seemed to be constantly grazing. The count, though rarely present inside the château, was often seen skulking in the shadows of the garden or pacing out in front of the stables.

One evening, he grabbed me by the arm after supper and steered us into the salon. "Does your father have some reason to hate you? Does it seem strange to you he has not yet tried to communicate? To let us know when to expect him with the lace?"

"Would you try to communicate with a daughter whose actions had so reduced your estates? Would you not be happy to be rid of her?" In spite of the impulse that had sent me here, I prayed I was not speaking the truth. I dropped my gaze from him and wrapped my arms around my chest.

"Then if you expect no communication, I will need you to have a talk with my father."

His father? The marquis? "Why?"

"At the moment, he is threatening to disinherit me in favor of this babe who is soon to be born. I am unwilling for that to happen. He seems to think you might be favorably inclined toward me should I happen to press a suit for your hand."

I felt my brow fold as I tried to understand what it was he was saying. "*My* hand? You?" He despised me. And he had made no show of hiding it.

"It doesn't matter what you think. What matters is what he thinks. I need you to persuade him to be kind to me. Listen!" He grabbed me by the elbow, pulling me toward him. "He's a man, just like any other man. And he's been known to take the things he wants, even when he has no right to them. My stepmother can't satisfy his needs at the moment. So if you please him, he might just give you anything you ask for."

He wasn't—! He didn't—! "Are you telling me to—?"

"He's already decided you might be able to redeem my degenerate soul. All I ask is that you find some way to have a private audience with him. And when you do, you need to encourage him to be merciful to your poor, pitiful Julien."

I shrank from him in horror. "I won't do that. Not to the marquise." We had quickly become friends. I had not had one before. She was everything I had been born to be, and she had everything I'd always desired. And yet, in spite of all those blessings, I did not want to be her. It cheered me I was not so vain, not so selfish as I had feared.

"Have you so quickly forgotten our agreement?" He

whispered this into my ear. The marquis had once more reappeared. The count bent and kissed my earlobe.

I flinched. "Don't touch me."

"I don't plan on it becoming a regular occurrence. Remy is much more suited to such things than I am."

"Do you threaten me?"

"Are you telling me you won't do as I ask?"

I raised my chin as I glared at him. "I can't."

He smiled in the marquis's direction and then pulled me along with him toward his father. "Unless you receive a letter from your father soon, telling us of his coming, then you must."

I had tired of being subject to this man's schemes and whims. "And what if I refuse?"

"Then I plan on delivering your father's head, on a platter, to the King."

God help me! My teeth clattered together with fear as I walked down the hall to the marquis's chambers. I clutched my hands together in front of me to keep them from trembling. Was there no other choice than this?

The marquis's servant opened the door at my knock. He bowed and announced my presence to his master.

The count's father peered at me from the chair in which he was sitting. "My dear girl! You're so pale. What has befallen you?" He rose and turned to his manservant. "Bring her some spirits. Quickly!" Then he walked over, took me by the hand, and gently pulled me into his chambers. They were large and warmer than my own. A fire had been lit in the hearth, and it lent a golden glow to the place. A collection of jeweled objects and serving pieces crafted from stone glittered from the mantel. There was a brilliant lapis pitcher with a silvered Neptune posing as a handle. And a glowing jasper bowl, scalloped in shape, with a golden fleur-de-lis sitting atop its lid. In the place of honor, at the center, sat a jeweled dagger.

I quite forgot my mission and my fears as I walked toward a cup that could only have been made of rock crystal. It was a standing cup, poised on a tall, thin, fluted column of gold. The crystal itself was a swirl of patches, both transparent and opaque. With its drinking edge covered in gilt, it brought to mind the mists of Souboscq.

"It's beautiful, isn't it?" The marquis took it down from the mantel and offered it to me.

"Oh. *Non.*" I put my hands behind my back. "I couldn't."

"Yes, you can. You must. Such craftsmanship is meant to be appreciated."

I shook my head.

"*Tenez.* Take it. You won't break it."

How did he know I would not? My fingers ached to touch its base and stroke its clouded sides. But how could he trust me when I did not trust myself?

He put a gentle hand to my arm and drew my own hand from behind my back. Then he placed the cup into my palm, closing my fingers about the stem.

"There now. A little beauty does the soul good."

"I am used to admiring from afar."

"Beauty is meant to be lived with, not just admired."

The marquis put the cup back on the shelf and pulled a chair from his desk toward the fire. "Come. Sit and warm yourself."

"I didn't mean to—" I could have finished the sentence with a hundred different phrases. I didn't mean to disturb you. I didn't mean to destroy the lace. Or my father. And yet I had done all of those things…and I had one thing yet to do. All I wanted was to free those I loved from the curse of my presence. I had not meant to give them another reason to despise me.

"Please, do not worry yourself. Only tell me why you have come."

He was looking at me with such kind solicitation, such genuine concern, I nearly turned and ran from the room. But I did not dare to. I had already torn from my father everything of value. The only good I could do him now was to keep the count from revealing Papa's secret.

"You seem troubled."

I almost wept from vindication and relief. At last, someone who saw things as they truly were. Someone who did not pretend I was anything other than I was. We had never talked at Souboscq of that night when everything had changed. Papa and Alexandre took such great pains not to bring it up, they might as well have spoken of it daily.

"Is it...Julien?"

I could not answer.

"Has he done something...?" There was a note of judgment and outrage in his voice.

"It's nothing."

He reached up and grabbed hold of the dagger on the mantel. "By God, if he has harmed you in any way—!"

"No. Please! He has not."

"What has he done, then?" The blade flashed with the fire's light.

"Nothing!" He had done nothing at all. He'd left everything up to me. I rose and walked toward the old man as his son's words rang in my head. *If you please him, he will give you anything you ask for.* My own father's words followed after them: *Sometimes the past has the power to devour the future.* Was my own worth so very great that I could

179

not sacrifice myself for the sake of my father? Had he not sacrificed so very much for me? "Please. Put the dagger down. He's done nothing."

He swung away from me toward the door, and for a moment I thought he did not hear me. But then he stopped. His shoulders drooped as he sighed. "Julien has always been good at doing nothing. Nothing I've ever asked him to do, in any case."

I led him toward the same chair he had just offered me. The warrior who had been brandishing the dagger just moments before had disappeared. Left in his place was a tired and stooped old man. He collapsed into the chair. Resting his elbows on his knees, he turned the dagger between his hands. The hilt was encrusted with glittering jewels in a multitude of colors. They seemed to capture and then return the fire's light as the marquis turned the dagger round and round.

"It wasn't supposed to be like this." He glanced up at me. "I fought in the Spanish Wars, you know. With the King's father."

Good King Henri.

"He was the best of men. King Henri knew what it was to be a nobleman. And he never required any of us be other than what we were. " He sighed as he looked at that dagger. "During the wars, I met up with a man near Troyes, at the Battle of Fontaine-Française. We became true brothers, united by combat and bound by blood. We swore our sons would never want for anything if it were ever in our power to help them. I owe everything, my life, to that man. Quite literally." The dagger kept turning between his hands as he spoke. "A Spaniard very nearly killed me at Ardes. He would have, had it not been for my friend."

His eyes had drifted toward the fire, though they did not seem to reflect any of its light.

"At Fontaine-Française, the King himself became encircled. My friend and I saw him, and we broke through the Spanish lines to save him. He rewarded us with titles and lands, granted side by side, at our request. My friend begged to be sent to Amiens to continue the fight. Before we parted, he entrusted his lands to my care. We had these daggers made." He held it out toward me. "But that was the last I ever saw of him. He wrote me several years later that he had fallen in love with a Spanish woman."

His teeth flashed in a smile.

"After all of that!" He shook his head. "Who can reason with the heart? He said they'd had a son. And then I never heard from him after that." He sighed a long sigh that spoke of regrets and lost opportunities, turning to me with a sad smile. "Julien wants to be my heir. He ought to be my heir. But things being as they are…I've often wondered what might have happened if I'd never had a son." A veil of sadness fell over his features. "I've tried to understand him…"

I reached down and placed a hand on his arm.

"Half of what Julien thinks I have is not even really mine. I hold it by proxy…for my friend." He sighed once more and looked up toward the mantel. He tried to stand, holding up the dagger.

"Let me." I took it from him and put it back.

"Thank you, my dear, for listening so graciously to the musings of an old man. Now what is it that you came for?"

Why is it I had come? I had come to save a man just as old and tired as the marquis. I had come to save what was left of my family. The marquis had spoken of nobility and honor. Perhaps he would respond to a request for those very same things. "I wanted to speak to you, in fact, about your son. He's unsettled by the coming birth of your child."

"My son. So many disappointments Julien has brought

me. I do not know that I could survive anymore. You know how he is, don't you?"

I hesitated only for a moment before nodding. I could speak nothing less than the truth to a man who had bared his soul to me.

"I left him alone too long with his mother. Such a beautiful girl she was…only she did things to him…to punish me." His voice trailed off, and then he blinked and seemed to return to the conversation. "I thought…She made it quite clear, at the start, how she felt about me. I thought… She practically gave herself to me. Why did she then despise me for the…" His eyes drifted toward the fire as I read a thousand sorrows in his eyes.

I shivered in spite of my proximity to the fire.

"Julien desperately needs someone to save him. I used to think I could do it…maybe—do you think you can? Can you save him from himself?"

"I don't…" I did not want to disappoint him, but neither did I wish to promise him something I could not undertake. "I do not know."

He seized my hand. "You can do it. You must do it. He is anathema to all that is right and true, and yet…I find myself hoping. You see why I must have a new heir. A real heir. But I will not abandon my son. I will make provisions for him. If you stay with him, I will see neither of you lack for anything. Please…you could be his salvation."

If he weren't so bent on destroying me! There was nothing more to say. I had accomplished what the count had requested of me. I curtsied. "Thank you, my lord, for your kindness."

"You will consider what I said, won't you?"

I returned to my chamber and was helped from my basque and gown by a maid. She had hardly turned me into my night clothes when the door opened. Startled, I clutched at my nightshift.

It was the count. He stalked into the room. Settling himself into a chair beside the table that held a looking glass, he propped his chin in his hand. "You weren't there very long. What happened?" His gaze fastened upon my face.

My eyes fell from his as I felt a blush rise to my cheeks. "I…"

"Yes?"

What did I have to be ashamed of? I had done nothing wrong. Raising my chin, I took a breath. "I did not have to do as you asked. He has already planned to make provisions for you." Now maybe he would leave me in peace!

"Provisions! I don't want *provisions*. Before his arrangement with the cardinal, that might have sufficed, but now, I want it all!" He swept a fist across the table, spewing the glass and a hairbrush onto the floor. "I want everything! I want all the world to know I am his son. If he won't be proud of me, at least he must claim me." He snarled at the maid, who left without even a backward glance. Then he came at me, his dark, flinty eyes reflecting no light at all. "I want everything, and I will have it. You must return to him at once and find some way to secure it for me."

I took a step backward toward the door. "I can't."

"I don't care whether you can or can't. You must."

"He thinks I can…I can save you. He thinks you have an interest in me. And he wants so badly to believe it…"

"Yes. I've heard all that before. He used to have special masses said for me. For the benefit of my eternal soul." He stared at me with such malevolence, I began to tremble. "I warn you. Unless you save my inheritance, there will be no hope for your own."

✑

"You are so pensive, Lisette. I need you to be amusing and gay." The marquise looked as if she were trying to smile. "Though I can no longer see them, I feel certain my feet have swollen to twice their size. I can no longer wear my stays, and my back aches abominably. I must be distracted from my thoughts, not forced to face them." Exasperation was evident on her face, and reproach embroidered her words. She set her needlework on a table and put a hand to her back.

"My apologies, my lady."

"Is it Julien who has distressed you?"

If only I could have kept that smile on my lips. "I'm sure there can be nothing but celebration here once the babe is born."

"I wish he would hurry!"

"Do you think it's a he, then?" If it were a girl, then the count could cease his scheming...but the marquis would be sorely disappointed.

"Of course I am! I've been sleeping on my right side for months. And look. Don't you think my right eye shines brighter than the left?"

It was difficult to tell in the afternoon's gray light.

"It has to be a boy. If we can find a bucket of water, I shall slit my finger, and you'll see that my blood sinks. Straight to the bottom!"

"No, please. Don't worry yourself." I had not meant to annoy her. Indeed, aside from the beauty of the château, her company was my only pleasure.

"It must be a boy. Don't even *suggest* it is not!"

"I have always thought it must be." I'd only prayed that it would not.

She smiled as if to reassure herself. "It will be a boy. And all will be well during the bearing of him, and afterward, I shall finally be able to dance again! How dull it has been here in the country. I'm sure I've missed a thousand things at court since we've been gone." A scowl creased her fine features as she pulled her fur stole up toward her chin.

I was not performing well at the task she had set before me. What would cheer a creature like her? She was a hundred times removed in nature from me. She seemed to live for songs and chatter and dancing...things I had all but renounced. I lived for peace and solitude, in a perpetual state of penance. She skipped through a life filled with grace and mirth. She was who I might have been.

There were some thoughts better left alone. "I suppose... you'll need new gowns before your return to court."

Her eyes brightened. "Yes! I shall ask Julien to help me. He'll tell me what Marie de Hautefort was wearing when he last saw her. And what sort of lace the Queen had at her collar. Not that I could wear its copy, but it would be nice to know. I do so wish the King would relent with his edicts. I don't see why the rest of us shouldn't wear exactly what we'd like!" With very little encouragement, she chattered on about this thing and that thing until it was time for dinner.

I lent her a hand then to pull her away from the chair. I tugged, perhaps a little too strenuously, for she found her feet with a grunt and immediately put a hand to her back.

"I'm sorry! I didn't mean to—" How many times had I said those words?

"It's nothing. It's just that I'm such a stupid, ugly, old sow." She burst into tears. "I can't do anything right anymore."

I shuttled her toward the door, ignoring her tears and reassuring her of her worth. "You're the apple of the marquis's eye. It's not what you look like. He doesn't care what you've done or what you can't do. It's who you are that's important, regardless of everything else."

"It's the child that's important, regardless of everything else. Regardless, even, of me." The look she gave me was fraught with resignation. And pity. As if I must be provincial, indeed, if I did not realize the truth of her words. "As long as I have a boy child, then all will be right."

CHAPTER 20

The Count of Montreau

CHÂTEAU OF ERONVILLE
THE PROVINCE OF ORLÉANAIS, FRANCE

THE TWO GIRLS SPENT THEIR DAYS PRATTLING ABOUT this thing and the other. When the weather was clear, they sat together in the garden, enjoying autumn's warming sun.

"They seem to be getting on like sisters." Remy came to stand beside me at the window where I was looking down at them. He carried a glass of brandy in his hand. For once, he was not on a hunt, out with his falcons, or riding through the godforsaken countryside. In fact, it made me wonder why he was not. He must know he could expect no solicitation from me. The good doctor's enemas didn't seem to be working.

As I took the brandy from him, I looked him straight in the eyes.

His gaze dropped away from mine.

"Gabrielle can get along even with my father."

"But isn't this what you wanted? To please the marquise in order to appease your father?"

"Yes." But my father was a stubborn bastard, taking every opportunity these days to remind me he intended to disinherit me.

The sound of laughter, carried by the wind, pierced the glass, reaching our ears.

"Your plan must soon start working, then."

Not quickly enough! If I could not persuade my father

from his designs before the babe was born, then all was lost. Unless…the babe turned out to be a girl.

Remy was watching me. "What?"

"If the babe turns out to be a girl…"

He raised his glass in my direction. "Then all of your father's plans will have been for naught."

"Precisely." And if it were indeed a girl my stepmother was spawning, things were not quite so bleak as they appeared. My father could not risk his annulment unless he were certain of having another heir. Was he certain? How did one tell about such things?

I took another look at Lisette from Souboscq. She wasn't the worst of females. She didn't talk overly much, and mostly, she kept out of sight. If my father thought I were truly reformed, then perhaps he wouldn't be quite so bent on pursuing his course.

Father plucked at my arm as I tried to leave the hall after dinner. I offered it to him as if that were exactly my intention, watching as Remy disappeared up the stair. Later, I would find him. I only hoped he wouldn't want what he usually did. I cringed from the thought of another disappointing encounter. I aided the count to standing and then matched my steps to his. It used to be he could easily outpace me. Now his stride was less than half of my own. War wounds, he said, though I imagined that to be an excuse for old age.

"We need to speak. In private."

Well. That was something. He could hardly stand to look at me. I would never have hoped he might desire to speak to me. I walked him up the stair and into his chambers. Leaned against the mantel as a servant lit a taper and the count settled himself in a chair. The dagger that lay on the mantel winked at me, its many-colored jewels reflecting the taper's light.

"I hope you understood me, Julien. When I spoke to you about the annulment."

I tried to smile. "I understood you wanted to wash your hands of me."

He sighed the tired, heavy sigh of an aged and wearied man. "Nothing could be further from the truth. I only wish that…"

I stared at him, daring him to say what I knew he'd always thought.

"I only wish I had never married your mother. How can you fault me for that?"

Fault him? For wishing to erase the very circumstance of my birth? "Then perhaps I ought to say I wish you had never been my father."

He recoiled as if I had slapped him.

"How can you fault me for *that*?"

"I can't." He shook his head as he spoke. "How can I? I've failed you, Julien…in every way possible."

It was the truest thing he'd ever said. "You may have hated her, but I loved her."

"No. Don't say that. Never say that!" That old look of fire and wrath, the one that had always given me pause during my youth, had come back into his eyes.

But I didn't care what he thought anymore. "She loved me."

"She cursed you. She twisted you."

"At least she knew what I was."

CHAPTER 21

Alexandre Lefort

RURAL FRANCE

I GATHERED THE DOG IN MY ARMS AND STARTED OFF through the night. But this was not the forest of my youth, where I had known the shape of every tree and the turn of every brook. I did not know in which direction I was walking, knew only that we had to get away from this place of death.

I'd been waiting in France with the dog runner when a great restlessness came over me. I tried to ease it by surveying the tools of his cooper's trade. When that didn't work, I helped him feed wood shavings into the fire.

"The dog likes it."

"…the wood shavings?"

"The fire. I treat him well over on this side of the border. I tend his wounds. I feed him meat. And cream. Keep him warm."

"And how is he used to being treated?"

The man laughed. "He's used to being whipped and starved and beaten by my cousin."

"And this is the dog that's to deliver my lace?" What madness was this?

"My cousin trained him. Dressed himself up in the uniform of one of those border soldiers whenever he beat the cur. Worked like a charm. He wraps the lace around the dog and dresses him up in a fur coat. When he lets the dog go, it runs straight to me."

"He beats the dog? On purpose?"

The man shrugged. "It's the only way that seems to work. *Mon cher argent*, I call him. My little purse. An easy way to make my fortune."

The restlessness had grown into a pronounced distaste of my host. And fear. If anything happened to my lace, then Lisette and the viscount were doomed. "I need some air." It was partly true. The smell of pungent, freshly worked wood only partially overcame the fetid stench of his person. The place seemed to close in about me: airless and oppressive.

The man looked up from the fire. "Don't…the dog might not—"

I closed the door on his objections. If that dog had not been carrying my lace, I would have warned him far away from here.

Out in the night, only the breeze whispered. But here, too, there was a restlessness. It was a countryside unknown to me, and the night might have held any manner of creatures, but I turned from the yard, and walked behind the house toward the wood. I had always felt safest in the forest. Even at Souboscq, I found myself often wandering past the fields toward the trees.

As I entered the wood, I heard a shifting in the space before me and the scuff of a boot against the earth. Remembering the lessons of my youth, I pressed my back against the nearest tree trunk and held myself as still as I could.

"You hear something?" The voice sounded anxious. And uncertain.

"It's the sound of me, pissing." That voice was supremely confident.

"You sure this is the place?"

"That's what De Grote said."

"It wasn't one of the other smugglers?"

"It's this one." There was silence for a few moments. Then came the sound of a man spitting. "How many dogs you think are trying to cross the border this night?"

"Twenty? Thirty?"

"I bet there's hundreds. At least we have it easy. De Grote tells us who, and he tells us when. Those other bounty hunters have to take their chances."

De Grote. Again. He hadn't been content just to take my money. He wanted my lace, too. And these men wanted the dog.

My dog. Who was carrying *my* lace.

I didn't make a habit of antagonizing people. I had not purposefully set out to make De Grote my enemy. I had approached him honorably, intending to conduct our transaction in an honorable way. Even after he'd had me beaten, I had turned the lace over to him for the smuggling…and I had left him in possession of my father's dagger. I had not wanted to harm anyone.

Not even him.

But now, he intended to steal my future. Our future: the viscount's, Lisette's, and mine. I would not allow that to happen.

As my resolve hardened, I felt a brick settle at the bottom of my stomach, and the hairs at the back of my neck began to prickle. I had experienced another night like this one, a lifetime ago. Back when I had lived with my father in St. Segon, the village priest had made it his duty to dog me, to harass me, to taunt me.

The forest had been my haven, a near-perfect paradise, where there were none to mock me but the birds, and none to hiss at me but the tortoises who lived by the brook. But one night, when I was ten years old, the priest had decided to follow me home.

I tried to lose him by leaving the path and dodging through the trees, but always he had reappeared like some tormenting spirit. I plucked a small stone from a stream and placed it into my slingshot. I wanted only to turn him from his course. I took aim at his arm, and I let the stone fly.

But he moved.

The priest moved, the stone hit him in the forehead, and he fell over, dead.

❧

I never told anyone what I had done, though I knew God had seen me. I dragged his body across the stream and over a hill, where I left it in front of a wolf's den. Then I ran home to the cave my father lived in.

I wanted to tell him. I yearned to tell him.

But I did not want him to hate me.

So I talked to the only one who knew what I had done. I talked to God. I begged him to forgive me. I promised him I would be good for the rest of my life. I would do good. I would never hurt any man again.

And I hadn't.

But this De Grote was different.

He was my village priest come back to haunt me. He would not leave me be.

❧

My fight was not with the bounty hunters, and so I let them go about their business. I watched as they shot the cooper. It was only when they turned their guns on the dog that I showed myself. And then, it was only to chase the dog from them. I ran after it, pushing through the trees into the unknown. I had come to the cooper's cottage by way of a road. But now, in the shifting shadows of the moonlit night, I did not know if I was running away from the border or toward it. I risked losing my self in that forest, but to have lost the dog and the lace would have been worse still.

I had to pause after nearly every step, to hear which way the dog was headed. Finally, I came upon it, curled into itself and panting, nestled within the roots of a tree. It was resting easy in my arms now, though that did no good in helping me find my way through the wood.

I looked toward my left. Looked to my right. Before us, the black shadows of the forest seemed to ease. I set out in that direction. Following the thinning in the trees, I finally walked into a clearing. Beyond it lay a shack.

The dog stirred, clawing at my arms.

I let him down.

He whined for a moment and sniffed at the air. Trotted over toward a box.

I followed him.

The box reeked of excrement and stale urine. Though the dog stretched out his neck and sniffed at it, he did not approach it. But he did go up to the body that lay in the dirt of the yard. He growled at it. He turned his back to it and kicked dirt at it with his back paws. And then he barked.

I understood then: we had come back to a place the dog had known. A place of beatings and whippings and starving. We had passed back into Flanders.

A path that meandered away from the shack eventually led us to a road. As much as I wished I could reverse my path and return to France, I had no confidence I could do it. I had no choice but to follow the road. I had regained the lace, but it was useless to me until it was in France. We walked back into the city of Kortrijk as the sun woke. I went into De Grote's store once it had opened and addressed myself to the clerk.

The dog slunk behind a barrel.

"I wish to see De Grote."

"He's not here. He won't be here for another hour. Maybe two."

"Then I'll wait for him."

"Come back later, I'll tell him you've been by."

I walked toward the back of the store where I knew De Grote's office to be. The dog followed at my heels. "I'll wait for him in his office, then." I put a hand to a door.

"It's locked."

I turned to face the clerk. "Then perhaps you'll give me the key."

"Only De Grote has the key."

I lunged forward, grabbed the clerk's collar, and threw him over a barrel, pressing his throat against the edge of the lid. "I'm sure it won't take you long to find another."

"I don't—"

"It would be a shame for me to break your arm for want of a key."

"I can't—"

"I've been marked by De Grote since I got here. Would you like to tell me why?"

"It's not you."

"It feels like me." I gave him a shake.

He yelped. "It's not you. It's what he does, if he thinks he can. He charges for the smuggling, and then he recoups the lace and charges for its smuggling again."

"Pity. I was beginning to think I was somebody special." I pulled the man off the barrel and threw him toward the counter at the front of the store. "Get me the key!"

✑

We waited for some time in De Grote's office, the dog and I. Eventually, there came the sound of shouting and the scuffling of feet upon the floor.

"What do you mean he's here? He can't be!"

"But he is, De Grote…he's—"

The door flew open, and De Grote stood in the doorframe. The dog slunk behind the chair I was sitting in.

De Grote strode into the room. "I did not expect to see you again."

"Because you thought me dead?"

"It doesn't pay to toss accusations about in Kortrijk."

"So I've discovered. You've made a profitable business out of cheating your business partners."

"I'm not accustomed to entertaining in my office. How can I make you leave?" He took another step closer to me.

I rose. "You can get my lace across the border like you promised to."

"I already did."

"You did not."

"I was assured, in fact, that the lace made it into France."

"I wonder how it is you come by your knowledge?"

"It's not my fault you brought it back across the border. But your lapse in judgment can be dealt with. We can make another arrangement. You can make me another payment. And I can deliver your lace once more."

"I will not pay twice for the same service."

Behind me, the dog whined.

"It is not the same service. I delivered once already. Now you're asking me to deliver again. One and one will forever make two, Frenchman."

"I see my own dagger there in your belt. As you said, one and one make two."

De Grote's hand closed upon the handle of the dagger. "It's a very fine piece of workmanship."

I took a step closer to him. "For the favor of using your services once more, I'd like it returned."

"And I'd like to never see you again."

"I will guarantee it. Just as soon as you get my lace out of Flanders."

The dog growled and came to stand beside me. De Grote took a step away from us as his face went white. "Call off your dog."

"Get my lace out of Flanders."

"Call off your dog! I've a horror of the beasts."

"My lace...?"

The dog barked with a sharpness that made me wince.

"Meet me at the cemetery of Sint-Maartenskerk on Friday night at eleven o'clock. I'll have it put in a coffin for you. Cross the border and deliver it to the priest in Signy-sur-vaux. It's a bit of a journey to the Ardennes, but the priest is willing, and no one will suspect you so far from the border."

"If you are not there, then I warn you, I will hold your life as forfeit."

CHAPTER 22

Katharina Martens

LENDELMOLEN, FLANDERS

ISTER HAD GIVEN ME A NEW COMMISSION ON THE Monday, just as I had expected.

"We have an order for something different. I told the Reverend Mother the only reason I could accept it was because I knew you would be able to do it."

Something…Had she said something *different*? I could not hear for the buzzing in my ears. I couldn't make something different.

"…I'll pin it just here."

I sat as she took my pillow from me and pinned the pattern upon it. I sat as she settled the pillow back on my lap. Sat as she patted me on the arm and then walked away. There was nothing to do. I couldn't see to know what to do. And I knew then what my fate would be. How could it be any different than Mathild's?

I set about twisting and crossing my bobbins for one cycle and then untwisting and uncrossing them in the next. All day long, I worked at undoing my work, praying Sister would not notice.

She did not.

The next day, Tuesday, the day of Heilwich's visit, I told my sister I was done.

"Not with the lace!"

"I finished it on Saturday."

"But you can't be done with the lace. I haven't got the money yet!"

"Sister gave me a new pattern."

"And…?"

"I can't see to make it. I've been pretending. All day yesterday and all day today I've been pretending."

"You must keep pretending, Katharina. Promise me you'll keep pretending."

"I don't know how long I can. And what if Sister sees me?"

"I'll pray she doesn't. This very afternoon, once I get back to Kortrijk, I'll pray the rosary for you in Father Jacqmotte's own office."

"The rosary? For me?"

"Just…whatever you do…don't leave the abbey. Don't let them throw you out."

❦

I tried not to. I tried not to let them throw me out. But the next day, Sister discovered I'd been pretending.

"What—!" She grabbed my pillow from me. The bobbins clattered to the floor. "What is the meaning of this?"

As I sat there, as I listened to the lace makers at work around me, I made a decision. I decided I was not going to be like Mathild. I was not going to let Sister shriek at me and pull me out of my clogs, following along behind her as meek as…as…a lace maker. "What happened to Mathild?"

A pair of shoes scuffed against the floor as Sister's footsteps halted. "What did you—?"

"What happened to Mathild!" I spoke the words as loudly as I dared.

There was no sound in that place save for the animals crunching hay below. Had I not known differently, I would have guessed myself to be alone. But then Sister wrenched my arm.

"Ow! What happened to Mathild? You threw her out, didn't you? She made lace for you, and when she couldn't see anymore, you just threw her out!"

"Hush. You will not speak of such things here—! You will not speak at all!" She tried to snatch me from the bench, but I let my pillow fall to the floor and leaned back on my heels so stubbornly she had to relent.

"Do you know what will happen once they've done with us?" I tried to speak so loudly even the children across the room would hear. "They'll throw us out onto the street."

One of the younger girls began to cry. "I want my *moeder!*"

"Hush now." Sister's whisper was vicious. "Look what you've done!"

"None of you will escape. You'll all go blind. Just like me. And Elizabeth and Aleit and Johanna. Beatrix, Jacquemine, and Martina."

"She lies."

"I don't! I swear on the Holy Mother. I was the youngest of the lace makers when I arrived. And now I'm the oldest. What happened to all of the others?"

"Lies!"

"What will happen to all of you?"

Sister seized me with such force I had no choice but to do what she wanted. What she wanted was to drag me from the room. I nearly tumbled down the stairs. I would have, but for the grip she kept on my arm.

Once we cleared the workshop, she began to yell. "Help! Someone help us!"

I twisted to free myself from her. "What happened to them, Sister? What happened to Elizabeth? And Aleit and Johanna?"

"Help me!"

I heard doors being thrown open. Heard the slap of shoes against paving stones. Heilwich's warning clanged in my mind. I broke free from Sister and ran to the only refuge I knew: the dark, looming shape of the chapel. Grappling with the doors, I threw them open and then ran straight for the Holy Mother herself. Hands brushing along the row of columns, I didn't stop running until I knew she must be there before me. And then I pushed around behind her. There was a space back there I had run to before. I felt for the ledge of the pedestal with my hand and then threw my leg onto it and pulled myself up. There was just room enough to wedge myself between the statue and the wall. And no room at all for anyone else to stand up there beside me. If I was to come out, it would be my own choice, and not anyone else's.

Once settled, I began asking questions once more. In the chapel, my voice seemed to vault up to the high ceiling and rebound from the walls. Instead of one question, it sounded as if I were asking ten. All of them at the same time. "Where is Elizabeth?"

Where is Elizabeth, where is Elizabeth, where is Elizabeth...?

"And where is Aleit?"

Where is Aleit, where is Aleit, where is Aleit...?

The chapel had filled with people now. I couldn't see them, but I could hear them.

"Hush, girl!"

"What is she talking about?"

"Can't somebody make her stop shouting?"

When I spoke next, I tried to make my words even louder. "What happened to the other lace makers? Where is Johanna?"

"There's no reason to speak of such things. I'm going to tell Mother. That's what I'm going to do." Sister's voice. It seemed to be coming from in front of the statue.

"Tell her! And then ask her. What happened to Beatrix and Jacquemine?"

Sister was true to her word. It didn't take long for Mother to appear. I heard her come several minutes later, her skirts brushing against the floor. I smelled the cool scent of her perfume as it invaded the air around me.

"Come out this instant!"

"*Nee.*"

"You're being obstinate."

"Tell me what happened to Mathild."

"To whom?"

"Mathild. And Elizabeth and Aleit. And all the other lace makers that aren't here anymore."

"They left of their own choosing. They're most of them married now. With children."

"Lies!" I knew they were lies. It had something to do with the sound of her voice.

"Come out. Now!"

"*Nee.* I'm not coming until you bring them here."

"Who?"

"All those lace makers. With their husbands and their children."

I heard nothing in the sudden silence but the grinding of teeth. And then Mother's retreat as her shoes struck the floor. "Have one of the novices stay here with her. She'll tire soon enough. Once she comes out, bring her to me."

I had not tired. It had been two days, and I had not tired.

CHAPTER 23

Heilwich Martens

KORTRIJK, FLANDERS

ON TUESDAY EVENING, AFTER I SAID THE ROSARY I'D promised Katharina, as I was finishing my sweeping in the kitchen, I had a visitor. I didn't know it, though, until he spoke.

I gasped as I saw him: De Grote. Had he been summoned by my thoughts, like some vengeful ghost? I crossed myself. He smiled, as if he really was the gentleman most of the city thought he was.

I frowned. Bit my lip. I didn't know what to say to him. So I started to sweep around the hearth. It was a sin just how sooty it got…and how sooty it would be not two hours after I finished the sweeping of it. If heaven had any rewards to offer, the one I hoped to receive was a perpetually clean fireplace with enough wood to heat even the coldest of winter's nights.

"I know I told you I wouldn't come here again, but I need you. Something's happened. And there's no on else who can help me."

No one else? There was no one else in any of those other parish churches? There was no one else who could bring themselves to do what I had done? I glanced over at him. "What makes you think you can change my mind?"

He stared at me a long moment, and then he sighed. In

that sigh I read surrender. It was the sigh of defeat. The sigh
my father had offered up when the nuns took Katharina and
disappeared with her into the abbey. De Grote took a purse
from his pocket, loosed the strings, took up my hand, and
emptied the contents into it.

My prayers had been answered! "This is twice as much as
you ever offered before." And if I had added it up right, it
would be just enough to buy my sister back from the nuns.

"I need you twice as much as I've ever needed you before.
I've a customer I need to be rid of. It's all yours if you can
deliver me a body. And I promise you I will never come to
you again."

I took the pouch from his hand and let the money slide
back into it. "The same way you promised before?" Father
Jacqmotte would cast me out of his house if he ever found
out what I was about. But still, I did not return the purse to
De Grote.

He noticed. "You don't need the money, then?"

Oh, I needed the money.

He must have read the indecision in my eyes. He dug
deeply into his coat and pulled out one coin more. He took
the purse from me, opened it up, and let the coin fall into it
with a clink.

Ja. I needed the money. I nodded.

He smiled, secured the purse, and put it back into his pocket.
"When?"

"Tomorrow."

Tomorrow! I shook my head. "It's not possible." Though
how I wished it were! I wished I could give him what he
wanted. Right that moment. "I can't promise tomorrow.
These things take thought. And planning."

"The next day, then."

"The third day."

He dabbed at the glaze of sweat that covered his forehead. "*Nee.* Two days or not at all. I want to be done with this commission."

Two days. Surely someone would die in the next two days. "Fine."

He left me as he had found me: sweeping. Two days from now. That would work. Somewhere, someone should die. And if nothing else, if no one else, if I hadn't misread the signs, there was old Herry. He would be long dead by then. And what he couldn't have any way of knowing had no way of hurting him.

When I went to call on old Herry, Marguerite pushed past me through the door. "It took you long enough! And where were you yesterday?"

"I was taking care of Father Jacqmotte. It's my work, you know."

"Well…I just…" She lifted her chin, stretched her cloak tighter about her shoulders. "I'm going out."

I let her go. And then I went to see to Herry.

Poor man. In the day since I'd seen him, he'd gone raspy in the chest and grayer in the cheeks. I rolled him over and changed out his pallet and blanket. Spooned some potage into his mouth…or tried to.

"You've got to eat it."

His gaze lingered on mine.

"You've got to. You wouldn't want to save it for Marguerite. I'd lay down money there's some young man bent on buying her supper this night."

He blinked.

I held the spoon to his lips.

He opened his mouth and might have taken it if he hadn't had to search for a breath.

I grabbed him by his shirt, tugged him up to sitting, and then beat upon his back until he stopped his gasping. Then I lowered him down to the pallet.

"What's to become of us, Herry?"

His only reply was a wheeze.

"I've got to save my sister." Anyone would understand that. "She was given to the nuns, you know. The ones over there in Lendelmolen, who make lace."

If I wasn't mistaken, I saw sympathy in his eyes. "She has over thirty years now. You know what that means. They'll throw her onto the streets soon. They always do. How many of those poor lace makers have we seen in the streets, begging for food, tossing their skirts over their heads for a bit of bread?"

I knew he'd seen them just the same as I had. But bless Herry Stuer, I'd known him only to take up with honest whores. The kind who were willing.

"I offered them money for her. Offered to buy her back as if she were a cow. Do you know what they said? They said I didn't have enough money. That was five years ago. You know what I've done since then? I've worked to make up the difference…and it was quite a big difference, just so we're clear. I've done things, Herry. Things you wouldn't want to know about." Things I didn't want to think about.

I pushed up from the floor and took up a broom. If I were going to spend my time here, why should I spend it in a sty? I pushed it around. Stirred up a nest of mice. I chased them out the door and then swept their mess out behind them.

Pausing when I got to Herry's pallet, I leaned the broom against the wall and sat down beside him. "I would never have done it if I hadn't needed the money. You'd have understood. Some people you'd do anything for. Katharina is the only family I have left. Think if she were your sister. You'd not let her walk the streets, giving herself away for a piece of bread. Not if you could do anything about it."

Of course he wouldn't.

"It wasn't that difficult, the thing I've done. And it didn't really seem like it would make any difference."

Poor Herry, lying there silent, without anyone to cover up his feet. If I were his wife, I'd be ashamed to have him seen with a hole that size in his hose. I wondered how long he'd been walking around the city like that. You could pay a girl to warm your bed, but she wouldn't darn your hose for you. I straightened the blanket so it covered his feet.

"You wouldn't want to know, Herry, but Father had given all of them their last rites. Not that he had anything ever to do with it. He never has. He doesn't know. He can't. It weighs on the soul. More than I thought it would. It's just not quite…right."

I sighed. Put a hand to my coif and pushed it farther back on my head. "Some things just shouldn't be done. And I wouldn't have done them, Herry. Really, I wouldn't have. I only did them for Katharina. And I only have to do it this one last time. That's it. I'm done with it. I made a promise to myself." Although, I'd made a promise to myself the last time, too.

Promises. They were made only to be broken.

"I hope…Do you think God forgives people…for doing things like I've done?" I would have gone to confession, but it was Father Jacqmotte who would hear it. And I wasn't sure he would forgive all the things God might. Maybe this time I would go to one of the other parish churches. One of those, way across the city, where few knew who I was, and no one recognized my voice. But really, who had I ever actually hurt? And if it all worked out as I hoped, then Katharina would be saved.

No one hurt.

One person helped.

Perhaps I hadn't done as great a wrong as my conscience wanted me to believe.

༄

That night, Annen was delivered of her babe. She sent a boy to fetch me, so I was there for its birth. A long, plump boy. A healthy boy. Once it cried, once I knew it had breathed, my work there was done.

There would be no coffins made for this family. Not this night.

Later, before the sun rose, Father got called to the home of a mason. He asked me to come along. I didn't know what had happened until we got there, but I knew it must be something terrible. Father called for me to go with him only when he thought I might have to lay someone out.

When we got there, we were told the mason had been working at a job, cutting at a stone, that his tool had slipped and cut his leg instead. It was sliced to the bone. Father performed the last rites. It seemed the only thing that could be done. Then he left.

I stayed. I had to. Actually, wanted to. I was hoping that mason's misfortune would be my own good luck. I might have prayed for it, but that seemed too much like cheating. I did, however, hope very hard. I needed a dead body, and his seemed the only one likely to come my way. Indeed, he lingered between life and death. His face was drenched in sweat, his voice low and distant when it came at all, as if he had already glimpsed the flames of purgatory. But near about noontime, he asked, in a voice quite unmuddled by delirium, for a sip of beer.

Miracles abounded in my parish in Kortrijk. But none of them blessed me.

Is it a sin to pray for someone to die?

It wasn't as if I was praying death on any person in particular. It wasn't as if I *wanted* someone to die. But no one lives forever, and death was a regular visitor to the streets and alleys of Sint-Maartens parish. If that dark angel were going to visit us in any case, then why couldn't I just ask him to speed things along? Was there anything wrong with that?

It felt like it. It felt very much like there was. I'd told De Grote I'd have a body. I needed the money he would give me, and De Grote was not a man who was familiar with disappointment. Though some of us were born to it, others, never having had the taste of it, grew testy in its presence.

Nee, I could not disappoint him. I had to have a body. Surely someone would die.

I had work to do in preparation. The coffin to be got. The grave to be dug. The burial. And then once the burial was over, there was the coffin to be brought up again. I stopped in at the tavern to catch Big Jannes before he'd drunk a cup too many.

It had always been a bit of a trick to coax Big Jannes from his cups. And he was always vexed about it. I might have gone in and just spoken to him, but I didn't want any to remember our meeting. I passed by the window twice, three times, before I caught his eye. Inclined my head out toward the square.

He put his cup down and rose, setting his cap on his head and settling his belly over the top of his belt. After ducking through the door and peering round the square, he joined me. So to speak. As I stood by the corner, back to the building, he turned into the alley and made quick work of loosening his breeches to piss against the wall.

"Do you have to do that? I know what you've got without having to be shown it, don't I?"

"What is it, then?"

"Thursday. You'll be wanted."

"Same as—?"

"Same as always. And bring your own shovel this time."

I was gone before he was done and no one the wiser. I just had to find out who the body would be.

By the tolling of the church bells at Nones, still I had found no body. No one in the parish was in danger of dying. Not the new babe, not the Lievens's daughter. Not even the mason who had nearly sawn his leg in two. Even the butcher's widow looked better than I was used to seeing her. There were two babes yet to be born this spring, but neither of them due to be delivered until next month.

I'd sought out the youngest in the parish and the oldest. I even nosed around the former lace makers who lived in the darkest alleys and plied their new trade in the most hidden of places. Not one cough, not one sniff among them.

Panic started to clutch at my innards.

Surely someone would die. Someone always had. Always. I'd never had to go looking for a body like I'd looked this day. Only one hope was left me. I went to see old Herry.

I sighed as I looked at him lying there on the floor. "You

have to understand, Herry, I'm doing this for Katharina. She's a lovely girl. I'm not a bad person. I would never think to do a thing like this, but it's Katharina's only hope. Can you imagine what those nuns will do to her if I don't? They'll throw her out onto the streets. And she knows nothing. Least nothing about any of *that*. She's not like Marguerite. Pardon me for saying what's only true."

His eyes rolled about, showing the whites as they slid from side to side.

"You've not long, Herry. We both know it. You'd be doing me the biggest of favors by letting me kill you now rather than dying later."

That was my plan. The only option I had left.

So how was I going to do it? I couldn't just wring his gullet as if he were the father's chicken I was to cook for dinner. I couldn't do that. His neck was too big, my fingers not long enough. I looked around the room for something. *Nee*, not a knife. I wouldn't do it with a knife as if I were some murderess. Something else. A kettle. I could dash him in the head with a kettle. That would finish him off.

Nee.

Nee, I couldn't see myself doing it like that.

"Couldn't you just die, Herry? And save me the trouble?" I didn't bother to turn round as I asked him. He couldn't answer me anyway, could he? That was one good thing. He wouldn't cry out when I did it. He couldn't.

I stood there, not knowing what to think. Not knowing what to do. Really, it shouldn't be so hard to kill someone.

There was the slightest of sounds. The dribble of liquid over straw. I knew what it was before I smelt it. "Shame, Herry. You've gone and soiled yourself again."

I rolled him off and made him a new pallet. Got him settled once more.

"I really don't want to do this. You know that, don't you?"

I patted his hand and then pushed up from the pallet. It was one thing to decide to kill a man, but another thing entirely to do it. What was I supposed to do? I could throw a rope over a beam and string him up, but he was terrible heavy, and then no one could say he'd just drifted off in his sleep. Not with the burns from a rope around his neck. There had to be some other way.

I needed inspiration, but I didn't feel as if I could pray for any.

Maybe...I could feed him something. In his potage. But, *nee*. Who knew how long it might take to work? And how much to give him? I'd just have to...do it. But, dear God, how?

His long, raspy breaths began to grate upon my nerves. Why did he keep so busy breathing when he was supposed to be dying? And why should I have to hear him? I unfastened my apron and threw it over his head.

There.

I wouldn't see him staring at me anymore. And maybe I wouldn't be able to hear him quite so well.

He gasped again.

But then he breathed again, and it was such a terrible sound. If he would just shut up his mouth!

I withdrew the apron and did it for him, pushing his jaws together.

They didn't stay.

He took another gasping breath as they fell apart.

I'd just have to tie them together. I took up my apron and knotted it at the top of Herry's head. "There now. Much better. If you don't mind my saying."

With Herry quiet, I could get back to my thinking. And so I did. But soon enough there came a great snorting sound.

And how was I supposed to concentrate on finding a way to kill him when he kept distracting me like that?

I turned around and knelt down to find tears trickling from his eyes. Using the hem of my skirt, I dabbed at them. "It's not so bad, Herry. You know you've one foot in the hereafter already. What's the bad in going one day sooner? Or two? I don't think it would be more than three, if you pardon my saying."

That sound came once more. He was trying to breathe… and having trouble with the doing of it.

"Could you just…do you mind? I have to think, Herry, I really do." I pulled him to sitting and shoved a pot behind his head to keep it from falling back against the wall. "Better?"

It sounded better. He was breathing easier. And that set me to thinking. Breathing easier is something I wanted to do too.

I needed the money, but I didn't need it that badly, did I? Badly enough to murder poor Herry Stuer?

I reached out and took up one of his hands. Could have sworn he flinched. "There now. I haven't been in my right mind, Herry, and that's the truth. How could I hurt you? You'll live to die an honest death. And that's the best I can do for you. I'm just going to have to tell De Grote 'No.'"

No.

The word rang in the stillness of the room.

"Have you ever known anyone to tell the man 'No'?"

Herry closed his eyes.

"Thought not. I haven't either. Least no one who lived to tell about it. But why should I tell him 'Yes'? I've done too many terrible things for him to agree to do one thing more."

Herry sighed.

"I know it. Katharina's stuck in that abbey. And they're sure to discover her secret any day now, if they haven't already. But if God can't save her, then what kind of God is he? That's what the priest says. And I find I have to agree with him. 'On the mountain of the Lord it will be provided.' That's exactly what Father Jacqmotte always says. I'm just going to have to tell De Grote 'No.'"

⁓

I had the coffin for De Grote. Everything was ready. Ready as it should have been. Except I had no body. Big Jannes came. I saw his shadow flitting between the gravestones. I called him to me and told him he didn't have to dig. He had only to drag the coffin over from the side of the church. Empty or no, it was going to have to do.

De Grote and his customer arrived soon after, their forms veiled by the clouds shifting across the moon. De Grote rapped upon the coffin. "Anyone in there?" He laughed one of his strange, silent laughs. Turned toward me. "Open it up, then."

Big Jannes glanced at me.

I nodded.

He prized the lid off with a chink of his shovel against the nails, and then a pull that distorted his face with the effort.

I turned away. Couldn't bear to look at De Grote's face.

There was a hissing intake of breath. An explosion of cursing. "There's no body!"

I shook my head.

"There's supposed to be a body there. The one I told you I'd pay for."

"No one died. I don't have one."

"You don't—!" It was as close as I'd ever come to hearing De Grote yell. Good thing he didn't. The priest might have woken. He stepped closer. "I ordered a body."

Somewhere out in the darkness of the cemetery, a dog

216

whined. A strange, rolling growl of a whine. It made the hairs at the back of my neck stand on end, and the strings in my belly tighten.

"Nobody died."

"And yet, here we all are."

I shrugged. There was no body. What else could I say that I hadn't already said?

He took another step closer. So close I could feel his heat. "I asked for a body. You agreed to get me one. De Grote never gets cheated."

"I don't—"

"Say nothing."

I sent a glance toward the other man, De Grote's customer. One hand had gone inside his coat, and he was reaching toward De Grote with his other.

De Grote turned toward his customer. "Don't even think—"

"You promised to get my lace across the border."

"And I'll do it! There will be a body for that coffin. One way or another." He grabbed me by the arm and motioned to Jannes. "Bring that shovel here."

"Don't—! You can't—" I tried to wrench my arm from him. When that didn't work, I dug my heels into the ground. But the rain had turned the graveyard into a mire. My heels slid right out from under me.

"'Can't' isn't a word I use. I thought you understood that. No one crosses De Grote."

His customer grabbed hold of his shoulder and spun him from me. De Grote dropped my arm to grapple with him. From the darkness, that strange, growling whine came again. It was followed by a bark.

"Unhand me!" De Grote pulled a glittering dagger from his waist and advanced upon the man.

As the man retreated, stumbling over a gravestone, a streak of snarling fur swept past him. It leapt at De Grote, fastening his teeth about the man's throat. De Grote fell, arms flailing as he tried to beat off the dog. The creature tore at him as if he were an avenging angel come straight from God.

I wanted to look away, but I couldn't. I'd never seen such a sight. The creature ripped De Grote's throat out by the roots. And then he deposited it at his master's feet and sat there, wagging his tail, as if he'd done some clever trick.

Big Jannes gagged.

The man bent to pat the dog on the head. "Well done, *mon cher.*"

The dog writhed for a moment as if in delight and then trotted away into the darkness.

The man walked over to De Grote and kicked at him. "There's your body."

I crossed myself. Least, I tried to. The trembling of my hands made hard work of it.

Big Jannes slunk out of the shadows. "What do I do with this?" He brandished the shovel.

"There's no need for it." There never had been. *On the mountain of the Lord it will be provided.* I turned toward the man.

The customer plucked De Grote's dagger from the mud, wiped it on his coat, and then shoved it into his belt.

None of my business. I turned my attentions to the work at hand. "Move that lid away from the coffin, Jannes. So we can throw him in there."

Big Jannes crossed himself. "What? Just like that? Without a word from the priest?"

"He never did anything worth blessing."

"It's a wicked thing. I don't like it."

"And God didn't either. You saw what just happened to him."

He finally did as I'd said, propping the lid against a grave-stone with a mutter.

I gestured toward De Grote. "Here, Jannes. You take up his feet while I take his hands." Before I could do it, the stranger had stepped in front of me and lifted De Grote's hands himself. He and Jannes settled him in the coffin, the way I settled my dough into the oven. A tuck here, a poke there.

"Have you got the…lace?" I didn't mean to be pushy, but I didn't want to spend more time than I had to with this particular body, looking at a bloody hole where his throat ought to have been. It wasn't natural.

The customer withdrew a packet from his doublet. "Where should I…?"

I shrugged. I'd always been charged with the bodies. Hadn't wanted to know about any of the other business. I had usually found my way back into the kitchen by this point. "Just put it in there somewhere. Where it's not so bloody. Someplace it won't be discovered if those border guards decide to have a look."

He bent over the coffin and then paused. Slipped the hand holding the packet inside. When he straightened, the lace was gone.

I motioned for Big Jannes to put the lid back on. But then I remembered something. "Wait!"

Plunging my hands inside the coffin, I patted De Grot's doublet. First one side, then the other. Ah! There it was. I pulled the purse from its hiding place, coins inside it clink-ing. I gave one of them to Big Jannes. It disappeared inside his fist. The rest I left in the pouch, and then I tied it to my apron's strings.

How about that?

De Grote was dead. I'd told the man "No," and I'd done the city of Kortrijk a favor besides. The specter that had haunted us was gone. The wages of sin may have been death, just like the priest always said, but it was also the payment for Katharina's life. I might have given that dog a dish of cream for his trouble…if I weren't half convinced he was a demon come to life.

. CHAPTER 24 .

Denis Boulanger
THE BORDER OF FRANCE AND FLANDERS

TODAY WAS THE DAY. I WAS LEAVING FOR SIGNY. I had risen early, as had been my custom, and I had gone to say good-bye to the lieutenant. And now, as I walked back into the house where I had been billeted, the family turned from the table toward me, brows raised.

I nodded. "Please. Don't let me disturb you."

They turned back to their breakfast meal. All but Cecille.

I grabbed my pack, hefting it to my back.

"Denis?" Cecille's voice had gone high with alarm.

"I've been ordered to Signy-sur-vaux."

She rose from the table. "Signy-sur-vaux? Where is that?"

"To the east. And the south. A good walk from here."

"But…for how long?"

I shrugged. Swallowed.

"But…Papa, do something!"

Her father turned round to look at me. Bit off a hunk of bread. Chewed. Glanced back toward Cecille. "What do you want me to do?"

"Say something!"

He swallowed. Nodded at me. "*Bonne route.*"

"*Merci.*" I stepped past them and went out the door.

"But, Denis—wait!"

I stopped.

She leapt from the door and flew into my arms. "What about us?" Tears had fallen from her eyes onto her cheeks. They looked like tiny drops of dew. The kind birds liked to sip from flowers of a spring morning. "What about me?"

"You're...very pretty, Cecille." She was. Quite pretty. She was lovely, really. She had hair the color of wheat. And she smelled like freshly baked bread. I'd always been partial to that smell.

"What am I supposed to do?"

Do? Well...what was it she normally did? I only ever saw her in the mornings and in the evenings. And she was usually doing what I did. She was eating. And then after, at night, she sometimes sat beside me while I cleaned my musket. "I don't...I don't know what you're supposed to do."

"I thought we had an understanding." Now the tears were gliding down her cheeks like rain off a flower's petals.

"You did?"

"You didn't?"

Another question I didn't know whether I should answer. *Non...non.* Definitely not. It was a question I didn't know how to answer. There was really nothing to understand about Cecille, was there? And if there was nothing to be understood, then...I suppose...maybe we had a misunderstanding? "What was it I was meant to understand?"

"That I...that you...that one day...I thought we would be together!"

Together? When I was walking down the road that would take us apart? "I'm a soldier."

"That's right."

"Soldiers get posted. And reposted. How can we be together when I'm leaving?"

"How can we be together when...?" She began to cry harder.

222

"I don't understand."

"He doesn't understand! All these months, and he doesn't understand!" Now she was wailing. Her family had come to stand in the door.

"I meant…I mean…" I hadn't meant anything at all. And now it had come to this? To Cecille standing in the road, crying? I looked past her, at the door. At her father and her mother, her brother and her sister, staring at me—at us—while they ate the last of their meal. I looked off down the street in the direction I was supposed to be going. And then up the other way. That was when I saw it: a single late-season flower, poking its head out from a puddle of mud. "Look there." I moved past her and bent to pluck it. Turned around and offered it to her.

She just stared at it.

"For you. It's the same color as your hair. Not exactly, of course, it's much brighter. Yours is lighter. A little duller. But it's yellow. Here." I offered it to her once more.

But she didn't take it. Instead, she threw herself up at me, pressing her lips to my own. Before I could even think what to do, she pushed away and went back into the house. But she'd left the flower behind. I held it out, meaning to leave it to her family, but they had already disappeared and shut the door behind them.

What was it she had thought I understood? I stayed there for a while, trying to work it out. When I couldn't, I started off down the road, twirling the flower between my fingers. I wished she would have taken it. She was such a pretty girl. It would have been a shame to have thrown it into the street, so I tucked it into a buttonhole instead.

As I walked, the streets began to awaken. Hands reached out toward me from darkened interiors as they parted shutters. Waterfalls of slops poured toward me as maids cleaned out the night's chamber pots. Dogs eyed me as they sniffed at piles of refuse. I even beat some of the merchants to market. And most of the other travelers out of the city.

I had liked this place.

Liked it more than Signy-sur-vaux.

∽

I wasn't two miles down the road before I overtook a man with a coffin. He was making slow time of it, walking beside an ox-drawn cart. And because I had nothing better to do, because it was only Signy-sur-vaux that awaited me, I slowed my pace to match his.

The dog who'd been trotting beside the man turned and snarled at me.

The man's hand went to his waist as he looked over at me. He had the look of a man who'd traveled much and fallen upon hard times in the doing of it. His glance took in my hat. My coat. My musket. "The dog doesn't like soldiers."

Ah! He spoke French like a Frenchman. Not like those who crossed the border from Flanders. As he spoke, the dog was moving from the road into the wood.

I shrugged. "I don't have anything against dogs."

A growl rolled from the wood at my words.

"My name is Denis Boulanger." I gestured toward my hat. "A soldier in the King's army."

He glanced at my hat. "I am Alexandre. Please excuse the dog. He's had a hard time of it."

We walked in silence for a while. The dog kept pace with us. I could see him peer out at us every now and then, his dark head a stain against the grasses.

"What's wrong with him?"

"Who?"

"The dog."

"Nothing."

"He has no hair."

"Oh. That! He had…mange. You have to shave them. If they have mange."

We kept walking. At this pace, it would take a full five days to reach the village. "Why is that?"

"Why is what?"

"Why do they have to be shaved?"

"Because it's what has to be done. Listen. I'm grateful for the company, but I know I must be holding you back. You must have somewhere to be, a King's soldier like you."

"I do." Eventually. "Who is it?" I lifted my chin toward the coffin.

"It's my…cousin. He's to be buried. In Signy-sur-vaux."

"Signy-sur-vaux? But that's where I'm going! We can go together."

I might have expected pleasure in the man's face, but he sent me a look I couldn't interpret.

We walked on. And on.

The man must have been very sad, because he said nothing at all. I began to think about that coffin. How extraordinary there were two of us who had left Signy-sur-vaux, both returning at the same time. Of course, I was alive, and the dead person was not, but still. Hardly anyone ever left the village. And that got me to wondering. "How did your cousin come to leave?"

Again I saw that odd look reshape the man's features. "Well, he…died."

"*Non*. I mean leave Signy-sur-vaux. Maybe I know him."

"How could you know him? Are you from Kortrijk, as well?"

"Kortrijk? *Non*. Why would I be?"

"He was from Kortrijk…and you said you might know him."

But I had thought he was from Signy-sur-vaux. "He's from Kortrijk? But he's being buried in Signy?" That didn't seem right.

He sent me another look from beneath his brow. "*Oui*. Family plot."

"A family plot? When he was from Kortrijk?"

"I don't know that he was *from* Kortrijk. By birth."

"You don't?"

The man shrugged.

Either the dead man was from Kortrijk or he was from somewhere else. And a relation ought to know that kind of thing. "He was your cousin?"

"*Oui*. I mean...of sorts. Distant."

We walked farther, dodging mud puddles and the sort of oozing, sliding muck the rain had brought. That dog kept pace with us from the wood.

How could a man not know where his cousins were from? Me? I even knew where all of mine were living. "I have twenty-four cousins."

"Pardon me?"

"Twenty-four. Eighteen live in Signy-sur-vaux. That's where I'm from. Three live in Signy l'Abbaye. And three in Dommery."

He said nothing.

"Two of them are fourth cousins."

"Large family."

"*Oui*. But I know who each of them are. And where they are from. Three are Anne. Five are Jeanne. Four are Jean. Six are Pierre. Three are Jacques and two are Michel. One is Louis." All in all, a fine, respectable group of people. Except for me, who had just been removed from my post. And one of the Pierres, who had once stolen some apples from the lord's estate. "What was this one's name?"

"Name?"

"His name. What was he called?"

"It was…Paul."

"Paul…? *Non. Non*, I know no Pauls. I would remember if I knew a Paul. It's not so usual a name. Are you certain he was Paul?"

"Why wouldn't I be?"

"It just seems like an odd name. For someone from Signy-sur-vaux."

We walked along some more.

"So he is a Paul to be buried in Signy."

"*Oui.*"

"With which family?"

"What?"

"I may not have known that Paul, but I ought to know his family."

The man, Alexandre, stared at me for a long moment. "There's a certain sadness I feel about this whole death. Do you mind not speaking of it?"

"Oh. *Non. Non*. I'm a bit sad myself."

It was several miles before the man even said anything at all. And then it was about stopping to relieve himself. I took advantage of the opportunity and joined him in the wood. "I was posted to the customs officer at the border, but now I'm being sent to Signy-sur-vaux."

The man buttoned up his breeches.

"I'm being sent there because I couldn't find any lace."

"Lace?" His head snapped toward mine at the word.

"It's being smuggled into France. By Frenchmen. Not that I ever noticed any." I had to speak over my shoulder to make sure he heard me. He was already walking back toward the coffin. "That was the problem. I never found any." I'd raised my voice so he could hear it.

He'd started up the ox and was down the road a ways before I was able to catch him.

"Why do you think people would do that?"

"Do what?"

"Smuggle lace. The King has strictly forbidden it."

He shrugged.

"I don't understand why they would do it." I took off my hat and scratched at an itch behind my ear.

"People do many things even they themselves don't understand."

"What about you?"

"Me? What about me?"

"What if you were going to smuggle lace? What would make you do it?" I gave my head a final scratch and then put my hat back on. Much better! Cecille's mother would have picked out my nits tonight, along with the rest of the family's. Another bad thing about leaving. Ah well. I'd just have to suffer until I reached my own mother at Signy-sur-vaux.

"Honor."

"What?"

"Honor would make me smuggle lace."

"You would do something dishonorable in the name of honor?" That didn't make much sense. "You know, if you were smuggling lace, I could shoot you. Or have you arrested. That would be very dishonorable indeed. And the magistrate could fine you."

"But what if someone had asked me to do it because his very life depended upon it?"

"Why would his life depend upon it? And how could you respect someone who asked you to do something dishonorable?" That's what the lieutenant had asked me to do: the dishonorable. And what had I done? I'd walked away. To Signy-sur-vaux. The reward for good works didn't always come in this life. That's what the priest in Signy had never tired of saying.

"What if I owed my very life to that person?"

"As if he…saved your life?"

"*Oui.* As if he rescued my life."

"If he rescued your life…" I thought on that for a while. Just how much did someone owe a person who had rescued their life? Very much. Quite a bit, in fact. "So…if you were going to smuggle lace, then it would have to be at the request of someone who rescued your life."

"*Oui.*"

"But if that person rescued your life, if they considered you were valuable enough to save, then why would they treat you so poorly?" There was something in all of this I didn't understand.

"So poorly as…what?"

"They must not value you very much at all if they asked you to do something so bad."

"Bad?"

"They would be asking you to disregard the King's law."

"*Non.* Not really. The man would be asking a favor for me in return for the one he bestowed upon me. That *I* should rescue *him.*"

"By defying the King?" That made no sense at all. "How?"

"How what?"

"How would smuggling lace allow you to do that?"

"What if he needed to do a favor for someone else?"

"A favor." There were too many people involved in this conversation. I had wanted to know what would make *him* want to smuggle lace. Not him and…two other people. There were three of them now.

"*Oui,* a favor. And what if this favor would lead that other person to stop some action that would have ruined the man?"

"Which man?"

"The man who had rescued me."

"A piece of lace? Would keep some man from ruin?"

"It might."

A piece of lace. A piece of lace that was contraband. A piece of lace that was so insubstantial you could see light pour through the spaces between its threads. "And why should you entrust your reputation to some man who's a smuggler?"

"Some man who's a smuggler? Is that not supposed to be me?"

"Is it?"

"That's what you asked me. What would make me do it."

"Ah. *Oui.*" That was so. I had asked him. But I still didn't understand his answer. "So you would smuggle lace for some man's honor."

"I might."

"But what about your own honor?"

"What about it?"

"You would exchange your own honor for the sake of someone else's?"

He frowned. "I suppose...is that what I am saying?"

"Isn't it?" Isn't that what he had been saying? I thought it was. And that's why it made no sense. But then, maybe he didn't really understand it himself. As he said, I was the one who had asked the question. I had asked what might make a person smuggle lace. He didn't smuggle lace, so how would he know? Definitively?

∽

As the sun began to sink, I began to hurry my pace. It wouldn't do to be found along the road, far from a village, as night fell.

The man with the coffin, however, seemed to feel no such urgency.

"Orchies is ahead of us. And it's not such a very great distance. If we hurry, we can reach it before nightfall."

"You hurry. I don't intend on sleeping anywhere but with the coffin."

"*Bien sûr.* With the coffin in the village. Some innkeeper will let you sleep in his stable." Though why would he want to? It wasn't as if anyone would steal a dead body.

"*Non.* No villages for me. I intend to just stop along the road. Or maybe even keep on walking."

"Along the—? But it's dangerous. Treacherous! There are bandits who lurk in the woods."

"And which of them would want to bother a man sleeping beside a coffin?"

Any one of them. But then…he had said he was overcome with sadness. Perhaps grief had stolen his good sense. "Truly, we should speed our pace. I must insist."

Alexandre gestured to the beast pulling the cart. "This old ox won't move any faster."

I eyed the animal. He rolled his own eye back and took a look at me. *Non.* He probably couldn't move more quickly. Not even if he'd wanted to. "Then…" I clutched my musket more tightly as I eyed the trees surrounding us. "I'll stay with you."

"What? *Non!* I mean, why should you be made to suffer for this animal's great age?"

"It would be like having your own private guard. I am, after all, a soldier."

"And a soldier deserves better than a piece of hard ground on which to spend the night. I don't even have a blanket to spare you."

A soldier didn't need a blanket. "It's not necessary."

"But you can go into the village and demand someone house you for the night."

I could. It was a right granted any of the King's soldiers. But I wouldn't. I never had. It didn't seem very polite. "*Non.* My place, as a traveling companion, is by your side."

"There's not room enough in the cart."

And I wouldn't think of sleeping in it. Not beside a body! "I shall sleep beside it."

"In the mud?"

I eyed the countryside around us. The dog's face suddenly appeared once more. "Perhaps I can find some shelter beneath a tree in the wood." Where the outlaws slept. And lived. And practiced their thievery. Perhaps I wouldn't sleep tonight. Perhaps I'd stay awake. That seemed like the wisest thing to do. "I'll stay awake for both of us. I'll stand watch."

He shrugged. "As you wish."

He didn't seem very grateful for my company. And truly, I was sacrificing quite a bit to stay with him. Hot food. A place on a dry floor somewhere beside a warm fire. But then, perhaps, he was stricken by grief. A man overcome by such emotion couldn't be depended upon to look after himself.

We continued on for a while, and when we found a widening in the road, we pulled the ox off to the side. The sky went gray then blue then black. The stars flickered like distant candles, too far away to provide any warmth, too distant to shed any but meager light. The moon, though, was resplendent in all of her glory. A pretty, plump maiden smiling down upon us. A breeze rattled the trees and startled shadows from the wood.

∽

I woke with the cold blade of a knife pressed against my neck. I was astonished I had fallen asleep.

"Your money." The voice that spoke was hoarse and smelt of beer.

"I don't have any."

He turned the blade. I felt a sharp prick from its point.

"Not much of any."

"Not much sounds like quite a bit to me."

"Please. I don't have very much." And what I had, I meant to keep.

"Your money."

"If you would let me rise, then I would get it."

"Just tell me where it is."

"It's…well…it's…" Did I truly want him to go digging around in my pack by himself?

The knife took a bite at my neck.

"It's in my pack. Right side. At the bottom."

The pressure of the knife eased.

I heard the sound of the pack being dragged across the ground. The clink of coins. The knife was withdrawn. I began to breathe more easily and sat up, only to have the knife put to my chest. "Take off your boots."

"My—?" My boots? Truly? "I would, but I can't quite move, can I?"

Moonlight glowed from the face of the knife. The man retreated, just a bit, though he brandished his weapon. In the uneasy silence, I heard the cocking of a gun.

The thief heard it, too. His eyes went wide, rolling first in my direction and then in the direction of the cart. He took one last look at me and then vanished into the wood.

I pushed to my feet, considering whether to pursue him. Better not. He'd taken my money, but I still had my boots. And who knew how many others like him there were out in the cavernous reaches of the wood.

Alexandre had jumped down from the cart. He took my jaw in hand, turning my chin toward the moon.

"You saved my life!"

"At the very least, your boots. Give me a look at your neck there."

"He took all my money."

"That's why you should carry it in several different places."

I hadn't thought of that. He pressed a finger where the knife had gouged me.

"Ow!"

"He nicked you."

"I felt it."

He drew the neckerchief from my collar, wound it round my neck, and tied it off over the wound.

"You saved my life."

"Perhaps I did. But it wasn't to hear you exclaim about it. It was to be able to get some sleep."

Sleep? Now? After I'd almost been killed? When I was shivering like a wet dog?

"Pull yourself together."

"He might have killed me."

"But he didn't."

"He might have."

"I would have killed him first."

Though I was clutching at my own arms to try to keep my wits about me, his words gave me pause. "You would have killed him?"

"*Oui.*"

"How do you know?"

"How do I know what?" He'd already climbed back into the cart, looking as if, indeed, he was planning to go back to sleep.

"How do you know you would have done it?"

"I had my pistol out, didn't I?"

"And I had my musket. And I never, not once, thought of picking it up."

"But then you were surprised out of your sleep." His head disappeared as I heard a rustling in the straw lining the bed of the cart.

"But even if I hadn't been, I don't know if I could have done it."

"You're a soldier. Of course you could have done it."

But how could he know that about me? How could he know that, when I didn't even know it myself? I was shaking my head, though it jerked up and down, side to side with my shivering. "I wouldn't have done it." I'd failed at soldiering, just like I'd failed at baking.

"You would have had to. He might have killed you otherwise."

"But even so…"

A cloak flew over the side of the cart toward me.

I caught it up before it hit the ground. Wrapped it about my trembling shoulders.

"You're a soldier."

A soldier who couldn't kill a man when it came down to it.

CHAPTER 25

The Dog

ALONG THE ROAD TO SIGNY-SUR-VAUX, FRANCE

I DID NOT LIKE THE MAN. THE ONE WHO HAD COME upon us on the road. He was wearing one of those glinting hats. Men who wore those hats were bad. And yet…a person who wore a hat just like it had killed my bad master.

How could a bad man do a good thing?

I took another look at him through the grasses that grew between the edge of the forest and the road.

He glanced over toward me.

I sunk down until my belly touched the ground, and I watched them walk by…he and my new master.

What was he planning to do to me? He didn't have a box. I didn't see a switch.

I crept forward on my haunches, keeping my head well below the tops of the grasses.

Was he a good person or a bad one?

I whined with indecision.

If he was bad, then I must leave; if he was good, then I could stay. My nose told me there was water somewhere near. I sat up to scratch at an ear. Perhaps I did not have to choose. I could let them walk away, and I could go find the water.

That is what I would do.

But though I would not mind losing the one with the

hat, I did not want to lose the other. My master. It was he who had carried me in his arms that terrible night through the woods. And he who had freed me from the burden of my brother's hide.

He did not have any cream.

There had been no warming fire.

No welcoming lap.

But he knew my name. He had called me Moncher.

Moncher.

I whined again and scratched at my other ear.

Perhaps he was walking toward a place where there would be some cream. I took a step forward.

The sun reached down and touched the other man's hat.

I stopped.

What good could come from going anywhere with a man who wore a glinting hat? But what right did I have to leave my master?

Perhaps…if he did not see me, the man in the hat would forget about me.

I turned and trotted toward the forest, keeping well behind the fall of the shadows, where the sun did not dare to challenge the chill in the air. I shivered. I could not see the men any longer, but I could hear them.

The ground was softer to my feet.

I brushed past ferns and padded over fallen branches. I stopped, once, to stare at a squirrel. It scolded me, buried a nut, and then scampered away into the wood. After a while, I crept close to the edge of the shadow to pull at some of the grasses. They came back up a short time after I swallowed them, but at least they had eased the pains in my belly. I trotted ahead of the men and lay at the meeting of sun and shade to warm myself while I waited for them. I sighed from pleasure and rolled over to expose my belly to the heat.

The man with the glinting hat did not sound so terrible when I did not have to look at him. There was no meanness, no malice in his voice.

Not like the bad master's. And not like that man called De Grote.

⌒

I snorted, rolled over, and pushed to my feet. Licked at the place where the bad master's razor had bit me. My master and the man with the hat had passed by, so I raced to catch up with them, and then I went on past. Lay down to wait for them once more.

If only I had not been so afraid.

If I had not paused at the edge of the field that terrible night, then I might have been able to save my good master. I might have been able to warn him about the men wearing glinting hats. I could have leaped at them. I could have knocked them to the ground. If I had not been so afraid, I could have protected him.

I would not let this new master be harmed. I would not fail him.

Some day…one day…I would show those men who wore glinting hats what I thought of them. I would punish them for beating me. For starving me. For taking me away from my good master.

I topped a ridge that overlooked the road.

The man with the hat spied me.

I slunk back into the wood.

Some day I would do those things… but not today.

⌒

I ran ahead and waited and ran ahead again until the sun began to fall asleep. But I started to wait for my master closer and closer to the road. Began to care less and less about what that man with the glinting hat might do to me.

There were things out there in the forest, following us. I could hear them rustling and crackling as they moved. I bit back a whine, for I did not want to betray my own presence. But I sped my pace, and then sat on my haunches as I waited, raising an ear to listen. And I trembled as night fell dark about me.

. CHAPTER 26 .

Lisette Lefort

Château of Eronville
The province of Orléanais, France

AT SOUBOSCQ, I HAD BEEN MISERABLE AMONG THOSE I loved. Here, I had no such comfort. The entire household was waiting for the birth of the child, but that wait had become interminable. The marquise was no longer attentive to anyone's condition but her own. The merriment had left her, and only impatience and irritation had come to replace it. The marquis had taken himself to hiding away in his chambers. Remy stalked me relentlessly, and the count never ceased to watch me.

I had but two hopes: that the expected boy child would miraculously turn himself into a girl and that the Count of Montreau would die. The first hope was new; the second, ever burning, born from that first encounter with the count ten years before.

Eventually the marquise was confined to her chambers by the family physician. Without the protection of her presence, I did not dare to walk in the gardens, day or night. The count pushed me into a servant's hallway one evening as I ascended the stair from dinner.

He reached out and took hold of my hair with a jerk.

"Ow!" I raised my hands to his wrist.

"Your father still has sent no word. You cannot think he intends to rescue you with the lace."

I felt tears pool at the corners of my eyes.

"You're going to have to rescue yourself. Do you understand? I can make your life here pleasant, or I can make it an unendurable hell."

"Please…!"

"Here's what I want you to do…there is one thing yet I must ask of you."

What more could I do for him? "I have done everything you have asked of me." I could do little more than whisper from the pain his hold was causing.

"And to no avail. I can expect only *provisions*. Without that lace, I am left with only one choice. If I cannot influence my father's decision, then I must be assured there is no heir."

"Who can say whether it will be a boy child or a girl?"

"I can say. I *will* say. A girl may live…a boy must die."

Die?

"You can't mean—!"

"My father is not going to let me anywhere near the cursed thing. He may be old and decrepit, but he's smart. You're the one who is going to have to do it."

He…Did he want me to kill a baby? "I can't. I won't!"

He released my hair, though he did not move to let me pass. "'Show me six lines written by the most honest man in the world, and I will find therein reason enough to hang him.' Does that statement in any way resemble the predicament of your father?"

My shoulders dropped with the weight of the threat.

"Do you know who once said that?"

I knew. Everyone knew.

"I believe it was Cardinal Richelieu himself…the King's chief minister. And I doubt very much your father is the most honest man in the world."

I backed away from him in horror. "If you want…I mean, if you intend that I…" I felt as if I were going to retch. "I cannot do such a thing."

He advanced upon me. "Neither can I. I abhor the sight of blood. Always have."

"I can't—"

He gripped me about my arm. "There are a thousand ways to kill someone. If you cannot take a knife to the babe, then smother it. Or leave it out in the garden for the weasels to find."

"I won't."

"Oh, yes, I think you will." He would not let me escape, but lifted my chin with his other hand so I had no choice but to meet his eyes. "Come now. We're both the same, you and I. Nobody really loves us. And why should they? I'm the son of a hard-hearted old bastard and his bitch. You're the contemptible daughter who led to her father's downfall. I would have given my inheritance ten times over to be told, just once, someone liked me for what I was. But fathers will yell, and mothers will, well…in the end, none of it really matters anyway. We're alive still, the both of us, and we ought to get something for our pain."

Something for our pain…and there was so much of it. There was so much pain in living.

"We understand each other, don't we?"

There was too much truth in his words and too much desolation in his eyes for me to look away. His beauty, in spite of all of his malice, was alluring. It was a beauty that made one want to believe him. He was right: we did understand each other. He might have been the only one in the kingdom who comprehended what I had had to endure. The only other person who knew what guilt will do to a soul.

I felt something inside me crumple against the smoldering

rage in his eyes. What did it matter anyway? It was too late. Father was too late. Alexandre was too late. There were no other choices left me. Not if my father's life was to be saved.

His hand slipped from my chin to my throat. As his fingers closed tight about my neck, he kissed me.

Hate gave way to fear, and fear to dread. I despaired that nothing was left for me, that there was no soul but this depraved and depleted man, who could possibly understand me. And so I found myself seeking refuge, begging comfort from him. But there was no warmth to be found in his kisses, no shelter in his embrace. I wanted empathy, I craved absolution, but even those eluded me.

He slammed me into the wall, and I pushed back as his hand contracted about my throat. But his kisses were bleak and desolate. The more I begged for empathy, the more I sought myself in him, the more he retreated, until I found myself as I had always been. Completely and utterly alone. My mortification was complete.

I pushed him away with a cry.

He laughed at me. Then he wiped his mouth with the back of his hand, looking at me with such contempt I felt the last of my dignity fall away. The corner of his lip lifted in a sneer.

I could not keep myself from trembling. Self-loathing seized me. If I'd had a knife, I would have cut off my lips and thrown them into the nearest fire.

"You're just like my mother. I was never good enough for her, either." He turned and walked away.

I pushed past him and continued on my way to the marquise's chambers, taking up a chair beside hers. Though I was quaking, I tried my best to hide it. The man was evil. I closed my eyes, trying to rid my mind of the memory of his touch, of the hiss of his words. But I could not. They rang through my head.

A girl may live; a boy must die.

He wanted me to kill the child!

I didn't know how I could do it. But then I did not know how I could not. In giving myself to the count that day at Souboscq, I had aligned myself with a devil.

The impressions of his fingers about my neck, the feel of his lips against my own threatened to leach through my skin. Even in his absence, he seemed to reach inside me for my soul. I had made mistakes, I had caused those I loved much grief, but he had asked me to do something more terrible, still.

Was he right? That no one loved me?

If no one loved me, then what did it matter? And why should I care?

I closed my eyes against a world gone mad. There, in that deep and awful darkness, Alexandre's eyes stared back at me. His hand reached out across that chasm of time and space to touch me.

Me.

Could it truly be as he had said? Could he want me?

A thousand times I had teased him as a child. A thousand times I had seen his shoulders relax and his lips lift in a smile from my presence. If I closed my eyes tighter, I could hear him shout as the count's carriage trundled me away from Souboscq.

"No!"

He had not wanted me to go.

He had tried to stop me, hadn't he?

He had tried to save me.

What I would give to feel the brush of his fingers against my cheek once more! I would give almost anything, but I would not destroy a child. I would not do it. I could not do it. I had thought I would have to, to save my father. I had thought there remained no other choice but obeying the count's commands. But I did have a choice.

I could refuse.

Though he may betray my father to the King, and though he threatened to turn me over to Remy, still, I would not do it. I would rather have my own head cleaved from my body than harm a child.

. CHAPTER 27 .

The Count of Montreau

Château of Eronville
The province of Orléanais, France

I SLAMMED INTO MY CHAMBERS, STARTLING REMY. HE turned from the window and, spying me, dismissed my manservant. Then he went to the table and poured a glass of cognac brandy. I slumped into a chair, staring into the depths of the fire. Fire and damnation. That's what hell was supposed to be. To my mind, even those would be better than the pain of living.

Remy handed me the glass. Such kind solicitation, such a pleasing and genial companion. He deserved more attention than I could give him, and I increasingly suspected he was finding it somewhere else. He walked around behind me, placing a hand on the back of my neck. It paused for a moment before sliding around front, and down the neck of my shirt.

I stopped him with a hand on his. "I think…I'd prefer…not."

"You'd prefer not…"

In the past year, I'd preferred not more times than I cared to remember.

He took his hand away from my chest, but he ran it through my curls, humming a child's tune as he did it.

~

Tell me yes, tell me no,
Tell me if you love me so,
Tell me yes, tell me no,
Tell me yes or no.
If you love me, there's hope,
If it's a no, there's suffering.
Tell me yes, tell me no,
Tell me if you love me so,
Tell me yes, tell me no,
Tell me yes or no.

⚮

He raked my scalp with his fingers as he finished.

I drew his hand away and held it over my shoulder as I sang a tune of my own.

⚮

Ah! Will I tell you, Mommy
What is tormenting me?
Daddy wants me to reason
Like a grown-up person...

⚮

When my tune petered out, he finished with the remaining words.

⚮

Me, I say that sweets
Are worth more than reason.

∽

Sweets worth more than reason. I wished they were. His hand released mine. "So you would rather not."

What did it matter what I would rather? I couldn't have done anything had I wanted to. I'd only ever been taught to be ashamed of myself. Whatever life I'd once had down there had long been snuffed out. Nothing could provoke it into being. Even that, the essence of myself, disdained to obey me.

"Then you won't mind if I go out for a while?"

Why shouldn't he? I couldn't keep him closeted in my chambers when I had nothing left to offer him. I waved him toward the door.

He bowed and then left, whistling his tune as he went. *Tell me yes, tell me no, tell me if you love me so.* He didn't seem as upset as I would have been.

I threw my glass into the fire after he'd gone. Felt a grim satisfaction as it shattered, and the flames danced blue for a moment.

I stood from the chair and took up my looking glass, regarding the image that stared back at me. Eyes firmly set, just the right distance apart, peering out from a finely molded brow. A nose protruding just so much as to be noble. Lips so ripe and delectable they had once been called red plums. And a chin ever so minutely tipped at its end. A head full of dark, thick, shining curls that fell past my shoulders like a curtain of the finest brocade. A face so finely featured and well-proportioned, there had only ever been one word to describe me: beautiful.

Then why did no one want me?

I cursed as I turned and threw the mirror into the fire.

My reflection laughed at me as flames licked at it. Then it shuddered and melted away to be consumed by the fire.

❦

Remy had left me. Or he was trying to, in any case. I found him in the stables with one of the groomsmen.

"Julien!" He snatched his hand away from the boy's arm.

"It looks as if I've taken you by surprise. My apologies." Was it my fault I could no longer please him? Was it my fault I couldn't do what he wanted? Syphilis had stolen my manhood just as surely as my mother had tried to all those years ago. "I hope you have not betrayed my trust."

"What? No. No! I would never do that. I was just…I mean…it's quite plain that… I would *never* even think—!"

I turned on my heel and stalked toward the door as he hurried to keep pace beside me.

"What did you expect me to do? We've been months in this godforsaken place with nothing to relieve the tedium. It was an innocent flirtation. I was lacking in amusement. You know I would never betray you. Had there been any girl worth the—"

I stopped and pulled out the pistol I kept in my coat. I wondered what it would be like to shoot him. I'd attended a duel once, but the shots had gone wild. Neither had hit the other. I knew what blood looked like, though. My mother's blood, in any case. And that memory made my stomach churn. "Leave. Now."

He put out a hand as if to touch me, but I swung the pistol up and pointed it at him.

"I've been faithful to you. I swear it!"

I toyed with the hammer, wondering if that had ever been true.

"I've put up with you and your schemes and…and your father. *Mon dieu!* And this business about the inheritance. You've become embittered. When we first met, you were…

different." His mouth softened as he seemed to plead with me to remember. "For God's sake—you could have settled this long ago. You could have just taken a wife to keep him from harping! And then it would never have come to this."

"You never really understood, did you? I'm not like you. I can't just take a woman now and then to feel better. I can't feel *anything*. And I can't stand women. I can't even *be* a woman."

"Listen! Marry that girl, the one from Gascogne. It would be so simple. Just think. It would solve all of our problems!"

"Women can never be pleased." Had I loaded this pistol? I couldn't remember. "No matter how hard you try, they whip you and beat you and dress you up in skirts, and bind your manhood, and still they can never be pleased. You can *never please them!*" My hand was shaking. "You can do everything they demand, and still you can never be anything other than what you are." I'd tried so hard to please my mother. Why hadn't she liked me?

"I don't—"

"I always *wanted* to be a girl, didn't you know that? God cursed me with a beauty my sex never deserved." That was the tragedy of it. I had been born beautiful. Why couldn't I have been what my mother wanted? "I was born while my father was at war. Fighting all those damned Spaniards. When he came home…it was seven years before he discovered I was not Julienne. That's what my mother called me, *Julienne*. And do you know what he said when he found out?"

Remy was backing away from me toward the door.

"He said…he said I was a disgrace. A *disgrace*! I didn't…I hadn't known. I was just doing what my mother had told me to. After…after all the…" My words dissolved in my throat as memories overcame them, as I tried to fight back the nausea at all of those things she had made me do. "She tried to take me away with her. She said my father didn't understand, he didn't realize I was meant to be her girl. But I was afraid, so I told my father." I didn't know why my hand was trembling so. I wouldn't be able to shoot anything if I couldn't steady my hand. "He shot her through the heart in the hall as she was trying to pull me toward the door."

There'd been so much blood.

"It was an accident." That's what Father said when the priest came to record her death. An accident: as if what she'd done—what she'd made me—hadn't ever truly mattered.

Revulsion crept over Remy's face. It was a revulsion I always knew I would find there. How could he not revile me? I had disappointed my father, and then I had betrayed my mother into his hands.

I realized quite suddenly I was sighting the pistol at Remy. I couldn't remember how it had gotten into my hand. "It was all for the best. She was mad—she always had been. Father sent me away to court to become part of the King's circle..." It was worse than a disaster. I hadn't understood any of them, living to hunt, lying in wait for servant girls, talking about their *things* as if they were something to boast about. As if that which made me most ashamed made them the most proud. I had not understood at all.

What had I been talking about? Ah. Yes. My mother. "She called out to me as she was dying. Called me Julien. It was as if she finally realized..." Why did I always have to disappoint everyone? "You can never be anything other than what you are." Even the girl had pushed me away.

Remy had slowly removed himself from me and the barn. Now, he was eyeing the château over his shoulder.

All I'd ever wanted was for someone to love me. Why couldn't I make people love me?

"What's happened to you?"

Me? Hadn't we been talking about him? "I trusted you. I thought you were different from the others. I thought you understood."

"I am. I do. I just—"

"Would you leave now, please? I would hate to have to shoot you." Truly, I would. He'd always been so pleasant and so genial. It would be a pity if things got bloody.

He paled at the advice as his eyes rolled wildly.

"I suggest you make haste."

He left, heading toward the château, and not once did he look back.

He did not stay for dinner. And he did not even take his clothes. I clapped the lid of the trunk down on them. All those fine, lovely clothes I had bought for him. Even after all the work I had done to raise him to the level of chevalier, he despised me. I ordered a servant to take the garments into the village and distribute them. If Remy dared to send for them, he would find himself disappointed by the result.

Just the same way I had been.

Had I not been the soul of patience while he was riding about the countryside? Had I not looked the other way when he had to satisfy his needs elsewhere? With women? And had I not always settled his debts…or had them added to my own accounts?

I poured myself a cognac brandy, and I would have drunk it had my hand just once ceased its interminable shaking. I raised it to my mouth anyway, but only succeeded in soiling the front of my shirt. I threw it to the floor to hear it shatter.

The sound of shattering glass. It brought to mind so many memories.

"Non, *Julienne! Mon dieu, who do you think you are? Slowly, gently, lightly. You must walk like a lady, not some wicked, evil, sniveling boy.*"

Emotions of pride and shame often competed within me. If my mother were yelling at me, then at least she actually saw me for who I was. But if she were berating me, that meant she wasn't pleased with that person. Was it my fault the stirrings in my nether regions that marked my sex brought only shame and the impulse to hide myself? Was it my fault I hated the very essence of who I was? I'd trusted Remy, but in the end he only echoed what Mother had always said.

You are not enough.

God damn her if He had not already!

I strode to the bed and ripped away the hangings that had sheltered us from servants' watchful eyes.

What a mess my life had become. Threatening to shoot my lover. Fighting for what was owed me by virtue of my birth.

I should kill the marquis.

It wasn't the first time I'd considered it. His death would solve all my problems in a most satisfactory way. But it was the principle of the thing that always stopped me. Why should I have to plead for what was, by rights, already mine? He *had* been married to my mother. Didn't my very existence prove that? How could he simply erase all those years of shame and torment? How could he just pretend none of it had happened? How could he say neither of us mattered?

I had happened. I ought to matter.

By God, I would make him pay for me! Somebody should pay for all the pain. Somebody…*he*…should have to say they were sorry. Mon dieu, *Julienne! Who do you think you are?*

It didn't matter who I was.

The Fates made you beautiful, but God made you a boy. So

now, we must try to fix God's mistake. It will be our secret, and we must never tell anybody. If you're careful and very good, then no one will ever know, and you will always be my little girl. Maman *needs you to be her little girl. Such exquisite beauty should not be wasted on a wicked and evil man.*

Wicked and evil: a man. That is who I was.

By some curse and accident of birth, I was born a man. But all was well. I needed only to be what everyone expected me to be. If I could just be named the heir of the Marquis of Eronville, then all would finally come right.

CHAPTER 28

Alexandre Lefort

ALONG THE ROAD TO SIGNY-SUR-VAUX, FRANCE

I HAD NOT KILLED DE GROTE, BUT I WOULD HAVE. IF the dog had not done it for me, I would have killed him as if I were ten years old again. What was it that made people torment me?

De Grote had not been the first. That honor belonged to the priest of St. Segon.

I tried not to think of him, but my sin always haunted the darkest recesses of my soul. My earliest memory included him. It was the memory of a mass.

Shortly after rising one morning, my father had made me walk into town along with him. Me in my best clothes; he in his worst, helped along by a crutch. He warned me not to walk close to him, using the end of the crutch to prod me away when I veered too near. I remember, as we left, the village grave digger had crept into the house behind us.

"Papa, what is he—?"

My father had stopped and turned. Put a hand up to his eyes. Saw, as I did, when the grave digger carried out one of our stools. "It's fine. He's fine."

"But—"

"We're expected, *fiston*. At the church."

Indeed, he was right. But though we were expected, we were not allowed to enter. Others had been, though, and they had congregated in front of the massive doors, atop the steps.

The priest raised his hand at our approach. "That's far enough."

My father fixed the end of his crutch in the dust at his feet. Leaned upon it. "But the boy."

"He shall have to live with you, as he has done these past years."

"He shows no signs."

"Not now. Not yet. But he might."

Father glanced over at me. Reached out his arm toward me...but then he let it fall to his side. He looked back up at the priest. Nodded.

"Over there is your grave." The priest pointed with a long, bony finger toward the churchyard.

Father turned toward me. "Stay here. When this is over, we will go back together...we'll go home." He started off in the direction the priest had pointed.

"Him, too."

Father stopped. Looked back at me. "Not him."

"Him, too."

Father looked at me, sorrow in his eyes. And suddenly, for the first time that morning, I was frightened. But when he beckoned me, what could I do but go? So we walked together past the gate—he in front, I some way behind—until we came to a hole that had been dug into the earth. I knew the place well. I had knelt just there whenever I had visited my mother's grave.

The priest and the rest of the people followed us, though they had kept their distance, stopping on the far side of the gate. All but the priest. He was moving toward us, hand extended, holding out some sort of cloth. "Here." He flung it in Father's direction.

Father hobbled over to it, pulled it from the earth,

shook the dust from it, and draped it over his head. Then he straightened and stood facing the priest, crutch wedged under his arm.

"Stand *in* the grave."

"I can't." He shifted his weight and lifted his crutch.

"Beside it, then." The priest turned his attentions to me. "You, too."

I looked at Father. He nodded. "Just stand on the other side."

And so we stood, the two men of the Girard family, facing each other across a shallow grave.

The priest raised his arms and began the Mass of Separation. "I forbid you to ever enter a church, a monastery, a fair, a mill, a market, or an assembly of people. I forbid you to leave your house unless dressed in your recognizable garb, and also shod. I forbid you to wash your hands or to launder anything or to drink at any stream or fountain, unless using your own barrel or dipper. I forbid you to touch anything you buy or barter for, until it becomes your own." He paused to cough. Spat at the ground. "I forbid you to enter any tavern, and if you wish for wine, whether you buy it or it is given to you, have it funneled into your keg. I forbid you to share a house with any woman but your wife. I command you, if accosted by anyone while traveling on a road, to set yourself downwind of them before you answer. I forbid you to enter any narrow passage, lest a passerby bump into you. I forbid you, wherever you go, to touch the rim or the rope of a well without donning your gloves. I forbid you to touch any child or give them anything. I forbid you to drink or eat from any vessel but your own."

The priest then lifted a clod of earth and threw it at Father. He missed. It struck me in the forehead instead. I felt my chin pucker as I began to cry.

The priest threw a clapper in our direction, which my

father went on to use to warn others of his approach. Then he rolled a wooden bowl our way. "Nicolas Lefort, you are dead to man and alive only to God. Go in peace now."

Peace. The only peace I could remember had fled when the priest said those words.

CHAPTER 29

Katharina Martens

LENDELMOLEN, FRANCE

I DIDN'T COME OUT FROM BEHIND THE STATUE. I wouldn't. And no amount of coaxing made me. They tried to have compline in the chapel, but I kept shouting questions.

No one came the next day. The bells still tolled the hours of prayer, but they must have been said elsewhere. As I alternated between standing and sliding myself down the wall into a squat, I was alone in the chapel all day with God. And with the novice. She was there all the time. I could hear her breathing. I could hear the rustle of her robes and her whispers as she knelt in front of altar. But I wasn't worried. I knew no one could reach me, and no one came near.

Not until the next day.

Two sets of footsteps came down the aisle that morning.

"Katharina?"

"Who's there?" The voice had been so faint, I wasn't sure I had heard it at all.

"It's me. Mathild."

"Mathild?" But…I thought. Hadn't they thrown her out?

"*Ja*. It's me. They said…they said if I came back, they'd let me stay."

"Here? After they threw you out? They *did* throw you out, didn't they?"

"*Ja.*"

I knew it! But…"If they threw you out, then why would you want to come back?"

I heard her quiet sobs. "You don't know. You don't know what it's like out there. The things they make you do…"

Vile things. That's what Heilwich had said. I pressed myself closer to the chapel wall. "Why are you here?"

"They want me to tell you… you have to come out. You have to stop saying those things."

"Why? They're true. And weren't you made to do… vile things?"

"*Ja.*"

I could scarcely hear her. "Then why can't I say what's true?"

"There's no point. It won't change anything. It will only make it worse."

Worse? For whom? There was a whispered exchange as I stayed hidden.

"Please. Come out. Please, Katharina! For my sake. If you don't come out, they won't let me stay. I don't want to leave. Don't make me leave!" That last was directed at someone other than me. Mathild had already turned away from the Holy Mother, away from me. She was protesting. As her voice diminished, as I heard footsteps retreating, I caught a whiff of scent. And then I knew who had been her escort.

"I'm not coming out!"

Sometime that night, someone must have come into the chapel. When I woke, I smelled the scent of bread. My hand soon found its origin. Beside me, on the ledge, someone had placed a loaf.

I ate it all, brushing my hands against my skirts once I was done, to free them of crumbs. I flexed my knees. Slid down along the wall until I was almost sitting. It was sheltered there within the confines of my prison. And warm. No wind found its way into the chapel, and nothing disturbed the peace. It was not a bad place to be...much better than the workshop had been.

All I had to do was last three more days, until Tuesday. Then Heilwich would come to get me.

CHAPTER 30

Heilwich Martens

LENDELMOLEN, FRANCE

THE VERY NEXT DAY I WENT TO FETCH KATHARINA home. A Friday it was, and a good four days before I was due to visit Katharina again. I was three days early. I began my trip as the sun woke, just after they opened the city's gates. It was a good day. A sunny day with some warmth in the wind and the promise of mild weather. But still I had to wade through the muck left by the rains. And I stood aside in mounds of it whenever a cart or a horse came along.

But I had the money now. All of it.

There was no delay in seeing the Reverend Mother; not like the last time. They let me right into the abbey and led me straight to her quarters. Didn't even knock on her door before they let me in.

I walked toward her desk, purse heavy in my hand.

She lifted her head. Such an odd expression she had as she looked at me. When she finally spoke, it was just one word. "You!" She did not even wait for me to approach her. She met me halfway, took me by the hand, and led me back the way I'd come. She was walking so fast, we were nearly running.

"I'm here for my sister, Katharina."

"I know it." She pulled me out into the courtyard and then through it toward the chapel.

I paused to dip a hand in the holy water, but she tugged me forward so quickly, all reverence fled. My hand plunged to the bottom of the font, searching for balance before I was pulled along after her, splashing water out onto the floor. "Forgive me for saying, but—"

"Just take her!" We'd come to a stop right in front of the Holy Mother herself.

"Take…who?" They wanted me to take the statue? How on earth—?

"Heilwich?" The voice seemed to rise from the Holy Mother's lips.

I crossed myself in horrified fascination and bent to throw myself at the Holy Mother's feet before I recognized that voice. It couldn't be…could it? "Katharina?"

"Heilwich! Is it really you?"

"It's really me. But…where are you?"

"I thought you were going to come on Tuesday." I saw my dear sister's face peek out around the edge of the Holy Mother's skirts.

"What are you doing up there? Get down this instant! Of course I was coming on Tuesday. I'm just a little…early."

"Ask her if she'll let me go."

"Why wouldn't she let you go? I've the money she asked for right here. All of it."

"Ask her, Heilwich!"

There was no point in trying to talk sense into my sister. Ideas always seemed to get stuck in that funny head of hers. I turned toward the Reverend Mother and tried to take up her hand to kiss it, but she pulled it from me. "Take her and go."

"Hear that, Katharina? She says we can go."

The Reverend Mother leaned toward me, her veil flutter-ing about her face. "And don't ever speak of this to anyone!"

I don't know why she had to be so mean about it. I'd brought the money she wanted, hadn't I?

I marched forward, reaching up to take Katharina's hand. As she slid from the pedestal, her skirts rode up behind her. It's as if she'd never stopped being a girl! I pulled them down behind her. "Let's go home."

I made it out the gate and into the street before I realized I hadn't paid the Reverend Mother…but then, she'd never asked for the money, had she? And she'd told me not to speak of it to anyone. Anyone included her, didn't it?

What was the right thing to do?

I turned from the abbey toward my sister. "You've a peaked look about you. When was the last time you ate?"

"Just this morning. Someone left a whole loaf of bread. Just for me!"

Just for her. As if she hadn't ever merited one before. That decided it. If they hadn't been in the habit of feeding my sister a decent meal, then I didn't feel especially obligated to give them any of my money.

"Heilwich, I was wondering, can we go…?"

"Where? Home? That's where we're off to." And Father Jacqmotte would just have to manage it. Manage us. In truth, he probably wouldn't even notice her.

"*Nee*, Heilwich. There's a man out here somewhere. He sells fish. Can I…could we…get some?"

We got some herring and an eel, as well. Even though we were very nearly run down in the doing of it by Pieter, that urchin I'd paid to tell me if Katharina had been let go by the abbey. Poor boy—I'd have run, too, if I had a mother like his chasing me about!

Katharina was as good as blind. And she was hunched as an old woman. Beside me, gripping my hand in hers, she chattered on. Was there no word the child did not know? One word she could keep herself from speaking? There seemed no end to the things she said.

"Am I talking too much?"

"What?"

"Am I talking too much? We were never allowed to speak. Not in the abbey. But I don't want to bother you."

"What strange thoughts you have. *Nee*. You do not bother me."

She talked nearly the length of the journey home. And then she paused. "I hope…" She squeezed my hand.

"*Ja?*"

"I hope that… it wasn't too much trouble, Heilwich…to take me from the abbey."

Trouble? "Do not worry yourself, child. It was no bother at all."

CHAPTER 31

Denis Boulanger

ALONG THE ROAD TO SIGNY-SUR-VAUX, FRANCE

ORNING DAWNED SLOWLY, AS IF IT WERE TOO early for the sun to want to rise from his bed. But we were already on the move by then. I hadn't been able to sleep, and Alexandre said my pacing had kept him awake. We'd gone quite some distance, when he stopped so suddenly the ox plowed right into his shoulder. "Do you hear that?"

I heard nothing but the drum of my heartbeat in my ears and the labored breath of the beast pulling the cart.

"There's a stream nearby."

It would not have surprised me. The Ardennes may have been forsaken by both God and man, but it was blessed with any number of streams.

The man cocked his head first one way and then another. "It's over there." He pointed off into the wood toward his dog. "I'm going to find it. It will just take a moment."

For a man who would not be parted from his coffin for even a few hours' sleep, it was odd he would leave it on the road, by itself, for even a few minutes. I hesitated. Should I stay, or should I follow him?

I decided to follow him. I did not want to be left alone any more than that mangy dog did. By the time I'd found the stream, Alexandre had already stripped and was standing out in the middle of it. Like a bird he was, all quick movements and angles, splashing about, managing to wet his entire body before scrubbing at it with a brush.

"Why are you doing that?"

"Doing what?"

"Bathing."

"You should try it."

I glanced down at my hands. Dirt rimmed my fingernails, and grease lined the turn of my cuff, but what did it matter? "I'm clean enough."

"Can you hand me that?"

His cloak? It was flecked with straw and was coated by the dirt of our journey. "You'd stay cleaner if you dressed without drying."

"Habits have a long life. And besides, it's not the dirt that concerns me."

Not the dirt? But...? I didn't understand. Not one thing. But this man had saved my life. The least I could do was hand him his cloak.

∽

The next day, after we had passed Jolimetz, the road narrowed as it went down over a pass. The ox stopped at the top of the hill and refused to move. Alexandre talked to it. Pulled at the harness. Slapped him on the shanks.

It lifted its tail and defecated. Stamped its foot.

It wouldn't move, and I didn't blame him. The road was steep, and it leaned into a corner a little way after it started down off the hill.

Up there on top, I could see down into the valley. There was a suggestion, here and there, of a hamlet: some clearings in the trees. The knob of the hill we were standing on had gone bald. I walked to the edge and peered over. Rocks had tumbled from here down into the valley.

I heard Alexandre talking to his ox.

Time to start moving. I had no wish to spend another night on the road. I loaded my gun and then lifted it to my shoulder and took aim at the cloud-cobbled sky.

At the report of my musket, the dog barked and the ox jumped as if I'd shot off his tail. The wheels shifted, and the cart clipped the beast in the rear. That ox might have been a hundred years old, but it clicked its heels together and began to race down the road. With the front of the cart pressing into his hindquarters and the creature's heels rapping it with every step he took, it was no wonder the cart slipped a wheel.

Once the wheel had come off, it was soon enough that the harness slid from the ox's back and the cart continued down the hill on its own for a few moments. But then a freed shaft became impaled in the dirt, and the cart spun itself sideways.

The coffin, jarred by the motion, slid out and took to the air like a bird. Its flight came to an abrupt halt as one end hit against a stone. But even then, it catapulted end over end into the air before finally coming down, somewhere unseen, with a crash.

And a splinter.

"*Merde.*" Alexandre had gone pale, his hands clasped over his head.

I would have chosen a more descriptive, more particular word. The cart had come apart, the coffin had gone over the hill, and who knew how we were going to get that body to Signy-sur-vaux now?

The ox was standing down the hill near the turn, looking up at us, the lazy creature. I left Alexandre where he was and ran across the rocks toward the coffin, my boots sliding over the gravel.

As I was slipping down the hillside, he finally started after me, and in the end, it was he who reached the coffin first.

But once he reached it, he stopped. When I got there, I could see why he wasn't moving. The lid had levered off, and the body had come out. The stench was horrendous. Birds had settled on the corpse, and they were already pecking at his throat. One of them had begun to pluck a packet away from the man's coat.

"*Vas-y! Allez—ouste!*" I ran at them, waving my hands.

They rose with an indolent flapping of their wings, dropping the packet as they went.

I bent and took it up. It seemed to be sprouting string. I held it out so Alexandre could see it.

"Put it down."

I was going to, but whatever was inside slid out. I dropped the packet and reached to catch the contents with my other hand. It was…a length of…lace. And it was exquisite. I flattened my hands as completely as I could, holding out that offering toward him, unwilling that I should contaminate it. "It's…lace."

He said nothing, though he took it from me, picked up the packet, and tucked it back inside.

"What would a dead man want with lace?"

He just stood there, looking not at his cousin, but at me. Then he threw the packet back into the coffin. Gestured for me to take the body's legs while he reached for its arms. Once we'd returned the body to the coffin, he bent to pick up one of the boards for the top.

I picked up the other.

Lace.

What was it about lace? What made it so important that

272

people would smuggle it? For that matter, what made it so important the King himself would forbid its import? It seemed a lot of trouble for such a flimsy thing. But more than that, what did its presence mean? That had been quite a bit of lace. Quite a bit more than any dead man would need.

I beat the nails back into place with the butt of my musket and then, each of us taking an end, we carried the coffin back up the hill. We left it on the road while Alexandre went to the fetch the ox and I retrieved the pieces of the cart.

Some of the boards on the floor had broken off, but if the coffin were placed at an angle, and if the ox didn't make any more sudden movements, I thought it might just reach Signy without any more trouble.

Alexandre arranged the floorboards and then harnessed the ox to the cart.

There was just one thing I wanted to know. "Why did you do it?"

He slapped the ox on the shoulder to get him moving. Looked over at me. There was no surprise in his eyes, though I had expected there would be. "Do what?"

"Why did you smuggle the lace?"

"I already told you. For honor's sake."

"But—it's dishonorable. And now I'll have to have you arrested when we reach the next village." At least I'd be able to prove to the lieutenant and everyone else I was worthy of my uniform now.

The ox was pulling the cart down the road without us. Alexandre jogged a few steps to catch up. "You don't have to."

Don't have to? "It's my job." Or it was, in any case.

"But who will know any different? Whether you do or whether you don't?"

I ran to catch up with the both of them. "*I* will!"

"But what does it matter? Truly?"

"What does it matter?"

"Whom does it hurt?"

"Whom does it hurt?!" Whom did it hurt? It hurt the King. It hurt the border officers. And most of all, it hurt me. I had thought he was my friend. I swung my musket from my shoulder, grabbed a cartridge from my bag, and tore off the top of it.

"Put the gun down."

"*Non!*" I poured some of the powder into the priming pan and then poured the rest of it down the barrel.

Alexandre was still walking down the road with the ox and the cart.

I dropped a ball and the cartridge paper into the barrel. Tried to pull out the ramrod. It stuck.

"You don't need to—"

"Stay back!"

I freed the ramrod, tamped the ball, and leveled the musket. Drawing the cock back, as I pressed my cheek against the stock, I knew in that instant I would shoot. If I had to shoot him, I would do it. The shock of that realization nearly made me drop the gun. "Stop. Right now!"

The dog beside him snarled.

He put a hand to the ox and moved so the cart was between us. "Whom will it hurt if you let me go?"

"Whom will it hurt?" What did he mean? What did he mean whom would it hurt? Why did it matter whom it would hurt? I tightened my grip on the gun.

"What will happen if you don't arrest me?"

"I—what do you mean?" His form had begun to waver above the barrel of my musket.

"If you don't arrest me, what happens is I will go on my way, and you will go on yours, and no one will ever be the wiser."

"Except for you and me."

"You will know, and I will know. But does that really harm anyone?"

"It harms the King. You shouldn't have done it."

"*Non.* I should not have. But will the King care if it doesn't get confiscated? Will he even know? What do you think happens to lace like this? You must know that even if you turned it in, it would never reach His Majesty."

"I...I don't—" Suddenly the memory of a frill of lace at the lieutenant's cuffs filled my head, and a remembered conversation echoed in my memory. *Do you know how old this lace is? Six months old. And do you know why? It's because you haven't brought me any that's newer!* Alexandre was right: It would never reach the King.

"The King doesn't care. But the one who rescued me will. If you arrest me, it will mean his complete and utter destruction. And his daughter's, as well."

His daughter: a girl. Girls were such a mystery. A complete and utter riddle with no sense whatsoever. Thinking of girls made me think of Cecille and the way she hadn't taken that flower from me. Why hadn't she taken it? "A girl shouldn't be ruined."

"*Non.*"

"So if I let you go, you can rescue her. But...then who will save me?"

He blinked. "You?"

"Who will save me from my dishonor? In letting you go?"

"I already did. I saved your life. You said so yourself."

"I'm not talking about my life." I was talking about...I was talking about my soul. Who would save my soul? If I didn't arrest him, then what kind of person would I be? "Who will save me?" I didn't know what to do. I didn't know what to do!

275

Alexandre approached, hands raised. "Put the gun down. You have no need of saving. You will have done a favor for a pitiful and quite undeserving man. It would be to your credit, not your dishonor, if you failed to arrest me."

To my credit? I couldn't quite keep up with his reasoning. "I'll shoot you if I have to."

"I know you will."

"You—but how do you know?"

"You're a soldier, aren't you?"

Was I? Truly?

Now I understood everything. The lieutenant had thought I had no imagination, but he was wrong. Now I could imagine anyone could be a smuggler, just as anyone could be a soldier. A person didn't have to be wicked to disregard the law, and a person didn't have to wear a uniform to shoot someone. If I had this man arrested and confiscated his lace, then I imagined I would become just like the lieutenant. The lieutenant who had kicked a crutch away from a cripple and left an old woman sprawled in the mud. If I returned with this man to the border, I could imagine exactly what would happen. The lace would end up adorning the lieutenant's own wrists. And how would that be right? That the cruel should be rewarded and the poor mocked?

Coffins and uniforms.

Guns and lace.

What did it all mean?

I felt as if all knowledge had passed away. As if everything I had once known had been proved to be false. But if that were the case, then what was true?

Anyone might do anything all. Perhaps...perhaps this whole journey was a sign. Perhaps I had never been meant to leave Signy-sur-vaux. Much as I had wanted to leave, destiny had conspired to bring me back. I may not have been as good a baker as my father, but fate had proved I was much less of a soldier.

"Are you...going to put down your gun?"

"Oh. *Oui.*" It had grown so heavy. Too heavy to carry. I might have left it right there on the ground if it had been my own. But it was not mine; it belonged to the King. I tucked it under my arm with sweat-slicked hands.

"Are you well?"

Was I what? "Pardon?"

"Are you well?"

Well? What did it matter if I was well? I could shoot someone. I knew now I could. But I had just discovered I didn't want to. If I wasn't meant to be a soldier, then what was I meant to be?

Alexandre patted my forearm, pulled the ox into a walk, and together we started around the corner. Here, the road leveled out and widened. "Perhaps you can tell me when we get to Signy-sur-vaux, where Father Lemaire lives."

I glanced behind me at the coffin. "We are not so very big a village. We have only one church. But...does that man even belong in Signy?"

"No."

That thought bothered me less than I might have expected. "Do you know who he is?"

"He's an evil man who happened to die at just the right moment. It's probably the only decent thing he ever did."

A dead man needed a cemetery. "When we get there, I will show you the church." And then I would forget I had ever met Alexandre or seen his coffin. As we walked along, I pondered my newfound knowledge.

I had turned into a soldier; I could shoot someone. But I had also committed treason. I had let a man go free when I had every right to arrest him.

I had done the right thing: I had done the wrong thing. But the right thing seemed so wrong, and the wrong thing had felt so right. There was no wide chasm between yes and no, between right and wrong. There was just a wide, vast plain, and I did not know how I could live there, in the middle of it, without the absolute certainty offered by either side. It was so much easier when I had thought right and wrong were two separate countries. That there was some warning, some point when one crossed from one to the other.

But if the right thing meant obeying the lieutenant, and the wrong thing meant letting a good man go free, then I had done the right wrong thing. Given a choice between being a not-so-good soldier and a not-so-good baker, I would rather live with flour between my fingers than a gun between my hands. Then I could decide for myself: rye or barley. White or brown. An honest choice for honest pay. It would make life so much less confusing.

CHAPTER 32

The Dog

ALONG THE ROAD TO THE CHÂTEAU OF ERONVILLE

WE LEFT THE MAN WITH THE GLINTING HAT, ALONG with the ox and the cart and the box, with De Grote's terrible unlife smell. But then my master got a horse.

I didn't like him.

He went along much too quickly and paid no mind at all to where I was when he pissed. But the horse did make people move off the road. And if that let us pass them more easily, then I could not much complain.

Though I did bark at them a time or two.

At least the sun glared at us no longer. It had let us go, warming our backs and our behinds, though my master kept me plenty warm as I trotted to keep up with him and his horse.

One morning, before the sun had risen far, we overtook a group of men wearing glinting hats. Though a marsh bordered the road, I whimpered and slunk back toward the mire.

I could not help it. I wasn't brave.

I watched from the safety of the grasses while the men formed a line across the road.

One among them pointed a gun at my master.

I flattened my ears to my head.

"A traveler, lads!" the man with the gun spoke. "He's the look of a foreigner about him."

One of the other men stepped forward and grabbed hold of the horse.

The man with the gun prodded my master in the leg. "Got anything to drink?"

"I have a little."

"Care to share it?"

My master took a flask from his bag and handed it to the other man, who pulled the cork, took a sniff, and then a swallow.

The man with the gun was still pointing it at my master "You've got the beard of a Dutchman—"

"I'm not Dutch. I'm as French as you are."

"Oh—hoity-toity, too! Just listen to him speak." He brandished the gun. "Don't waste the accent on us."

I growled.

"I wonder if there's some gentleman up the road happened to wake up this morning and find his horse gone?"

I crept from the marsh on my belly.

"Why don't you come down off that horse? Have a little drink. And maybe a smoke."

My master got down from the horse.

The men with glinting hats gathered in a circle about him. "Best meal we've had all week, here in this flask. Do you know why? The damned peasants have eaten everything else. Every loaf of bread, every wheel of cheese. Every pig and chicken in the whole countryside. It'd be nice to catch some of them at it. You don't know where they'd happen to be, do you?"

"I'm just a traveler riding alone."

The man with the gun bared his teeth. Gave a lift of his chin to one of the men who was standing behind my master. "I'm afraid now you're just a traveler."

One of the men pulled at the horse's reins. Another man tossed the flask back toward my master.

My master did not catch it. It fell to the ground between them.

The man holding the gun picked it up, feeling the heft of it with his hand. "Silver, is it?"

My master said nothing.

"Did you steal this, too?"

"It was given to me by the viscount of Souboscq."

"At the suggestion of a knife, no doubt!"

All the men bared their teeth and laughed.

I growled.

"I suppose I couldn't leave a man without the means to collect a drink now and then."

"I would be most grateful."

As the man handed the flask back, my master pulled a knife from his belt, grasped the man's wrist, and pulled him close, pressing the tip of that knife against his throat. "I would be most grateful for both the flask *and* the horse."

"We weren't serious about taking the horse. Just having a tease is all."

"Then you won't mind dropping your pistol."

The man dropped his gun.

"And the rest of you won't mind putting your muskets and pistols in a pile beside me and then stepping off the road."

The man my master held shouted to the others.

"And you certainly won't mind donating to the expenses of my travel."

Several of the men put their hands into their coats and brought out coins, which they tossed in my master's direction.

"And I'd like you to remove your clothes, as well."

They stood there, blinking.

"Now!" My master pressed the knife into the man's neck. He cried out.

Each man took off his clothes and gave them to my master. They weren't so frightening as they cowered in front of my master without their glinting hats and shimmering clothes.

I took one step onto the road. Then another.

They looked just like regular men now. I took a third step forward. If they threatened my master, then I would kill them just like I had killed De Grote.

My master tossed their clothes toward me. I cringed and crouched, my belly to the ground. Carefully, I stretched out my neck to sniff at them.

They had bad smells. They reeked with that same sour stink of my bad master.

I blew the stench from my nostrils with a snort. I looked at the men. Growled. Stretched my neck out farther as I took one step closer to their clothes. I sniffed at them again and then growled. Reached out and snapped at one of the coats.

It did nothing.

I took it between my teeth and shook it.

The men without their clothes were not so terrible, and the clothes without the men were nothing at all. I went through all the clothes, ripping and tearing at them until they would grant no man power over me again.

When I was done, my master shoved the man he was holding toward the others. When one of them lunged forward, toward my master, I leaped at him, growling and snapping.

He retreated.

My master collected their coins and threw their guns into the marsh. Then he mounted the horse and started off down the road.

They yelled after us. One even started running at us. "*Bâtard!* It's nearly the middle of November! What are we going to do for warmth?"

"I'd suggest walking. Briskly."

We trotted along the road, the horse and I, where we could and walked where the mud was too deep. By the time the sun was high, we had reached a city.

My master went into a building. I went with him, staying close upon his heels. As he ate, I found a bone to gnaw upon. I took its knobbly end between my teeth and worked at breaking it open. There was a fire in that place. I couldn't feel its warmth, but I could see its light between the peoples' legs. If only I had some cream. I might have whined for some, but I had just managed to crack the bone. Now I could get at its insides.

I would look for cream later.

Sooner than I wanted, the master rose and walked toward the door.

I took the bone with me, leaving it on the street once he had mounted the horse. As we started off, a shout went up behind us.

I turned to see two men wearing glinting hats, heads bobbing above the crowd. As the people cleared around them, I could see they were sitting a horse. "That one! Right there!" It was one of the men we had left behind. He was pointing in our direction.

My master and the horse sped away down the road. I had to run quickly. It was hard to keep up with them, even though all the people on the street fled at their approach.

He turned first one corner, then another and another. Finally, he forced the horse to a halt, leaped off its back, and slapped him on the haunch. The horse flinched, and then he sprung past me with a snort. As people shouted, my master slipped through the crowds and turned, quickly, onto a different street.

I followed at a trot.

My master peered into each window he passed and sent glances down all of the alleyways. I barked once, hoping he would slow his pace, but he did not. At the end of the street, where different colors of clothes had been laid out across the bushes and a fire had been built beneath a large kettle, he paused. A woman was stirring the kettle. As she squatted to tend the fire, he reached out and snatched a cloak from a bush, drawing it over his shoulders and pulling the hood down over his head.

As he turned the corner, something happened. He went lame, favoring one of his legs over the other. And as he walked, his stature shrank.

I barked, tugging at the cloak. Barked again.

"Hush, *chiot!*"

I whined.

"I'm fine. I just don't want to be recognized."

I slunk along beside him as he entered a busy square. But the men were already there. They were stopping everyone entering or leaving.

We stepped into a shadow cast by a tall building, slipping by one of the men as he stopped to talk to someone. "Very tall, he was. With a dog beside him."

My master waved his hands at me, gesturing toward the opposite side of the square.

I looked toward where he was pointing. It was far, far away from him.

I sat on my haunches.

He gestured once more.

I lay down at his feet.

After casting a look up at the man, he walked back the way we had come, toward a quieter area of the market. Then he paused and bent toward me, clicking his tongue. "Come here, *chiot.*"

I lowered myself toward the ground and wagged my tail at him.

"Come here!"

Why did he sound so cross? I whined before I could stop myself. I could hear those men behind us. They were pushing through the crowd. They were getting closer.

"Come here, *mon cher!*"

Moncher! With a yelp, I threw myself at my master's arms.

He clasped me to his chest. Keeping the hood draped over our heads, he nestled me with one arm against his side. He used the other to settle the cloak about me, blocking my view of the square.

I didn't need to see. What I needed was a nap. And some cream.

My master started off with his strange, new gait.

There were people all about us. I could hear them, though I could not see them. Suddenly, my master stumbled, bumping into something.

"Pardon me. Sorry." His arm reached out, and I could see, for just an instant, as a woman bent toward the ground.

Quick as she bent, my master took hold of a pail and a ladle. As he lurched away, I dug into his side with my legs, trying to keep myself from tumbling from his arm.

"Patience, *chiot*. You saved my life once. I'm trying to return the favor. I'm going to turn myself into a leper. The only thing anyone would do with a leper's dog is kill it. With a little luck—"

That pail—it carried cream! I could smell it. I scrabbled against the constraint of his arm, trying to reach it.

"*Merde!* If they see you, we're both finished! Here." He shifted the pail to the hand that held me.

It *was* cream!

"Gently! You're going to spill it."

Some spilled over the edge before I could eat it. And then my master began to beat on the pail with the ladle.

"Sorry, *mon cher*. I need this for other things." He tipped the pail, dumping the cream to the ground. I would have

285

barked, but some had clung to the sides. If he would just stop beating the pail, then I could lick it.

"Stay away." Clang. "Stay away."

I timed my licks to his words.

Around me, people gasped. I could hear them. "Leper! A leper!" There came the sound of people running from us. The master paused in his beating, and I got in an extra lick.

"Stay away." Clang.

He almost clipped me on the nose.

"Stay away." Clang. "Stay away."

"Halt there!"

At last, my master stopped beating on the pail. I nosed my head into it and licked up what I could.

My master had turned toward the voice. "Stay away! I warn you."

"Take off that hood."

"I beg you—please—spare yourself the horror."

"If you're a leper, then show yourself."

My master bent toward the man, giving me full access to the pail. I tipped it toward me with a paw.

"Stop!" His grip on me tightened. "I'm a leper. Don't come any nearer. Just…"

My master dropped the ladle, took up my leg, and threaded my foot through his sleeve. He grasped my paw with his other hand and exposed it to the sun when it emerged. I did not wince much, though I was nearly hairless. I had almost licked the sores from the razor closed, but still they wept foul-tasting ooze.

"*Mon dieu!*" Someone else, some other man, gagged.

I paused in my licking when I heard it.

My master pressed me tighter against his side.

I went back to licking up the cream.

"Stay away!"

"Did any man pass by here just now?"

"I saw no one."

"If you do see anyone…any man. Quite tall…with a dog…"

"I shall tell him to stay away." My master banged at the pail with his knee.

I could hear the scrape of boots again as the men turned from us.

Once they left, their voices were replaced by others. "Get out, leper. Go away!" Though my master hurried from those voices, they followed us. "If they don't stop throwing stones at us, *chiot*, I'm going to start throwing them right back. And I have deadly aim."

Eventually, those footsteps and voices fell away. And soon after, they ceased all together. My stomach was full; the fat of the cream coated my throat. My master straightened and resumed his usual gait. To the rhythm of his stride, I fell asleep. I dreamt of cream and fires. And a hand stroking my fur. Moncher, Moncher, Moncher.

. CHAPTER 33 .

Lisette Lefort

CHÂTEAU OF ERONVILLE
THE PROVINCE OF ORLÉANAIS, FRANCE

UNFORTUNATELY, MY RESOLVE NOT TO HARM THE child did not solve my problem. The count had gone mad with desperation. His demand had proved that. If I did not kill the babe, then I would have to find some way to protect him. If, indeed, it were a he.

Pray God for a girl!

I would have gone to the chapel that next day and repeated Hail Marys for eternity, but just before dinner, the marquise cried out, placing a hand on her belly. "I think… I'm almost certain…I think it's time!" She looked at me with both dread and delight. And with her other hand, she grabbed for my arm.

I prayed the birthing would take just as long as it could to give my father time to return with the lace. But the hours seem to slow in their passing as she labored in her travail. The midwife rubbed unguent onto her belly and whispered soothing words. As a cock greeted dawn, still we waited. At some point, a servant brought us dinner and then came to take the remains away. As the birds in the garden left off singing and a wolf howled at the moon, I began to amend my desires.

"Does it usually take this long?" I whispered the question to the midwife as she changed out the bedclothes.

"Sometimes it takes longer."

Longer!

"Longer it takes, the worse it is for the child."

I had not considered the child might not live. Though perhaps in this case, it would be a blessing.

"Worse for the mother, as well."

I glanced toward the marquise. She had passed much of the time since dinner in a state of misery, moaning and tossing about on the bed. Her face looked pale, even in the dim-lit chamber. If the child died, might that not mean the death of its mother, as well? I could not pray that on anyone…save the count. He deserved the worst of all of hell's torments.

When the marquise next cried out, I went to the bedside and smoothed the hair from her brow.

"I'm so afraid."

I could have assured her I was more so. "There's nothing to fear. All will come right."

"What if it's a girl?"

May heaven be so kind! "If it's a girl, then she will be the most beautiful babe in the kingdom."

"What if…What if I…if I—?"

"Hush." I held a cup to her lips. "There's too much work yet to be done, and there's a babe still to be born."

The midwife sent servants to open all the château's drawers and doors and cupboards, to release the babe from the marquise's womb. I saw the marquis out in the corridor. The count must have hid himself away somewhere in the depths of the château, for I did not hear or see him.

As the cock announced the sun's coming that second day, the marquise's moans were uttered with new urgency.

The midwife unfastened the shutters and pulled them open. "Sometimes the sun draws the babes out." I went quickly to the other window and did the same.

"I think—I think he's coming!" The marquise's voice was a shrill and desperate shriek.

I went to her and offered up my hand once more.

Though she pushed and though I prayed, the only thing that seemed to come was blood. I swabbed at her forehead with a linen. She was gripping my other hand so tightly my fingers had gone numb.

So much blood.

The marquise cried out, more sharply this time. The midwife helped her to sitting and then took a hand and pulled her toward a stool. There she collapsed, panting, in the midwife's arms. "It's coming." She spoke the words with confidence, as a command, but a hitch in her brow proved no remedy for my anxiety.

The midwife tried to extract herself from the marquise without success. "My lady!" She gestured me toward the foot of the stool with a sweep of her chin.

Did I dare to? What if I could not catch him?

There was no time for hesitation. The marquise gave a wrenching cry as I knelt before her, and the babe dropped into my hands. It was slick as a newborn calf and warm as a chick. Holding it to my side, I hastily bundled it into a cloth.

The marquise slumped, threatening to fall to the floor.

"No, my lady. You'll do better back in bed." The midwife somehow pulled and pushed the marquise back onto her mattress. And then she turned to me, a single question in her eyes.

Just how much had she seen while she'd been struggling with the marquise? "It's a...It's a girl."

The marquise rallied, opening her eyes.

I went to the bedside and held up the babe. "You've birthed a girl child, my lady."

"A...girl?"

"It's a girl?" The midwife looked at me sharply.

A tear shimmered at the corner of the marquise's eye. "After all of that…" Exhaustion seemed to overwhelm her features, but even so, she stretched out her hand toward me.

I could not let her have the child, so I simply nodded and then took her hand up in my own.

"What must be done for you? You have helped me so."

In my arms, the babe nuzzled at my breast. "Entrust to me the care of your babe as you rest."

The marquise grasped the child's hand in her own for an instant before she succumbed to fatigue. "Take her. Please."

But the midwife was already reaching for the child. "I must insist I have it, my lady, to ensure everything is—"

"No!" It was on my word alone the child's sex had been declared.

"I must cut the cord."

Clasping the babe to my chest, I moved toward the door. "My lady gave the child to me."

"Just let me—"

"*I* will do it." A long-forgotten stubbornness stiffened the line of my jaw even as a queasiness sifted through my stomach.

The midwife handed me a knife.

I took it with one hand as I clasped the child to my breast with the other. "What is it—how shall I—?"

"Really, my lady!" The midwife stalked to the bed, beseeching the marquise.

"I shall do it. I do not need your help." I spoke the words with a confidence I did not feel. Placing the child on the marquise's desk, I unwound the cloth I had fastened about it. The babe was intemperate and squalling, its fists and tiny feet writhing in the air. Across its belly lay a tube, long and waxen. I could hardly bring myself to touch it, let alone cut it. I nearly laughed aloud at the absurdity of it. How could I have ever contemplated killing the child, when I could not even bear to cut its cord? Clamping my teeth together and taking long, deep breaths, I finally accomplished the task and then wrapped the child once more in the cloths.

"You must clean her, my lady." The midwife held out a bowl of some grainy mix.

"That is not how it is done at my estate." I tried to sound quite certain about it, though I had not the first idea. And the child did have an alarming amount of white curdles stuck to its skin. I nudged the woman away with my elbow as I made for the door with the babe.

What did one do with a child? I shoved aside my bed's hangings with an elbow and placed him on the counterpane. His tiny face furrowed, and he let out a hearty cry.

Picking him up, I put him to my shoulder and used a kerchief to rub him clean, then wrapped him back in the cloth

A knock sounded at the door.

I clasped him to my chest.

The maid entered, trailing a woman behind her. They both curtsied. "The wet nurse, my lady." Done with her announcement, the maid left.

The nurse looked around the room and then strode toward the chair by the fireplace. She sat and proceeded to unlace her stays, pulling down the front of her shift, from which tumbled two enormous breasts. She extended her arms toward me.

"I can't—"

She rose and pulled him from me and then put him to her breast, where he began to suckle.

The maid soon returned bearing clouts. "For the babe, my lady." She curtsied once more and left.

Once the child had finished feeding, the wet nurse returned him to me, laced herself up, and left us, as well. It wasn't long, however, before the count entered without a knock, pulling the door shut behind him.

I moved to the front of the bed, leaving the babe safely sleeping behind me.

He pinned me with a look. "They say it's a girl."

"It's indeed a girl, my lord." And may God forgive me for the lie. It was better, in my opinion, than the alternative.

Looking at me through narrowed eyes, he closed the distance between us. "Let's have a look, shall we?" He pushed me aside and reached for the child.

I fell onto the bed, hand splayed toward the child. "Don't, my lord! You'll wake it."

A cough sounded by the door.

He spun from the bed.

I rose. When I saw it was the marquis, I curtsied.

He nodded. "The marquise says she's given you charge of the babe."

The count went toward his father, all smiles. "Congratulations. In spite of your schemes with Cardinal St. Florent, you find yourself, once again, without a proper heir."

The marquis ignored the count and walked toward me. I moved to offer the bundle up to him, but he shook his head and only looked down upon it, smiling sadly into that small, peaceful face. He put out a finger to stroke one of the babe's plump cheeks. "I suppose one must be thankful for what is. We must not be ungrateful for God's gifts."

"Indeed not." Triumph rang in the count's voice.

The marquis gave the babe a pat on the head and then turned, taking the count with him as he left my chambers.

Thank God!

I left the babe on the bed and stood a bit away from him, considering how I should proceed. I always seemed to harm those I loved. But this child's life depended on me. I had to keep him safe. At least he could not appeal to my affections; that offered him the best chance of protection.

In spite of all my best intentions, I fell in love with him at some point between that first day and the third. Between the comings and goings of that chaff-brained, buxom wet nurse. At some time during those long, interminable nights, when the child would coo away the hours, he wormed his way into my affections. With the babe beside me, I was no longer alone. I had found someone more vulnerable than I.

Someone who depended upon me completely.

I could not harm this child. I wouldn't.

Indifference became our best protection. The marquise never called for it. The marquis never asked after it. The count never visited.

'Twas only the wet nurse I had to be on guard for.

I was the child's sole guardian and arbiter. When he came down with a sniffle, it was I who discovered he had managed to kick loose of his cloths. When he began to wail long before it was time for the wet nurse to come, it was I who taught him how to be content with the sucking of my littlest finger.

The count seemed to have lost all interest in me once the babe was declared a girl. And yet, I could not leave. The child's life depended upon my presence. If I could keep my secret until the family returned to court, then I could reveal to the marquis the child's true sex. At court, there would be safety among the crowds of people. The count would not dare to harm the child with an audience in attendance. We just had to survive, he and I, until then.

CHAPTER 34

The Count of Montreau

CHÂTEAU OF ERONVILLE
THE PROVINCE OF ORLÉANAIS, FRANCE

IN SPITE OF MY FATHER'S BEST-LAID PLANS, I WAS STILL his heir. The irony is that for the first seven years of my life, my father did not even realize he had one. Not until the day he walked in on me as I was using a chamber pot.

"She's a…a boy!"

"Of course she's not." My mother had taken me by the hand and tried to pull me off down the hall with her.

But Father had followed. "But she's a—*he's* a boy." He said it with more certainty that time. And something within me cheered to hear him. *He* wouldn't mock the way I walked. *He* wouldn't constantly examine my face for signs of "wickedness" or pull the smallest of hairs from my neck. And maybe he wouldn't keep measuring me and then binding me around the waist.

"He's a boy."

Mother dropped my hand and whirled on him. "What if she is? You took everything else from me. All I wanted was a girl. A girl who wouldn't betray me, who wouldn't hurt me."

"Took? What did I ever take from you? You practically threw yourself at me from the moment we first met!"

"We were just children!"

"You weren't a child. You were a temptress. A seductress."

"I was just a girl doing what my mother told me to!"

"You bewitched me."

"I despised you. You hurt me! After that, I prayed for God to give me a girl. I prayed and prayed and prayed, because I didn't want my baby to grow up and ruin someone else's daughter. And you know what?" Her face was contorted. She was panting with rage. "She never will!"

"Because you've spoiled him. You've completely destroyed him!"

"I've saved her."

"*Him!* It isn't natural, what you've done to him."

"But now he'll never grow up and turn into you!" Perhaps she was a witch, just as everyone had always said, for her words had come true. I never had turned into him. She had exacted the ultimate in revenge.

She had turned me into her.

I'd burst into tears at that point.

"Look at him—he's blubbering like a girl!" Scorn and contempt dripped from the marquis's words.

"He *is* a girl."

"He's not."

"He is. I've made him into one."

"Enough of this! Come, boy. Shed that gown." He stripped me right there in the hall. "There, now. Isn't that better? Don't you feel like a man?"

I nodded simply because I knew that's what he wanted me to do. But I was lying. It wasn't better. I didn't feel like a man. I only felt naked. Stripped and exposed.

And here I was again.

Exposed. Alone. Stripped bare.

My father despised me, and my lover had deserted me. In truth, I was not much surprised. I had always known the former, and the latter had simply been a matter of time.

But as long as I was my father's heir, there was no reason

for me to care. There would be other men. I would find another man just as soon as we left this godforsaken place for court. My father's inheritance would ensure it. And once I had the lace, all would come right.

I needed everything to come right, but increasingly I had the feeling something had gone wrong. As if something had eluded me. But what? The outcome of the birth had been much better than I had feared. We gathered for the baptism of the child, though not a week had passed since her birth and though it seemed I was the only one inclined to celebrate. I had worn my best embroidered satin doublet, and I carried my court sword instead of my pistol for the occasion.

Cardinal St. Florent was there to preside, resplendent in his scarlet-colored robe. Though my inheritance was safe for the moment, who knew when my father would try for another babe. As soon as the girl's father returned with the lace, I would ensure it was safe forever.

Gabrielle was standing up in front by the altar, wearing a balloon-sleeved gown fashioned from yellow satin. New jewels sparkled at her neck and around her wrists. She was dreadfully pale, and she held onto the marquis's arm with a white-knuckled grip. The marquis stood beside her in his best suit of clothes, the medal he'd been awarded for saving King Henri gleaming at his throat. They were pathetic, the pair of them, trying to disinherit me. At least their plans had ended in a disaster.

A girl child!

The child I had always wished to be.

They stood before me: the cardinal, my stepmother, the marquis, and the girl with the babe in her arms. Such a detestably endearing family tableau. Everything looked gallingly perfect, but the feeling nagged that something was not right.

What was it?

As I stepped into the chapel, the girl looked at me. The color drained from her face as she clasped the babe closer to her chest. I supposed she would be named the child's godmother; the babe had been with the girl ever since the morning of its birth.

I mounted the steps to the altar and stood beside the marquis. In the girl's arms, the babe kicked out at the confines of its gown, filling it with air. As the material settled, the babe kicked out at it again.

I knew what it felt like, that space beneath a gown. I knew what freedom could be found beneath a skirt. I knew what it was to spin and spin and spin again, skirts and petticoats flying out around me.

I too used to be free of all constraints.

That babe was destined for everything I was not; she was everything I ought to have been. It didn't matter that the child wasn't a boy. Still, it mocked me. It threw a fist up and cuffed the girl on the chin. She only smiled at it and kissed the top of its downy head. Eyeing me, she leaned over toward the marquise and whispered something in her ear. Glancing back at me once more, she tightened her grip on the babe.

My stepmother's brow folded for a moment, but then she gave a small lift of her shoulder, nodding.

Why was it the girl had been given charge of the babe? Why hadn't it been placed into the care of a nurse?

I leaned over and asked the marquis.

He frowned. "Because the girl asked for it. Hush now. The cardinal is to begin."

She had asked for it? But...that was odd. Why would she

beg to care for a babe that wasn't her own? Normally a nurse would have taken charge of an infant. My gaze swung to the marquise. I looked at her, considering. Surely she wouldn't have wanted to care for the babe herself. If I knew anything about her at all, it was that she would have had a nurse already chosen. Why, then, the change in plans?

The cardinal pronounced his incantations, waving his arms this way and that. "What name do you give your child?"

My father opened his mouth to speak.

It made no sense unless…unless…as I looked from the child to the girl, she seemed to cower before me. There was only one case in which her actions made any sense. I shoved the cardinal aside, drew my blade, and then lunged toward the girl.

"Give me the child!"

Darting behind the cardinal, she shouted at the marquis. "It's a boy, my lord!" Her voice rang out, trembling but determined.

Gabrielle gasped.

"A boy, my lord!" I wished the girl would shut up her mouth. It was a boy I would destroy.

The marquis, fool that he was, did nothing but stand there gaping like some overfed goose.

I stalked the girl, chasing her from the cardinal back toward a steeply winding staircase tucked into the back of the chapel. It was built into a tower, with tall, open arches carved into its walls. With the babe clutched to her breast, the girl bolted up the stairs toward a balcony perched high beneath the vaulted ceiling. Meant for a singer or musician, the balcony was hardly bigger than a coffin. The stairs provided the only access.

"You run from me!" Enraged at her temerity, I dove for the skirts that were disappearing around the spiral of the stair.

She cried out as she stumbled. With another pull, she began to slide toward me.

"Julien! Enough!" My father was standing at the bottom of the stairs, wrath darkening his face.

I caught a flurried movement from the corner of my eye. The girl. With a gnashing of teeth, I darted upward again.

Her slippered foot kicked out and struck me on the chin.

The chit! I caught hold of her ankle and twisted, wrenching it. I felt my lips curl as she cried out in pain.

She fell on her back as I pulled her down the stairs toward me.

The babe squalled in the girl's arms as her head struck the stone steps. I would shut him up! Dropping her ankle, I raised my sword.

Before I could silence him forever and make certain my future, the girl turned onto her stomach, hiding the child beneath her. As I retreated to avoid the churning of her feet, she scrambled back up the stairs. In an instant she had already vanished around the turn.

"I want that babe!" I shouted.

My only answer was the child's cry. And a bellow from my father.

I charged up the steps, but she was standing there above me, blocking the way. I swung the sword at her. The broad side of the blade struck her on the head, but though she staggered, she did not yield. What had she done with the child? As I looked beyond her, straining to see up the stairs, she grasped my sword with both her hands and wrested it from me. She gasped as the blade ripped through her flesh. Blood dripped from her palms as she tore it from me and heaved it through one of the arches.

It clattered to the floor somewhere far beneath us.

"Let me pass!" Her fingernails raked at my neck as I pushed her toward the arch where the steps were wider.

Finally, I caught her hands around the wrist and tried to slip past her. As she wrestled with me, kicking out at my knees, she lost her balance, threatening to pull me with her through the wall.

I let go of her hands.

She threw out her arms and then, with a look of horror and a terrible shriek, she dropped away through the arch.

⁂

"What have you done!"

It was the marquis. And he was looking at me with such... loathing.

"Murderer!"

"I didn't mean—I only—" I'd only meant to kill the child. And I had not yet done it.

With a cry of rage, he charged me.

I put a hand to his chest and shoved him away. He stumbled against the rail. As I brushed past him, he reached out and grabbed at my sleeve.

"I never knew you."

At that moment, I realized the disappointment and disapproval he had always shown me were nothing compared to the hatred his eyes now held. As I looked back at him, I discovered that hell was not some place of torment or unquenchable flames; it was the chill oblivion of contempt and disregard. And then I felt myself being jerked from behind, dragged down the staircase, and flung out onto the floor. "You *bastard*!"

CHAPTER 35

Alexandre Lefort

CHÂTEAU OF ERONVILLE
THE PROVINCE OF ORLÉANAIS, FRANCE

I T TOOK TWO DAYS TO REACH THE CHÂTEAU OF Eronville. But once there, I strode up the steps, dog trotting beside me.

A servant met us in the hall.

I had not washed for two days, and my face was unshaven, but I lifted my chin and did my best imitation of my father, Nicolas Girard, the King's finest warrior. "The Count of Montreau, if you please."

The servant bowed. "They're all in the chapel, my lord. For the baptism of the child. You may not yet be too late."

Being too late was the greatest of my fears. I hurried through the halls behind him, and when I discerned the direction in which he was headed, I pushed past him down the corridor. I had waited too many weeks already. I would wait no longer.

As I crossed the threshold of the chapel, I saw a cardinal, as well as a man and a woman I didn't recognize. They were all staring at some stairs in the back, and as I followed their eyes my heart stopped. I saw the red-faced count and Lisette high on the staircase. He was pushing her toward an open arch. Before I could move, before I could even call out, she fell through it.

"No!" My cry joined her own as I watched her tumble, striking her head against the wall. My heart stopped beating as all my hopes turned to dust. No one could long survive such a fall.

I took the steps to the altar two at a time. As I knelt beside her, blood poured from a gash in her head and slashes in her palms. Mon dieu! Her limbs were so bent and twisted that I feared to touch her. I stripped off my doublet and folded it, placing it beneath her head. If only I could do something for the bleeding. The lace! I shook it from its packet and wrapped it about her head, praying that it might slow the bleeding long enough to let me bid her adieu.

And long enough for me to demand some measure of justice.

Leaving her, I sprung up the stair, grabbed the count by the back of his collar, dragged him down the steps, and threw him onto the chapel's floor. "You *bastard*!"

"I didn't mean—"

"You detestable, loathsome bastard!" I had not been forced to sell our estate, nor toil in the rain and mud; I had not been cheated and assaulted and nearly killed, to have Lisette murdered before my eyes by this...this...monster.

"It wasn't—"

Pulling the dagger from my waistband, I lunged at him.

Somewhere up near the balcony, a baby cried.

Rolling beyond my reach, the count recovered his sword and regained his feet. "My father wanted to give that babe everything that's mine."

An old man stumbled down the staircase. Had the count attacked him as well? I lunged at the count again.

He parried. "I only ever wanted your love." Though he was countering my thrusts with admirable skill, he was focused almost entirely on the old man. "Your love and your regard."

"And you had them! You have always been my son. But now...? You can be no son of mine. You're a murderer. And I'll see you hanged for it."

"Like some common peasant?" The count attacked me.
I parried.

"You're worse than common!" the old man cried.
"You're a disgrace. I could tolerate your gambling and even
your—your proclivities. But murder?"

The count took a slash at me.

The dog growled and sprang at him, biting at his boot.

He swore and shook the dog off.

The babe's cries rang through the chapel.

The count's face twisted with fury. "Will no one *shut him
up*!" He raised his sword toward the balcony as if he held
some hope of silencing the child.

His attention diverted, I threw myself at his side, rocking
him off balance. He fell to the floor, sword rattling at his feet.

As I moved to collect it, he swung his leg and tripped me.

Though I fell, I retained hold of my dagger. But the move
had given the count time enough to recover his sword.
Seizing it, he launched himself toward me. I crouched and
then sprang up to meet him. The dagger rent his doublet and
plunged into his chest.

His sword dropped to the floor.

I kicked it away from him.

Hands outstretched, he turned from me and staggered
toward the old man. Halfway there he paused, putting a
hand to the altar. He lowered himself to the floor and leaned
against it, panting.

The cardinal rushed forward, bellowing profanities.

The count seemed not to hear him. He put a hand to his
chest, clasping the handle of the dagger. Blood welled up
between his fingers. He sent a despairing glance in the old
man's direction. And then, with blood darkening the front
of his shirt, he looked up at me. His eyes blazed with fury,
as his hand dropped to his chest. "So much blood..." He

coughed, a pink-tinged froth burbling from his mouth. And then he let out a great sigh and died.

With a boot to his chest, I pulled my dagger from him, wiping it on my breeches and securing it in my waistband. Then I went to Lisette.

She still lay where she had fallen, though her limbs did not look so twisted and her neck was no longer bent to the side. And—she was yet breathing! I knelt beside her, brushing her golden curls from a face gone deathly pale. "My love."

"Alex...andre..."

I took up her hand in mine. It was so small. And so cold.

"My eyes...they betray me." Her words tore at my heart. If only I could hold back that eternal night. But she spoke without fear. Without panic.

"I have—I brought you something." The lace that I had wrapped around her had become a bloodied crown, though it seemed to have served my purpose. It had staunched the flow. But in doing so it had become joined to her wound. To tear it away would only cause more harm.

How fitting that the lace could not be taken from her. That which she had once desired she now possessed.

So much blood. So much pain, so much suffering for something so insubstantial. Just a handful of threads woven around nothing but air. "Here." I took the free end, wrapping it around her bloodied hands and then closed her fingers about it. They burrowed into the threads as if they could tell her the information her eyes could no longer convey. The suggestion of a smile curled her lips. "Lace." The word came out in a sigh.

I had done the right thing by killing the count, and I had done the wrong thing by leaving Lisette in his care. Now there was nothing left at all, and I did not know who could save me. I had become Alexandre Girard once more. I gathered her to my chest. The memory of her smiles and kisses and laughter was still so fresh in my senses. I closed my eyes as I lay my cheek against hers. I did not ever want to open them.

At that moment the count's father clapped his hand on my shoulder, jerking the dagger from my waistband. "Where did you get this?" He said it with great indignity, as if accusing me of theft.

There was no sin greater than the one I had just committed. I had taken a life in the sight of God's presence, again, in spite of all my promises never to hurt another man. And I could conceive of no greater grief than the one I now felt. It could matter no longer who my father was or how he had come to die. I laid Lisette back on the ground, and I pushed to my feet before him. "I got it from my father, Nicolas Girard. He brought it back with him from—"

"From the Battle of Fontaine-Française." He gestured fiercely toward some servant and then whispered into his ear. The servant bowed and then left.

I would be arrested for killing the count. There was no way around it. His own father had been witness to the killing. Closing my eyes, I prayed for the mercy of oblivion.

Several minutes later, the servant came back into the chapel. He handed something to the old man, who then extended it toward me. "I have here your dagger's match."

Find its match, fiston. Therein lies your destiny.

I could only stare dumbly. First at one of them and then at the other.

"You are Nicolas Girard's son."

I nodded.

"Then you have proved yourself worthy of his great valor."

I understood nothing at all about his words. I had just killed this man's son. In God's holy sanctuary. Valor? I expected nothing but to be cursed forever. And then hanged afterward.

The old man laid a trembling hand on mine. "There is

309

good news for you this day. I have been holding your father's lands on your behalf. They border my own."

My father's lands? Surely he was mistaken. "My father never owned any lands."

He pushed his dagger into his waistband, took my face between his hands, and kissed both of my cheeks. "Today, you have become your father's heir. You must now take his title and possession of all that is his."

He was offering me a title? And lands? I looked beyond him, toward Lisette. Why could they not have been offered when I could have used them? When they would have meant something? I could have paid the debt. I might have saved Souboscq. And then Lisette would not be lying on the floor, bent and broken. A laugh burbled in my throat, but when I opened my mouth, it was a sob that escaped instead. Wretched, vile lace! What use were lands to me now?

The dog approached the count's body. He took a sniff, pointed his nose at the ceiling, and howled. Then he crept toward Lisette.

"Come here, *chiot*."

He ignored me.

"Come here!" I wouldn't be able to bear it if he howled again.

He gave me a cursory glance and kept going.

"*Mon cher!*"

Though his tail wagged and his muscles bunched as if he wanted to spring toward me, he took a delicate sniff instead. He walked closer to Lisette and nosed at the lace clutched in her hands. Sniffed again. And then he lay down at her side and whined.

"Come here, *mon cher*."

He barked, tail wagging.

And as I looked at the lace in her hand, it seemed to tremble.

Acknowledgments

I AM OFTEN ASKED HOW LONG IT TAKES TO WRITE A book. This one took a long time. I stumbled upon the beginnings of the story in 2002 when I was researching a different manuscript. It went through lots of versions and several casts of characters before it emerged, in this basic form, in 2009. It is due only to the kindness and forbearance of three people that this book was even published.

My husband Tony encouraged me, even when the story wouldn't come together and it seemed as if it would never sell. My agent, Natasha Kern, graciously tutored me in a short course of How to Write a Novel and then tirelessly worked to sell the revised manuscript. My editor, Shana Drehs, saw some sort of design in the mess of structure and narrative I submitted, and with patience and grace, helped me to realize my vision.

Writing a book sometimes takes as long as it takes, and I am blessed beyond measure by those who have encouraged me, supported me, and aided me in the journey.

$\mathscr{Discussion\ Questions}$

1. Did you have a favorite character? Which one? Why did that particular character appeal to you? What was it about that particular storyline that drew you?

2. Is there anything these seven disparate characters had in common?

3. In your opinion, what was the most tragic part of Katharina's life?

4. Do you agree with Heilwich's opinion that she was a murderess? She certainly intended to murder Herry Stuer. Do you think she ought to have gone through with it? How would the story have changed if she had? How would she have changed? What other outcomes did her choice affect?

5. How do you navigate the world? In blacks and whites, or with a palette of grays? Which approach is more terrifying to you? Why?

6. What did Denis most want? Do you think he will achieve it? Should he? Was he asking too much from life?

7. Denis was meant to be a representation of all of us. At some point, we all have to take off our rose-colored glasses and face the world as it truly is. At what point did you have to do this? What did Denis lose, and what did he gain in doing this? In your life, what did you lose, and what did you gain?

8. A Flemish woman berates Alexandre in Chapter 14: "Are you too good for God? Is that it? You're only harming yourself. And besides, you can only be as clean as you are." What did she mean?

9. If you could tell the dog anything, what would you say to him?

10. What would you say to the count?

11. Was the count a sympathetic villain? Who made him the way he was? At what points in the story could he have made different decisions? What would it have required of him?

12. Did Lisette live, or did she die?

13. In some ways, Lisette and the count are mirrors of each other. What similarities did they have? What differences? Both face ruin, but they respond to the prospect in different ways. Why?

14. Can you take worth away from someone, or do they surrender it?

15. Whose fault was it that the lace smuggling industry flourished in seventeenth-century Europe? The King's? The courtiers'? The lace makers'?

16. Is the provenance of consumer goods important to you? Why or why not?

17. Katharina and the dog are both innocent victims in a world steeped in corruption. Did their lack of guile help or hinder their survival?

18. When has corruption knocked on your door? What was your response?

19. Is there an antidote to corruption?

20. What responsibility, if any, do you have for the corruption you see going on around you?

21. Is corruption a result of capitalism, or is it a result of totalitarianism?

22. Each character was offered a chance either to corrupt others or to aid in furthering corruption. What choice did each character make?

23. What might cause a good person to make a bad choice?

Author's Note

WHEN I FIRST STARTED WRITING THIS BOOK, I thought it was about lace. When I told my agent, she strenuously begged to differ. *How can a novel be about an object?* she asked. *It has to be about a person.* I thought about what she said, and I rewrote the story, realizing that, in fact, it was actually about corruption and how people became ensnared in it. And it *was* about corruption...for two rewrites worth of edits. But in the end, that wasn't really right either. It was during the third rewrite of this novel I finally listened to the conversation I was having with myself—for that's all a novel really is. I was grappling with the concept of worth. Why would a person feel unworthy? And what is it that makes them keep feeling that way?

If the stories of Alexandre and Lisette, the count and the lace maker, the sister and the border guard had anything to do with one another, and if you found the dog illuminated any principle at all, I hope you discovered the pattern being created was one of worth—an interplay between positive and negative moral spaces. As I was writing this story, I came to the conclusion that worth is a paradox. We are all of us creatures of the same God. So if you can convince yourself that your fellow man has no worth, then the only thing you've really managed in the end is to prove to yourself that you have none either.

There were strange things done in the centuries of old. It was not unheard of for mothers to wield their children's sexuality as a weapon. King Louis XIII's advisors several times purposefully encouraged him toward male favorites in attempts to stabilize his infamous moods. And the King's younger son, Philippe, was actively pushed toward homosexuality by his mother, Queen Anne.

King Louis XIII himself is an enigma, who just recently has begun to emerge from behind the robes of his much-celebrated minister, Cardinal Richelieu. It was their partnership that wrenched away the last remaining powers of the nobility and ushered into Europe an era of absolute monarchism.

At one point during the seventeenth century, Flemish bobbin lace was the most lucrative contraband in Europe. A network of lace smuggling, established in an earlier time for purposes of import tax evasion, was quickly enlarged. It used traditional methods, such as hollow loaves of bread, as well as coffins and dogs, to move lace from Flanders into France. Entire estates were sold for the privilege of purchasing lace, and reputations rose and fell on the amount and quality of lace a courtier wore. The smuggling practices begun in the sixteenth century would continue until the nineteenth century.

Lace makers were needed by the thousands to keep up with the demand. They worked long hours in workshops that were heated by animals housed beneath or beside them to spare their precious lace the possibility of being contaminated by soot or cinders. The work was painstaking and done in such poorly lit conditions that many went blind by the age of thirty. And when their usefulness had been exhausted, they were thrown out into the streets. In the interest of accuracy, I must say not all lace workshops and schools were run by nuns, and those that were did not necessarily treat their charges with such cruelty.

The story of lace is fascinating. That a frivolous piece of frippery could produce such heartrending consequences is both paradoxical and tragic. And the lives of these characters are mirrored by those working in the sweatshops of today's fashion and accessory industries.

Be careful what you wish for; your wishes have a way of reaching out to impact others in unforeseen ways. And remember that no matter how convinced you are to the contrary, you always have a choice.

A Conversation with the Author

Iris Anthony

Q: *Lace* smuggling? It doesn't seem quite right to put those two words together.

A: And that's exactly where this book started. I ran across a reference to lace smuggling as I was doing research on costuming for a different novel back in 2002. At that point, the idea of lace and the concept of smuggling were so disparate that it was hard to place them side by side. But they kept niggling at me. And finally, the thought of putting two such unexpected things together proved too great a temptation. I had to write about it.

Q: The novel is set during an era in France when lace was forbidden. Can you talk about that?

A: Sure. Louis XIII issued five edicts that placed prohibitions and restrictions on clothing, and on April 3, 1636, he forbade the wearing of lace altogether. That's the edict that provided for confiscation, fines, and banishment from the kingdom. Sumptuary edicts were enacted across Europe during this time period. The reasons were several. In France's case, money was being lost across the border through lace purchases in Flanders and Italy at a time when the King desperately needed money to fill his treasury due to expenses from wars and other pet projects. It was hoped that forbidding the wearing of lace would keep all that money in France and, therefore, available to the King.

Another reason is more difficult for our modern minds to understand. Europeans had a great need to keep everyone in their place. Most of these sumptuary edicts were very explicit about who could wear what: Princes of the Blood could wear cloth of gold; other princes were only allowed to wear cloth of silver. Dukes could wear gold lace; earls could only wear gold trim, etc., etc. Ever since Europeans first started visiting America as "tourists," they've been appalled that they couldn't tell who was who. Since our founding, part of being an American was the "right" to purchase and wear the things we wanted.

In Europe, even an extremely wealthy merchant couldn't wear cloth of silver, for instance, or lace in our case. In America, if you had the money, no one would stop you from buying (and wearing) what you wanted. These edicts seem very much like quibbling to us, but they were important tools for social control.

Finally, the King himself was quite ascetic. He did what he had to in order to be kingly, but he was austere. He wasn't into the whole musketeer look (floppy boots, huge hats, big ruffled lace collars). He was called "The Just" because he really did try to enforce the rules he made (when violations were brought to his attention). He killed the noble who plotted against Richelieu, for instance, in the Chalais Conspiracy. He also executed a court favorite who insisted upon dueling after he had forbidden it. The King was derailed from his natural penchant for justice when his mother and his brother started conspiring against him, but in general, he wanted order. And he didn't approve of conspicuous consumption. Obviously, many of those at court did since he kept having to issue sumptuary edicts, but that seemed to be how it went back then just about everywhere.

Louis XIV, his son, had a different focus. He loved glitz and glamour. The more of it, the better! He actively encouraged his nobles to partake in lavishness. He wasn't personally against lace and consumption the way his father had been. He did, however, have a huge need for funding his wars. Colbert (his minister) decided not only to forbid luxury goods in France (as Louis XIII had done), but also decided to encourage the creation of domestic rip-offs. For a while, the rip-offs were just that, but eventually, they became even more desired than the foreign goods they had been copied from. The association of France with luxury goods began during Louis XIV's reign under Colbert's guiding hand. All of the famous French laces date from that period. The French perfume industry developed then. The glass industry came of age, as did luxury textiles.

Q: Let's switch gears for a moment. I have to tell you that I hated the dog's story. Not because I hated the dog, but because the abuse he suffered was so terrible. It was difficult to read. Tell me you made those parts up.

A: I would give almost anything to tell you that I did. If the idea of lace smuggling fascinated me, it was the smugglers' treatment of dogs that forced me to write this story. If there were a stronger word, I would use it. The dogs *compelled* me to write this book! Envisioning what they went through outraged me. At first, the only mention of dogs I could find was in a French text that noted over 40,000 of them were killed during a fifteen-year period as they tried to cross the border between Flanders and France. So it wasn't an instance of one demented person abusing dogs. It was a whole industry.

I knew I had to write about it, but I didn't know how. How could you train a dog to sneak across a border, deliver a length of lace, and then return to you without being detected? I talked to a friend who raised dogs, and we had an interesting but inconclusive discussion about how they might be trained to do that. Obviously, there would have to be some sort of reward for the dog. We didn't arrive at an answer, but we knew that to cover that sort of distance, a dog, in effect, would have to be self-motivated. He would have to want to do it. I never dreamed what that motivation would be! It wasn't until several years later that I discovered the answer. I wish I could say there were no dogs harmed in the creation of this book. I actually cried when I wrote those scenes.

Q: So you're a dog-lover then?

A: Absolutely! In fact, my family adopted a dog from Mutts Matter Rescue in the summer of 2011. It breaks my heart to think that he was on a kill list. I look at his cute little pug face and wonder how anyone could ever have given him up. I wish I could have known him as a puppy. If only dogs could talk!

Q: How did you come to an interest in lace?

A: It started at the age of eleven. I remember it very distinctly because it was that year that my grandmother decided to teach me how to tat. (Tatting is a form of shuttle lace.) Unfortunately, that was not the year I actually learned how to do it. It took several more years and an infinite amount of patience on her part for me to acquire the knack.

When I lived in Paris from 1996–2000, I made several visits to Bruges, Belgium, and became enamored of bobbin lace. Another juxtaposition in this book akin to lace and smuggling is the exquisite, valuable bobbin lace made in the seventeenth century and the plight of the girls and women who made it. They worked in the fashion industry's original sweatshops.

Q: The structure of this story, having seven alternating first-person points of view, is very unique. Why did you write it the way that you did?

A: I wanted to tell the story of lace, and it seemed to me that in order to do it, I would have to follow the process from start to finish. Some of the characters would logically never meet each other, and there was no one person who would be present in every scene of the story. I knew I would have to have multiple points of view.

In its first drafts, the story was originally composed of nine parts (I included the perspectives of Lisette's father and the priest in Signy-sur-vaux). Beginning with the commissioning of the lace in France, I let each character appear once to tell his or her part of the story. That worked for the beginning, and it worked for the parts set in Flanders, but I quickly realized I would have to allow some characters to make a second appearance once the lace was smuggled into France. Several more drafts had Lisette, the Comte, and Alexandre resume their stories at the end of the book. That didn't quite work well either because Alexandre's story took place in both France and Flanders.

It took a brilliant editor to suggest that (1) lace was the whole point of the story and it would be more engaging to start the book with its creation, from Katharina's point of view, and (2) that the narratives should be broken up and alternated to create a more continuous sense of narrative. She was right, and I like the result!